RECKLESS DYNASTY

KNIGHT'S RIDGE EMPIRE #9

TRACY LORRAINE

Toby's demon

Tracy

TRACY
LORRAINE

Editing by Pinpoint Editing

Proofreading by Sisters Get Lit.erary

Photography by Wander Aguiar

1

TOBY

Pain like I've never experienced tears through my chest, ripping my heart into shreds as the ambulance Jodie was stretchered into speeds down the street with its lights flashing and siren blaring.

My knees ache from where I fell to them the second the paramedics slammed the door on us, cutting off my view of my girl.

I want to assume that they didn't give us an update because they thought I was just a stranger who rescued her, but I fear it's worse than that. That they didn't have time.

A pained roar erupts from my chest, my lungs burning from the smoke, but it's easy to push aside, allowing my anguish to take over.

"Toby." A soft hand lands on my shoulder, startling me. "We need to go."

Stella steps in front of me. Her face is a stone

mask in her attempt to take control of this situation and be what I need, but her eyes reveal how she's really feeling. And the concern within them does little for my fragile heart.

"She's going to want you there when she wakes up. And," she adds, her eyes dropping to my body, "you need checking out too."

"I'm fine," I hiss, barely able to feel the cuts and bruises from our escape from a different burning building not so long ago.

"Toby," she warns.

There's a loud shout from one of the firefighters working on the building behind me and my heart jumps into my throat.

Sara.

The only fucking good thing about this whole situation is that the Wolves who started it have fucked off, leaving us with the heart-wrenching fallout.

Although, they're not far away. I can hear gunfire in the distance, and the smoke from the burning estate is covering our heads, making the place look even more like hell on earth than it usually does.

"The others are coming," I force out, vaguely remembering that they told me they were going to follow me.

"They'll be fine," she assures me, although I don't miss the way her chest compresses at the thought of Seb still being in the middle of all that.

Getting to my feet, I pull her body into my arms,

quickly realising that she's trembling just as hard as I am.

"He could handle this in his sleep, Stel. You have nothing to worry about." Although, I can't help but wince at my own words because they were right behind me. So where the fuck are they now?

"Message them, tell them what's going on, and to meet us at the hospital. You got Jesse's number?"

She shakes her head as her eyes shift to the building, grief twisting her features despite the fact that she's never met the girl inside.

"They'll get her out. There is no other option," I state, forcing more confidence into my tone than I feel.

Stella nods, her eyes glistening with tears.

"Come on. Jodie needs you."

She grabs my hand and we run toward her car, abandoned in the middle of the road.

She stops being quite so compliant when I go for her driver's door.

"You're not fucking driving in this state," she asserts, her eyes dropping to my shoulder.

"I need to get there fast."

"Get the fuck in the car, Tobes."

She rips the door open and falls in without another word, and I'm forced to comply. I don't have time to stand here and argue over this.

"Message the guys. Call Jesse. I've got this, Bro."

I glance over at her and strap myself in, the deep rumble of her engine coming to life beneath us.

"Didn't Seb ever tell you about the night I drove Theo's Ferrari?"

Before I get a chance to answer, or even remember the night in question, I'm thrown into the passenger door as she spins the car on a dime and shoots off down the street.

"Jesus, fuck, Stella," I bark, pain radiating around my body.

"Whoops. You said you wanted to be quick." The grin she shoots me is pure trouble, and on any other day, it would light me up with pride, knowing that she's my sister. But right now, I feel nothing. Nothing but despair and unfiltered fear.

Dragging my phone from my pocket, I find the screen shattered into a million pieces. It illuminates behind the glass, but I can barely read it.

"Fuck," I bark.

"Use mine. It's in my ass pocket."

Stella lifts from the seat, allowing me to pull it free.

I hold it up to her face to let it unlock before diving into her messages and finding our group chat.

Stella: The bookies and the flat have collapsed. Someone needs to find Jesse NOW.

By some fucking miracle, the dots start bouncing

immediately and I breathe a sigh of relief that at least one of them is fucking alive right now.

Theo: We're on it. Where's Toby?

Stella: This is me. Stella's driving.

Nico: Jodie okay?

My heart jumps into my throat once more as the memory of her passing out in my arms comes back to me.

Stella: I don't know. They're still trying to get Sara out. It's fucking bad.

I squeeze my eyes shut, trying to force the image of watching that building collapse around them out of my head.

Theo: We'll be there as soon as we can.

The phone trembles in my hand as a million questions I need to ask them slam into me. Theo and Nico are breathing, but what about Alex and Seb? Are they anywhere fucking close to winning this thing?

"Everyone good?" Stella asks, the back end of the

car spinning out as she takes a corner at blood-curdling speed like a fucking pro.

Swallowing down my concern, I force some positivity into my tone.

"Yeah. They're gonna meet us at the hospital."

"Jesse?"

"They're on it."

Tipping my head back, I blow out a long breath and squeeze my eyes tight. Every single fucking inch of me aches, but I don't care. I'll happily take worse, so much fucking worse if it means Jodie will come out of this in one piece.

Stella takes another hair-raising turn that forces me to pay attention once more. The blood coating my arms and chest catches my eye, and my heart clenches at the sight.

Please let all of that be mine.

Everything was too much of a blur as I dragged her from that building. I have no idea if she was hurt —I didn't have time to look. I just knew I needed to get her free before shit got even worse.

Stella's warm hand lands on my thigh as if she can read my thoughts.

"She's going to be okay," she says softly, her grip tightening in support.

I blow out another breath, praying to anyone who will fucking listen that she's right. That I'm not going to have the one good thing in my life ripped away from me like this.

If I'd have fucking known she was going there.

Hell, if I knew Jesse hadn't got his girl out before all that shit kicked off...

My fists curl as Stella floors the accelerator and the hospital building appears before us.

I'm coming, baby. I'm fucking coming.

I've spent entirely too much fucking time in this place over the past couple of years. I'd hoped that with Mum's treatment coming to an end, I might get some reprieve. But with Stella being stabbed, both Seb and me getting shot, and now this, it doesn't seem to be the case.

She spins into a space and we both fly out of the car, damn near running toward Accident and Emergency. All my injuries are long forgotten.

"J-Jodie Walker," I spit at the receptionist, thankfully a different one to the one I barked at the day Mum was brought in a few weeks ago.

"They've just wheeled her in. If you can take a seat and..." I don't hear the rest of what she has to say as I back away and finally bump into a wall.

Resting my hands on my knees, I hang my head and suck in a deep breath.

Stella's hand lands on my bare back, reminding me that I'm standing here shirtless and covered in blood, cuts, and bruises.

"Come on, Tobes. We need to get you checked out." Stella's warm hand moves against me and I flinch as I begin to spiral into the darkness that the prospect of a life without Jodie in it causes.

"I'm fine," I state, slowly standing back to full

height and holding her eyes in an attempt to convince her it's the truth.

She quirks her brow as she puts her hands on her hips.

Her strength and sheer determination to focus on the issue at hand astounds me, and I cling onto it in the hope it gets me through the next however long until we find out what's happening.

"Tobias Doukas," a deep voice booms from the double doors, and when I look up, I find a nurse in dark blue scrubs staring right at me.

"Come on," Stella pleads, her fingers twisting with mine as she pulls me toward the nurse.

"You look like you've got yourself into some trouble, young man," he quips teasingly as I step up to him.

I hold his eyes, my lips pressing into a thin line as I bite back the need to ask him if he knows exactly who he's talking to.

The Cirillo Family owns an entire ward of this fucking hospital, and in an uncharismatic move, I have to force myself not to throw my weight around in order to get where I need to be—by Jodie's side.

It's usually Nico or Alex who pull the 'do you know who I am?' card to make almost anyone in the city bend to their wishes. I can't say I've ever really been in a situation before where I've found it necessary, but right now, the need burns through me like an inferno.

The nurse swallows nervously as he bravely holds my stare.

"Tone it down, Bro," Stella jokes lightly, but there's not really a whole lot of amusement in her tone.

"I need to know what's happening with Jodie Walker," I demand, walking beside the nurse as he directs us toward a bay.

"Let me get you cleaned up, and I'll see what I can do. Hop up here for me." He points to a bed in the middle of the space before reaching for a pair of gloves.

Pausing, I glance over my shoulder at Stella.

"Please," she breathes. "I promise I won't ask anything else of you. I'll do whatever you need," she bargains.

Unable to deny her despite the dread sitting heavy in my stomach at the knowledge that Jodie is here somewhere, I climb up onto the bed. I can almost feel her, the crackle in the air when we're close. It gives me hope. Hope that she's okay, that we're going to at least have a chance for me to win her back.

Stella lowers herself to the chair in the corner before pulling her phone out.

"Anything?" I ask when her brow wrinkles in concern.

She shakes her head and my heart sinks.

How am I meant to tell Jodie that we left while Sara was still inside that pile of bricks as the fire continued to consume anything in its wake? How am I meant to tell her that she's lost someone else that she cares about, if that is the outcome of this? Honestly, from the state of the place, the heat of the flames and the thickness of the smoke, I'm struggling to convince myself that she can be okay. My stomach knots as guilt assaults me at that thought.

"Shit," I hiss, letting my head drop back as the nurse wheels a little trolley over.

"Okay, so my name is Aaron and I'm going to check you over and clean you up. Are you okay with your visitor being present for this?"

"Yes. She's my sister," I say, keeping my eyes closed, my skin prickling with his attention.

"Is anything hurting other than the obvious?" he asks, his fingers pressing against a seriously painful spot on my upper arm.

"I'm fine. I just want to know where Jodie is."

"I beg to differ. You're dripping blood all over my clean bed," he deadpans.

"Toby, just let the man do his job. You're no good to Jodie with half your arm gaping open."

"Wha—" I lift my head once more and look down at my arm. "Jesus."

"Now do you see my point?" Stella says, glaring at me from the corner.

"All right, Mum," I hiss, letting my head fall back once more, and Aaron does something to my arm that sends a pain so strong through me that it makes my stomach turn over. "How long is this going to take?"

"Depends how good a patient you are. But from the amount of blood that's soaked into your trousers, I suspect it's not going to be a quick job. Would I be right in guessing you were in the Lovell Estate this evening?" Aaron asks.

I crack an eye open and assess him. He glances up, sensing my attention, but he doesn't cower or shy away.

"I grew up in the valley. I'm more than aware of what it's like down there and what the current situation is."

"Do you still have family there?" I ask, suddenly seeing a whole new side to him.

"Yeah, but they're not home right now."

"You have intel?" I ask.

"I've got a friend in the know. I got them out last week."

"G-good," I choke out as the image of the destruction we left behind fills my mind. "That's good."

Ripping my eyes from him, they fall on Stella, who's watching me with pain and fear etched into her features.

"They're going to be okay, Stel. They're gonna come back to us."

She nods, swallowing thickly as she looks back down at her phone.

"Come here," I say, holding my hand out for her.

She looks at Aaron, who nods in agreement.

"I think I'm going to be busy on this side for a while."

"Great," I mutter.

"You want a local anaesthetic?" he asks me.

"Nah, just stitch me up and point me in the direction of my girl."

2

TOBY

Turns out, the gash on my thigh is pretty serious. Mostly because it had been there so long now that it had damn near fused to my trousers.

I hiss behind my clenched teeth as Aaron does something that hurts more than getting shot in the damn chest.

"Stop being such a guy and accept the local, you hard-headed douchecanoe," Stella snaps at me, making Aaron snort a laugh.

"It's fine. I just want it done."

Stella's hand squeezes mine. "I know what you're doing," she warns quietly.

"Do you?" I grunt as Aaron stabs me, starting to put me back together.

"You're forcing yourself to feel every ounce of pain as punishment for all of this shit with Jodie."

Despite the fact that she hits the nail right on its

head, the next words that come out of my mouth don't confirm her suspicions.

"I have no idea what you're talking about."

Her brow quirks as she glares at me, but if she thinks it's going to make any difference, she needs to think again.

Jodie is... somewhere here, possibly fighting for her life. And Sara, the woman my girl wanted me to save is... well...

My teeth grind as the pain continues and I focus on my breathing, on getting back to Jodie as Aaron works his magic.

"You're all just a bunch of sadists really, aren't you?" Stella huffs in annoyance, continuing to watch me suffer.

"You're only just learning this, Princess?"

Her lips purse as an angry growl rumbles deep in her throat.

We hear the guys' arrival before we see them.

A loud ruckus comes from somewhere beyond the curtain and Stella jumps up from the chair.

"They're here," she breathes, her hand trembling in her lap.

The curtain is thrown back before Theo's cold,

hard mask of a face appears before us. Nico and Seb flank him as they storm inside my cubicle.

"Excuse me, but you can't just storm in here and—"

"Seb," Stella breathes, cutting Aaron off and practically launching herself across the room and jumping into his arms.

"Hey, Princess. Miss me?" he asks.

My heart clenches painfully as I watch the two of them.

Seb's covered in dirt and blood—I'm hoping other people's—but none of that seems to bother my sister as she slams her lips down on Seb's.

"Where are Alex and Daemon?" I ask when they don't appear with the three of them.

Nico rolls his eyes. "Alex got clipped by a bullet. Daemon's taken him to clean him up and stop him crying like a little bitch. How are you doing?" he asks, his eyes dropping to the stitched-up wounds on my arm and thigh as I sit here in just my boxers.

"I'll be fine when someone tells me where the fuck Jodie is."

"Still not heard anything?" Theo asks, although from my previous comment you'd think the answer was obvious.

I shake my head. "Did you get hold of Jesse?" I ask with a wince.

"Yeah, but not until it all calmed down."

The desperation becomes thick around us and I fight to drag in the air I need.

"Did they get her out?"'

"We don't know yet. We came straight here for you."

As much as I appreciate that, I think I'd prefer them to do whatever they could to get to Sara right now. Assuming there's anything they could have done.

"Is it over? Did Archer and his boys beat them?"

"Yeah," Theo sighs, dropping into the chair that Stella's vacated. He rests back, rubs his hands down his thighs, and rolls his head, cracking his neck. "The OGs have lost too many men to keep fighting."

I nod, not feeling as relieved as I probably should be.

"You need to get that looked at," I say to Nico as he cradles his arm to his chest.

"It's not broken," he states, pain lacing his voice.

"Oh, so you're a doctor now, huh?" I snark, taking in the deep frown marring his brow.

"I've dislocated my shoulder," he scoffs.

"I offered to pop it back in," Theo says as if it's nothing.

"It's fine, I'll go see—"

"Who said you could have a party?" Aaron snaps, slipping back into my cubicle with a set of scrubs in his hands.

"We don't need permission," Nico says, puffing his chest out.

"Stand down, man," Theo mutters. "Any chance

you could pop his shoulder back in while you're here?"

"I said I'm—"

"Sure. Toby is done, so hop up on his bed. Consider it a two-for-one offer."

Nico scoffs, rolling his eyes at Aaron.

"And make sure it hurts," Theo instructs with a smirk.

Nico glares at Theo. "Fuck you, man. This only happened because I was protecting your arse."

"Sure it was."

"Children," I snap, nowhere near having the energy for their bullshit bickering right now.

"I brought you something to wear." Aaron offers me the scrubs he's holding. My lip peels back, despite knowing I don't have another option after he cut my trousers off me to get to my thigh.

"Great."

"Aw, Jodie will love it. You can play doctor and she—"

"Where is she, Aaron?" I ask, remembering his deal from earlier.

"Bay twenty-two. But she's got the—"

I don't hear the rest of his warning as I take off with my new scrubs barely up my legs. The eyes of all the nurses at their station turn on me as I march past them, my gaze locked on the numbers of each cubicle as my heart pounds in my chest over what I'm about to find.

She's in a bay. That must be a good sign.

If the worst had happened, she'd be elsewhere right now.

My hands tremble and my palms sweat as I find the number I need, taking in the curtain that's closed around her.

Voices come from inside, but none of the words register. All I know is that they don't belong to her.

With my heart in my throat, I pull the curtain back and look inside.

I swear the entire world falls from beneath me at the sight of her laid out on a hospital bed, covered in stark white sheets, a line coming from the back of her hand and a mask covering her pale face.

"Jodie," I breathe, stumbling forward and only just catching myself on the edge of her bed.

"I'm sorry, sir, but we're in the middle—"

"Please," I beg. "I won't get in the way, I swear. I just need..."

I take her hand in mine, my heart shattering at how cold it is.

"Is she going to be o—" My word is cut off by the huge lump in my throat.

My eyes burn as I stare at her, taking in the dark stains covering her usually flawless skin and her closed eyes.

The doctor standing at the IV stand stares at me for a beat.

"Please, doc," I force out. "She's my girl. I pulled her from that building. I need to know—"

"From what we can tell, she's going to be fine."

All the air races from my lungs as a sob of pure relief falls from my lips. Someone pushes a chair behind me. My body seems to know what to do the second something touches the back of my knees and I fall into it, lowering down to press my brow to the back of Jodie's hand.

"Fuck, baby. I'm here. I'm right here."

With my head bowed and the realisation of just how easily this situation could have been different right now, I lose the battle with my emotions and red-hot tears fall free, landing on Jodie's dirty skin.

"Could we please have her details? We need to call her next of kin."

"Jodie Walker. Her mum is Joanne Walker," I force out, looking up at meeting the eyes of the tired-looking doctor. "I'd offer you her number, but my phone is fu—"

"We can get it," he assures me, holding my stare.

My stomach knots, able to read the hesitation in his eyes.

"You shouldn't—"

"Joanne won't have a problem with it," I say, hoping like fuck it's the truth.

His mouth opens to say something when we're joined by someone else. Theo's presence makes the doctor's eyes widen in shock.

"Mr. Cirillo," he growls in greeting. "To what do we owe this pleasure?"

I look between the two of them as the air crackles around us.

The other nurse backs out slowly without saying a word.

"Something tells me that you're going to be run off your feet tonight, Richard. I suggest you go and make yourself busy and leave us to look after our own," Theo suggests, the tone of his voice not allowing any space for argument.

"Right," Richard mutters.

"Does Jodie need any more treatment?" he asks, moving closer to the bed and coming to a stop at the end, as if he's about to lift her notes and read them for himself.

"Aside from smoke inhalation, we've stitched a couple of the deeper lacerations and given her some pain relief. We're waiting to send her for an x-ray to ensure nothing is broken, but I'm confident it's all surface injuries. She's been very lucky. A few more minutes and the smoke could have caused some serious damage."

"Thank you, Richard. We appreciate it. If she's going to need admitting, we'll require her to be sent up to the Cirillo ward."

"Of course. I'll get that arranged."

"Thank you. You're possibly going to have another patient coming through with the name of Sara Ashcroft. We're going to need the best team you've got on her."

"Has she been brought in yet?"

"We don't know," I say when Theo looks at me for confirmation. "She was in the building with Jodie.

When we left, the firefighters were still working to get her out."

"I'll see what I can find out."

Theo nods once and stands aside to let Richard out.

"You're welcome," Theo says with an amused grin from the end of my girl's bed.

"Prick," I mutter lightly.

"She's going to be okay, Tobes. You did that. You saved her."

I sigh, not feeling as heroic about that statement as I'm sure Theo thinks I should.

"She asked me to go back for Sara," I say quietly.

"Bro, the building was a wreck and the fire crew turned up. You did nothing wrong."

"But—"

"No, Toby. You did all you could," he assures me.

"You weren't even there."

"I didn't need to be. There's no doubt in my mind that you'd have run straight back in there for her if you could. You let the experts do their job. You saved your girl, and yourself."

I nod, fully aware of all of that but feeling the guilt gnawing at me nonetheless.

"You're a good person, Toby. And a fucking fantastic soldier. No one can question what you've done tonight."

I shake my head, resting back in the chair but keeping my hand locked around Jodie's as she sleeps.

Theo moves, squeezing my shoulder in support

before pulling another chair over and sitting down beside me.

"How are Archer and his boys?"

"Still breathing, as far as I know. But as I said to Richard, this place could be busy tonight."

"That's gonna fucking cost Archer."

"And us," he agrees.

"Who knew that the biggest cost of war was paying off the hospital staff instead of the loss of lives," I mutter, my voice low and pained.

Theo chuckles darkly, but it's forced.

"The rest of our guys?"

"No news is good news, right?"

I let out a heavy sigh. "I need this shit to stop for a bit, man. I need to take a fucking breath."

"No. What you need is to kill that motherfucker in our basement so you can focus on a future with your girl.

3

JODIE

Theo's words about killing the man they've got locked up for his crimes isn't the first thing I really wanted to hear. But then again, I didn't really have any plans to experience everything I did tonight... last night... either.

My head spins as I lay still, listening to Toby and Theo as they continue their conversation. If the situation were different, I might make it known that I was awake, aware of Toby explaining his wishes for me to be able to make a choice about what happens to the man with whom I, unfortunately, share DNA with. That thought makes my chest ache. The pain of losing the man I always looked up to despite the fact that I thought he had no input in my creation almost hurts more than the rest of my body. Almost.

Every single inch of me pulsates in agony. If I didn't know better, I'd think I'd been hit by a freaking articulated lorry. Unfortunately, one sharp breath in makes my lungs burn like a fucking bitch, reminding me exactly what did happen before I embark on a coughing fit that brings tears to my eyes.

"Fuck, Jodie. Baby, it's okay."

Toby is right there, gently pulling my fingers away from the oxygen mask I'm trying to rip from my face, calming me down, and placing it back over my mouth, allowing me to get the benefits.

His large warm hands hold the sides of my head, his dark, haunted eyes staring down into mine.

He doesn't say anything. He doesn't need to. I feel every single word that is right on the tip of his tongue.

"I'm gonna leave you to it. See what I can go find out." I startle at the deep rumble of Theo's voice, too lost in Toby's gaze to have heard him move. "I'm glad you're okay, Jodie," he says sincerely before gently squeezing my foot in support and disappearing from the bay.

The air crackles between the two of us even despite my lightheadedness. Our connection is like a living, breathing thing that's impossible to forget about or ignore, even when we're apart.

"I thought I'd fucking lost you, baby," Toby finally says, lowering his brow until he touches mine. It's an awkward move with the mask between us, but he makes it work. And it's not like I'm going to argue. I need this connection—his strength—just as much as I think he needs it from me.

"Same," I whisper. Attempting just that one word

feels like knives ripping up my throat, and I squeeze my eyes closed for a beat.

"What's wrong, baby? What do you need?" Toby pulls back, allowing me to see the cubicle I'm in.

My eyes lock on a jug sitting on an over-the-bed table and I stare at it.

"Drink? You need a drink?"

I nod, not willing to try speaking again until I've at least swallowed some soothing, cool water.

He quickly pours a cupful before lowering my mask and pressing a straw to my parched lips.

Relief floods me as it relieves the burning of my throat a little.

"Better?" he asks when I finally release the straw.

"Y-yeah," I manage to get out a little easier. A small smile twitches at the corners of Toby's lips before he places the cup back down.

A gasp rips past my lips at the state of his arm.

"Toby," I breathe, reaching out to gently brush my fingertips over the bandage.

"I'm fine, Demon. Just a little scratch." He winks teasingly, but it does nothing to lessen the concern that's pressing down so heavy on my chest it's making it hard to breathe.

My eyes shift, taking in the scratches, blood, dirt, and soot that cover his bare torso and then the blue scrubs he's wearing.

"You should be in bed."

His smile widens a little farther. "You're right, I should. Can you move?"

Guessing where this is going, I just about manage to shift over a few inches. Thankfully, it's enough, and only a second later, Toby climbs on the bed with me, laying on his side so he can watch me as if he's afraid I'm about to vanish into a puff of smoke.

"Y-you s-saved me," I force out through the emotion that clogs my throat and burns my eyes.

"Always, baby. There's nothing I wouldn't do to protect you."

Unable to fight the tears pooling against my lashes, two spill over, racing down my cheeks and soaking into the thin elastic strap of the mask.

"Everything is going to be okay, Jodie," he says sincerely.

My brow furrows as I think back to the horrors we experienced before reality slams into me.

"Sara?"

I know the answer long before Toby manages to say any words. I see it in the way his eyes darken, the way his gaze shifts from mine for the briefest moment.

"I don't know, baby. As I carried you out, the firefighters rushed in. I didn't see her... I don't know..."

"Oh God," I whisper, my hand coming up to cover my mouth but finding the damn plastic mask in the way as my tears begin to flow faster.

"Jesse," I cry, my heart shattering all over again. If she didn't make it, if they didn't find her... It'll kill him. It'll... "Fuck."

"We don't know anything. I got the guys to find him. Last I heard, he was heading toward where you were. As soon as Theo finds anything out, he'll tell us, okay? He's got the doctors and nurses in this place in his back pocket."

Well, I guess that's something.

Reaching out, Toby wipes my tears away with his dirty thumbs.

"Just get some rest, Demon. I can't cope with you in this place any longer than necessary."

"Have you called Mum?"

"My phone is fucked. They're doing it though," he says, casting a look at the curtain, indicating the people beyond.

I nod, unable to respond through the lump that's only growing in my throat as I think of Mum's reaction when she discovers I'm in the hospital. This is going to kill her. But what can I do?

"Is Stella here?" I ask, having a vague memory of her voice tonight.

"Yeah, baby. She's safe."

I want to ask if she'd go and get Mum, or even Maria, but my eyes get too heavy and I drift off before I manage to form any words.

The first thing I notice when the fog begins to lift once more is that the heat of Toby's body is still warming mine, and his fingers are still tightly twisted with those of my free hand.

I was sure that he'd have been given little choice but to get down by now. But then, I guess it's easy when we're in our little bubble to forget who he is and the kind of power he holds over this part of the city. I'm sure demanding he gets to stay by my side while I'm resting is nothing in the grand scheme of things.

A whimper across the room catches my attention, and I force my eyes open.

"Mum," I croak, seeing her sitting there, catching her tears with what looks like an already-sodden tissue.

"Jodie," she gasps, jumping out of the chair faster than I'm sure she has in years.

I try to pull my hand from Toby's so I can hold her, but I find it locked in his grasp. When I glance over, I find he's out cold beside me.

Lifting the hand with the cannula in, I pull the mask from my face so Mum can hear me.

"I'm so sorry," I breathe, my eyes burning once more.

"Oh baby, it's not your fault. You couldn't have known." She takes my face in her hands.

I shake my head. "I know. But getting that call... you must have been terrified."

"You're okay. You're here and you're going to be fine."

"Do you know anything about Sara?"

Her shoulders drop. "I don't, sweetie. I'm sorry."

I fight to force the lump in my throat down, but it won't shift an inch.

Toby shifts beside me, his fingers tightening on mine a second before he snuggles closer to me.

"Despite the circumstances, you two look cute," Mum says softly.

"Thanks, Joanne. I appreciate it," Toby whispers roughly, making me jump and Mum laugh.

"I hear you saved my girl," Mum says once Toby has woken a little more and opened his eyes. "Thank you." The sincerity in her voice makes me lose the fight with my tears once more. Her warm hands leave my face, but she doesn't move away, instead taking my cannulated hand in both of hers.

"Anytime. How are you feeling?" he asks, turning his attention to me.

"I think the pain relief has kicked in," I admit.

"I think they're going to move you soon," Mum says, obviously having found out everything while we were sleeping.

"I've got to stay?" I complain.

"Just for the night. They need to monitor your oxygen levels after the smoke inhalation."

"I won't leave your side, baby."

Twisting around slowly, I look into his heavy eyes. "I'm not sure you'll be allow—"

"You don't need to worry about that," he says, brushing his lips lightly against mine as if my mum isn't standing right there. "I'm not letting you out of my sight."

Suddenly, the curtain is pulled back with a flourish and a friendly looking older nurse bounds into the room with a massive smile on her face.

"Right then, Miss Jodie Walker. It's time to get you somewhere a little more comfortable. Although," she says, her eyes alight with amusement as she looks between the two of us snuggled together, "it looks to me like you've already got it pretty good there, girly."

Toby barks a laugh while my cheeks burn and the nurse's eyes drop to his body.

"Once you're back up and on your feet, you could wash laundry on those abs of his."

"Oh my God," I mutter, my face burning hotter.

"I'll let her do whatever she wants once she's at full health again," Toby confesses.

"Stop," I plead. "Stop it now."

But when I look over at Mum, she doesn't seem to care. She's too busy chuckling with the nurse.

Traitor.

"Don't look at me like that, sweetheart. She's got a point." Mum quirks a brow.

"Where are you taking me?" I ask with a sigh, my throat burning more with every word.

"Up to the Cirillo ward. We'll look after you like royalty up there, my dear."

"Damn right she will," Toby growls, finally sitting up and swinging his legs off the bed, albeit slowly.

"Grab everything you need and we'll get on our way. I've got two strapping porters outside waiting, although they've got nothing on your boy."

My eyes follow Toby as he reaches for the top he's been supplied with and pulls it over his head. But he soon comes to a grinding halt when he has to lift his bandaged arm through it.

"You want some help?" Mum offers.

"Nah. I can cope without. I like giving the nurses some excitement." He winks at the nurse I now know is called Claudia thanks to her name tag.

"Please ignore him," I urge in my croaky voice.

"Girl, he's the best thing I've seen all year." Her smile is so full of love and compassion, I can't help wishing that she was my grandmother. I've got a feeling life would never be dull with her as part of the family.

Claudia fiddles about with my drip and gets me ready to move.

"How long does she need to have that for?" Mum asks, gesturing to the bag of whatever has been slowly working its way into my body.

"There only seems to be about thirty minutes or so left."

"Good," I say. I might feel like crap, and every single inch of my body might still be aching and heavy, but there's no way I want to be connected to that thing for any longer than necessary.

Claudia writes a few things on the chart hanging on the end of my bed before she pulls the curtain all the way around, revealing the two porters she promised me who quickly descend on my bed.

"Are you okay to walk, young man? I understand you've been stitched up like a tapestry."

Concern for Toby sits heavy in my stomach. I've seen the bandage on the back of his arm, but what else am I missing?

"I'm fine, Demon. Just worry about getting out of here so I can look after you properly."

"Oh, he's a nurse as well. If I were forty years younger," Claudia teases.

"Looks like you've got some competition, Jojo," Mum adds as Claudia puts my mask back in place just as my bed is wheeled out of its space.

The second we turn the corner, we find a small, familiar crowd blocking the corridor.

"Jodie," Stella cries, rushing forward, quickly followed by the others. "Are you okay?"

"Yeah." I nod. "I'm okay."

"Where are you going?" she asks in a panic as if I might be lying.

"Just going up to the ward overnight as a precaution," Claudia answers for me. "Visiting hours are—"

"Are always," Toby interrupts. "We don't pay for that ward for nothing."

"Sara?" I breathe, desperate for some news.

Stella swallows thickly, and my heart drops into my feet.

"They've taken her straight to intensive care."

"Oh God," I gasp, and Stella dives for my hand as Toby takes the other. "Is she..."

"We don't know anything yet, but it doesn't look good. I'm so sorry, Jodie."

Ripping my eyes from hers, I focus on the pale wall ahead as I try to process what she just said. But it's like my body has entirely shut down, refusing to accept it.

"We'll keep you up to date, we promise."

"Is Jesse here?" My voice might be rough from the smoke inhalation, but it sounds even worse now.

"Yes. He's upstairs."

"Go be with him. I know you don't know him but—"

"We will." Her glassy eyes lift from mine and focus on Toby. "Look after our girl, Bro."

My heart swells at her words, that I've been accepted into their family just like that. On the outside, they might look like a fucked-up bunch of reprobates, but on the inside, there's nothing but love, support, and endless friendship. It's really quite incredible to be around such a close-knit group.

"You got it."

Seb wraps his arms around Stella and pulls her back against his chest while the other guys all offer me a smile of encouragement.

"Where are the twins?" I ask, unable to summon the brainpower to find their names.

"Gone to see their mum. Alex got grazed by a bullet, apparently." My lips twitch in amusement. These big bad mafia soldiers have gone home to have Mummy clean up their boo-boos. "He's not a big fan of his own blood. Or hospitals. It's just easier if Gianna cleans him up."

"How very brave of him," Mum deadpans with a snigger.

"We all have our vices." Toby shrugs. His eyes find mine, and I don't need him to tell me what his is. It's the whole reason for us colliding in the first place.

Our journey up to the ward is mostly in silence. Toby's hand is locked in mine the entire way as my heart continues to ache from the news Stella delivered.

I should have been expecting it. Hell, I was expecting it, but that doesn't mean it didn't cut through me like a million knives.

A sob rips from my throat as Mum pushes a set of doors open for the porters, thinking of Jesse sitting somewhere in this building feeling utterly hopeless as the love of his life's future hangs in the balance.

"Theo has the best doctors in the city for her," Toby assures me. "She's one of us, just like you are."

4

TOBY

My thigh burns as I drop to my knees to help Jodie push her feet into her boots.

"Toby," she grumbles, her voice still rough from the smoke. I know it's wrong, but every time I hear her raspy growl, it hits me straight in the dick. It makes me feel like an arsehole because I know she's suffering, but I can't help it. "I'm more than capable."

"I know. Humour me."

She glares down at me, but I don't let up.

Yeah, it hurts, but I know she's sporting a couple of bandages that match mine. Hers might hide fewer stitches than I needed, but that's not the point. I want to do this. I need to do this.

It's the exact reason I told Joanne that I'd be the one escorting her home from the hospital. I might have caved about letting her go home and not insisting that I lock her up in my flat, but I wasn't being talked out of this.

"Hard-headed idiot," she mutters under her breath as I pull her boot on and push to stand. Slowly. "Don't expect any sympathy if you rip those stitches," she warns.

"Wouldn't dream of it, Demon. You ready?"

I fucking well know I am.

After a night curled up in a hospital bed with her, with doctors and nurses coming in and out like the room had a freaking revolving door on it, I'm more than ready to go somewhere quiet, wrap my arms around my girl and let her get the rest she needs.

Her bottom lip trembles at the prospect of our first stop before heading back to Joanne's.

I told her it wasn't necessary, that she didn't need any more pain on top of everything else, but unsurprisingly, she was insistent on visiting the ICU before we left.

Sara shouldn't be having visitors aside from her next of kin—her parents, whom she hasn't seen since the day she announced she was moving in with Jesse —which is a fucking joke, if you ask me. But thankfully, we've managed to buy our way around those rules, allowing Jesse in with her whenever he wants, although he wisely disappeared when her parents did turn up for a visit this morning.

Jodie thinks that if she were awake, she'd actually ban them from being here at all, but while she's still critical there's not much she or Jesse can do about it.

"She's going to be okay, isn't she? Tell me she's going to make it."

Wrapping my hand around the back of her neck, I press my brow to hers, staring her deep in the eyes.

"They're doing everything they can."

Jodie's eyelids lower, and as they close, a lone tear falls from the corner of her eye.

The sight of it physically hurts me.

I wish there was something I could do. I wish I could wave some sort of magic wand and fix everything. But I can't. We just have to put our faith in the professionals and Sara's strength.

"Come on." I take her hand in one of mine and the small bag of things we accumulated during our overnight stay in the other.

With a heavy sigh, Jodie falls into step beside me. Silently, we make our way out of the Cirillo ward with a few grateful nods toward the nurses at the station before we head toward the ICU.

I tap a code into the pad beside the door that allows us the access we shouldn't have and push the door open for Jodie.

She trembles in my hold as I wrap my arm around her shoulders and guide her toward where I understand Sara is.

As we round the corner, we find Jesse sitting hunched over in a chair beside the door that leads to her room.

All the air rushes from Jodie's lungs and she rushes forward.

Jesse glances up just before she reaches him, and my own breath catches in my throat at the wrecked expression on his face.

It's the exact reminder I don't need about just how close I came to losing Jodie yesterday. If I didn't find her as quickly as I did, if the wall she was sitting against came down just a few seconds earlier...

A shudder rips down my spine, but it's hard to feel grateful for what I still have when his entire life is falling apart.

He wraps Jodie in a bear hug and tucks his face into the crook of her neck as his entire body shakes with his sobs. My heart breaks for the poor guy.

Walking over, I lower my arse to the chair beside him and place my hand on his shoulder, letting him know that he's got our support.

They stay in their embrace for the longest time while they hold each other together. As much as it pains me that I can't be the one to do that for Jodie right now, I understand, and Jesse needs this just as much as she does. I have no idea if Sara has any other friends or family aside from her shitty parents, so this might be it for her close support network. It makes me appreciate the family I have around me that little bit more again.

We might be all kinds of fucked up, but I know for a fact that when shit hits the fan, in whatever form, they'll be there for me.

My phone buzzes in my pocket, and it's just proof of how true my previous thoughts were. Seb and Stella turned up sometime after midnight last night with a brand-new phone for me. Not only that, but Theo had installed a backup of my broken one, so it was like I never lost it.

Stella: How's Jodie?

A smile twitches at my lips. It's the third time she's asked since we had little choice but to give up on the idea of sleeping this morning.

Toby: We're with Jesse.

Stella: Any news?

Toby: Nope. They're still saying it's just a time thing.

Stella: Jesus. I can't even imagine. I wish we could have done more.

Guilt tugs at my inside. If I went for Sara first, maybe I could have got them both out. If I was two minutes earlier. If I could have run a little faster...

All the what-ifs tumble around my head on repeat, but none of them help. It's too late to think about all the things that could have been different from the night before.

This is what happened, and this is now our

reality. Waiting to find out if Jodie is going to have to say goodbye to someone else she loves.

When they finally part, Jesse lifts his arm and wipes his face with his sleeve to clear the tears.

"Has there been any change?" Jodie asks hopefully.

He shakes his head. "Nothing."

Jodie grips his bloody, busted-up hand and holds it tight.

"She's stronger than this, Jesse. She's going to come back to us."

He sniffles, pushing his other equally dirty hand into his hair and dragging it back from his head.

"You should go and get yourself checked out," she urges him, just like I know the others have since they first found him up here.

He's got a bit of someone's old shirt tied around his arm to try to stem the blood flow from what I hope is just a graze and not a bullet wound. I mean, it seems to have worked because there's no fresh blood, but still. His face is black and blue, and his clothes are a mess.

The guys brought him a bag of everything he might need when they arrived with our things earlier today which is sitting at his feet.

"I'm fine," he says hollowly.

"Jesse," Jodie sighs. "Sara needs you more than ever right now. She isn't going to want to wake up to you looking like this."

"I'm not leaving her," he states, fear darkening his eyes.

"Jesse, please," Jodie begs.

"Go up to the room we just left. It has a private bathroom. You can have a shower, wash all that shit off you," I add.

"But—"

"We won't leave. And the second we're allowed inside, we'll be right by her side," Jodie assures him.

A million arguments are on the tip of his tongue as to why he shouldn't do this, but with one more pleading look from my girl, he finally concedes.

After giving him quick directions, he reluctantly grabs the bag and heads off once he's confident we'll call him if anything changes.

It's not until he's gone and the sound of a door closing behind him fills the silent corridor that Jodie speaks.

"He's not going to cope if—" She bites back the end of that sentence, not willing to say the words out loud.

"He will. You both will. Because if that happens, then it's what she would want."

"Fuck," Jodie breathes, leaning forward and resting her elbows on her knees. "This is so fucking hard. Losing Joe and... yeah... that was a shock. But it was done, it was quick. It was anything but painless, but this... it's not knowing. Fuck, it's heartbreaking."

"I know, baby." I know it's not the same, not by a long shot, but I felt a little of the uselessness, the desperation she's feeling now every time I sat with Mum while she was having treatment. She was with me though, talking to me, aware of everything. But still, we had no idea if it was going to work, if we were living on false hope.

It's nothing compared to Sara's situation now, but I get it, I really do.

The door beside us opens and a nurse walks out, quickly followed by a doctor and then another nurse. Their expressions are anything but hopeful, and a little bit of me dies inside and I've never met the girl. I can only imagine how it affects Jodie.

My girl hops to her feet faster than she should with her stitches and injuries. "Are there any updates? Improvements?" she begs, and my heart aches when they all turn to look at her with grim expressions.

"I'm sorry, no. She's critical but stable. She hasn't improved, but equally, she's not declining."

All the air rushes from Jodie's lungs, and I pull her into my arms.

"I wish I could be more helpful. We've done everything we can. It's up to her now."

"Can we go in and see her?" Jodie's voice trembles as she tries to fight the emotion swarming inside her.

"You can," the doctor says, his eyes locking with mine in warning.

"Where's Jesse?" one of the nurses asks.

"Jodie convinced him to go and get cleaned up," I explain.

"How did you manage that? We've been trying since the second he arrived. Hasn't even let us anywhere near that damn wound."

"My girl's got magical powers," I say, trying to force some lightness into the situation.

"You guys had better get in there then and see what you can do," one of the nurses says.

Jodie rushes toward the door as I catch the eyes of the doctor who is still lingering, I assume to answer any questions we have, but Jodie doesn't seem interested in the reality of Sara's situation. She just wants to be near her.

"Thank you for everything you're doing," I say as Jodie slips into the room, her loud gasp of shock filtering down to us.

"You're welcome. But I really think it's important you try to all prepare for the worst here."

I nod, taking his stark warning on board as I look toward the door.

"Go and support her. We'll be right out here," the nurse urges with a soft, sympathetic smile.

Turning my back on the three of them, I rush forward in search of my girl.

I find her standing at the end of Sara's bed with her arms wrapped around herself, as if she's hoping that will be enough to hold her together.

Her heavy breathing can easily be heard over the

beeping and whirring of the machines that surround her friend, keeping her alive.

Wrapping my own arms around her, I rest my chin on her shoulder.

"I'm right here, baby," I whisper in her ear as my eyes take in Sara.

She looks... peaceful. She's got pipes and tubes coming from her and a big white bandage on her cheek probably covering either a burn or a laceration, but other than that, she just looks... at peace.

"She's not going to make it, is she?" Jodie says quietly, her voice strangely steady.

"I don't know, baby."

"This probably sounds stupid, and I hope I'm wrong, but I kinda feel like she's already gone."

My heart pounds at her words, wishing they weren't true for both her and Jesse. But I fear she might just know what she's talking about.

The two of them have been close since they were young kids. They obviously shared a connection.

"Come sit." Tugging her to the side of Sara's bed, I lower down, placing her on my lap. She cuddles into me, although she keeps her eyes on her friend.

Her body trembles with pent-up emotion, but she doesn't do or say anything else, and I allow her the time and the silence—as much as we can get of it with the machines working away.

I have no idea how long we sit there. I guess it can't be all that long, because there's no way Jesse would leave for longer than necessary.

When the door quietly opens and he steps inside, he looks better. A hell of a lot better than he did earlier. Although, it's still easy to see the agony in his eyes. Just like Jodie, his grief is already etched into his every feature. It makes me wonder if he senses the same thing she does.

"Hey," Jodie breathes, uncurling herself from my lap. "Do you feel—" She cuts herself off, aware that there's no way a shower and a change of clothes could actually make him feel better.

"Clean?" he grunts. "Yeah, I guess. Anything?"

Jodie shakes her head while Jesse studies her reaction to this situation.

"You feel it too, don't you?" he says quietly, turning his attention back to Sara again.

Jodie climbs off my lap and goes to him, throwing her arms around his waist and resting her head on his chest while he clings to her as if she's his lifeline.

W e stay with him until a nurse pokes her head in to say that Sara's parents are on their way, and I'm forced to watch as both Jesse and Jodie say goodbye to her.

The lump in my throat is so fucking huge I can barely breathe as Jodie lowers over her friend and presses her lips to her brow, whispering all kinds of sweet things to her as Jesse falls apart.

I've been through some shit, but this is by far the most gut-wrenching.

After a few more seconds, Jodie stands and takes one long final look at Sara before turning to me and striding toward the door with her head held high.

Her strength astounds me as she slips past and steps out of the room.

I quickly follow but come up short when I find her staring at three guys all sitting patiently in a row on the chairs we were on not so long ago.

Jodie's brow wrinkles, having not met the scary-arse motherfuckers before. But something tells me that if she gets on with Jesse, it won't be hard for her to see something softer in each of them.

Each of them is sporting the evidence of the brutality they endured from the night before. Swollen eyes, split lips and bruised jaws are probably the least of the injuries they walked away with. But they're here, and that speaks volumes for how much they care about Jesse.

"Doukas," Archer says, clearly not expecting to find me here.

"Archer, Dax, Jace, this is Jodie. Sara's friend," I say as an introduction. "Jesse is still in there."

"Good to finally meet you, Jodie," Archer says. His eyes twinkle with amusement, but it doesn't show in his voice. The situation is too dire for that.

"How's our boy doing?" Dax asks.

"He's—" Jodie's words are cut off when the door closes behind us and the man in question joins us.

"Fuck, man."

All three of them are out of their seats and surrounding Jesse in a heartbeat.

Dax wraps his arms around him, holding him upright as the other two offer their sympathies.

"Guys," Jodie says, cutting through their moment. "We need to get out of here before—"

"Fuck, yeah." Jesse scrubs his hand down his face before rolling his shoulders back. "Her parents are at the main doors. We need to move."

The guys nod, and Jesse leads the way in the opposite direction to the ward entrance that he must have been shown to the last time this happened.

In less than ten minutes, we find ourselves in the hospital restaurant.

We move to follow them, but my concern for my girl is only growing. She's exhausted. I understand that she wants to support Jesse right now, but she also needs to look after herself.

"I should get you home, baby," I say, pulling her to a stop as the others head for coffee.

"But... Jesse," she argues.

Jesse steps up to us—I hadn't realised that he hadn't followed Archer.

"You should go and rest, Jodie. I promise I'll call you the second anything happens."

"I don't want to leave you here alone."

"I'm not. I've got those three bellends to keep me company." He forces a smile in the hope of convincing her.

She looks between the two of us, torn between what her body needs and where her heart needs her to be.

"I can get you back here in ten minutes from your mum's house," I assure her.

It takes her a few seconds but eventually, she nods in agreement. And after a long hug and hushed conversation with Jesse, he heads back over to his boys and I'm finally able to take my girl home.

5

JODIE

I feel nothing as I sit in Toby's BMW and he drives out of the hospital toward where I know Mum is going to be anxiously waiting for me.

With one hand firmly on the wheel, his other is locked on mine. His silent support means everything to me right now. I'm pretty sure I'd have drowned already if it weren't for him.

"Are you hungry?" he asks quietly so as not to scare me.

"Uh..." My throat burns once more and I swallow, hoping that it eases soon. That and the pain that shoots through my chest every time I suck in a breath. "Not really, but if you wanna hit up McDonald's, I could probably use a strawberry milkshake."

"Sounds like a plan, baby."

He shoots a left instead of taking the right that would lead us home. We're through the drive-through in only minutes and I'm clutching my ice-cold milkshake in my hands as if it might magically fix my life while a bag of food for Toby warms my feet.

Mum is at the front door the second we pull up. I don't even get to lift my hand to attempt to let myself out before she's there, doing it for me and taking everything from me.

Toby joins her in only seconds, pulling me from the car as if I'm made of glass and wrapping his arm around my shoulders, guiding me toward the house behind Mum.

"I've set the living room up so you should be comfortable. Your bed has new sheets and I've—"

"Mum," I stop her, resting my hand on her forearm. "Everything is perfect. It's just a little smoke inhalation. I'm okay," I assure her, ignoring the pain from the cuts and bruises that litter my body.

I was lucky, unlike Sara, that I somehow managed to stay away from the worst of the flames. The only burns I have are superficial and will be gone in days.

If by some miracle Sara does survive this, I fear that her life is going to look very, very different.

I may not have wanted to hear the details of her condition—the facts are just too much to process right now. But I do know that the burns to her hands and arms could have life-changing effects.

My heart aches at the thought of her surviving but not being able to create. From as early as I can remember, all she's wanted to do is draw, paint, anything that involved making marks on a page or a canvas. I can't imagine she'd want a life without that.

I let out a heavy sigh, and Mum pulls me into her arms. But I don't cry. I can't. I think I've run out of tears at long last.

"Mum," I sigh, emotion clogging my throat when she ushers me into the living room to find it exactly like it used to be when I was a little girl having a sleepover with my friends.

With Sara.

The sofa is covered in pillows and the spare duvet, there are candles flickering, drinks and snacks cover the coffee table, and she's even dug out some of my favourite old-school chick flicks that I used to love as a kid.

"Throwback to when things were easier?" Mum offers with a sad smile.

"Thank you," I whisper, unable to get any more words out.

"Now, you two go and get yourselves comfortable and I'll leave you to rest. But I'll only be in the kitchen baking, so if you need anything just shout, okay?"

"You don't need to," I say, knowing that she's going to go and cook up a storm of my favourite treats, most of which I'm probably not going to be able to eat for a few days with the state of my throat.

"Trust me, baby. I do. Stella and Maria are going to pop around later and take some of it to everyone else, to Jesse and his boys."

My eyes burn as I stare at her.

"It's the least I can do."

"Thank you, Joanne. I'm sure everyone will really appreciate it," Toby says gratefully.

With one lingering look at me, Mum slips out of the room. When I turn back to Toby, he's dragged his hoodie off, leaving him in just a fitted t-shirt that's damn near moulded to every toned inch of his body, and he's pulled the duvet from the sofa.

"Come on, baby. You need to rest."

I'm too exhausted to do anything but follow his orders.

I curl up with my head on the pillow Mum left on the armrest while Toby falls into the middle seat and pulls my legs over his lap.

He places his bag of food on top of them, the heat of it warming me through as he rips into it and throws a few chips into his mouth.

My eyes drop when his tongue sneaks out to lick a grain of salt or two off his bottom lip, and my stomach somersaults. It's the first time I've felt anything close to normal since I had coffee with Bri yesterday. Shit. How was that only yesterday? It feels like a year has passed since then.

"Want some?" he offers, noticing my attention.

I shake my head.

"Ah, so it's not the chips you want," he teases. "You get better and you can have every inch of me, baby."

My mouth waters at the prospect. It's been... too damn long.

After he let me go last week to get my head together, there was never any question in my mind that I would end up back at his door. But I also knew that I needed to make the most of the time and space he'd given me.

What we have... the connection we share... I think it's it.

No. I know it is.

But I also know that there was too much bullshit surrounding us for me to fully dive in headfirst until I'd processed everything.

Well, that was my opinion then.

Now, having almost died in a fire that has potentially claimed Sara's life, I've got to say I've found a bit of perspective.

"That sounds like a promise I might just hold you to," I whisper, my eyes already getting heavy now I'm lying down.

"I damn well hope so," he says, squeezing my thigh lightly. "I know it's probably not what you want to hear right now—there are other more important things—but fuck, baby. I missed you so bad."

Having lost my fight with my eyes, I reach out, searching for his hand, needing a connection with him.

"Me too, baby. Can you promise me something?" I ask sleepily.

"Anything."

"Never let me go again."

W hen I woke after that desperately needed nap, I was burning up. It only took me about three seconds to discover why. Toby had managed to slot himself between me and the back of the sofa. Both his injured arm and leg were wrapped around me, pinning my body as tightly to his as possible, and we had the duvet up to our chins.

But as much as I might have been sweating in my leggings and hoodie with my very own koala hugging me like I'm its favourite tree, I wasn't going anywhere.

We came too close to losing each other for good to worry about being a bit hot.

So instead, I focus on thoughts of the guy behind me and snuggle my head back into the pillow.

That was three days ago.

Three days of sleeping, healing, crying, and nothing but the heartbreaking feeling of utter uselessness and desperation that comes along with our situation.

I'm fine. I get a little stronger and my lungs seem to work better every day. I can even swallow now without wincing, which is good.

Toby's wounds are healing too, and the bruising

that seemed to cover every inch of his body is beginning to fade.

But as the visible evidence of our ordeal disappears, the pain that still lashes at my chest while Sara remains in the same state in her room in the ICU is about as unbearable as it was the day she was admitted.

There is still little hope. Every time I've visited or spoken to Jesse on the phone, the story is still the same. Keep praying. But they're worried that the longer this goes on, the less and less chance there is of her body pulling through.

I'm trying to remain positive, but I'm finding it harder and harder to hold on to. I know Jesse is the same. I see it in the deep lines of his face every time I see him.

He still hasn't left the hospital. He'll go as far as the restaurant when Sara's parents turn up, but that's it.

My heart aches as I think of his home. Of the one place that he might feel some kind of comfort right now. But it's gone. Every single thing Sara and Jesse had went up in flames in their flat. All their memories. Sara's artwork, her business.

I'm fighting back the tears once more when footsteps thunder up the stairs and a dark shadow fills my doorway.

"You nearly ready, baby?" Toby asks softly, his eyes dropping to my body as I sit at my dressing table in just my underwear.

"Yeah." Blinking away my tears, I quickly swipe some mascara onto my lashes. Brave, I know, but I want to walk out of the house in a few minutes looking as put together as I possibly can.

Pushing from my stool, I walk over to the bed and pick up the two dresses I've left out.

"Which one?" I ask, holding them up for him.

"You mean staying as you are isn't an option?" Toby quirks a brow at me, his eyes continuing to eat up my body instead of looking at the fabric hanging from my fingers.

"We're going to your parents' for lunch. No, it's not an option." I roll my eyes, and he finally glances at his options.

"Pink one," he states before pulling them both from my hold, taking my face in his hands and brushing his lips against mine.

"Why the pink one?" I ask, needing to know his reason for choosing my favourite out of the two before I let him distract me with his drugging kisses.

"Because." Kiss. "It reminds me." Kiss. "Of our first." Kiss. "Night." Kiss.

I can't help but laugh. "So we're going to be sitting around your parents' dining table while you remember nailing me in Hades?" I ask.

"Something like that," he confesses, taking a step closer so I have no choice but to feel what just one thought of that night does to him—or it might be the sight of me in my black lace underwear, to be fair.

His tongue plunges past my lips, seeking my

own out to play as one of his hands skims down my body, being careful of the fresh bandages he put on me after my shower not so long ago until he's squeezing my arse and ensuring there is zero space between us.

A deep growl rumbles in the back of his throat as our kiss deepens.

We haven't done any more than this since I was released from the hospital, and while I love that he's taking care of me and ensuring my wounds are healing as they should, I'm damn near desperate for the escape his body can offer me.

Now more than ever.

Losing Dad and Joe was hard, learning the truth about them even harder. But this unknown with Sara? It's unbearable, and I'd do just about anything to get out of my own head right now, even if just for a few minutes.

My hands slide down his sides until I connect with his waistband and I slip my fingers under the fabric of his shirt.

"Demon," he growls into our kiss as his skin pebbles from my touch, his muscles bunching as I work higher. "You're going to make us late."

I still for a beat before stepping back out of his arms.

"Well, we can't have that. Whatever would your mother think of me?" I say, putting on my most prim and proper voice as my eyes lock on to where his cock is trying to bust out of his trousers.

He chuckles, reaching down for my chosen dress.

"Rain check?" he asks, pushing his hand into his boxers to rearrange himself.

Without realising it, my own fingers curl as if I'm about to wrap my hand around his length. My breathing becomes more erratic and I bite down on my bottom lip.

"I'm sure we could be a few minutes late."

The most incredible smile lights up his face before he shakes his head at me.

"Demon," he says so quietly it sends a shiver racing down my spine. "Get dressed, and if you're a good girl at dinner, maybe I'll reward you for it later."

"Oh?" I breathe, my knickers getting embarrassingly wet at his words.

I love this. I love losing myself in him and, just for the briefest of moments, forgetting the rest of the world exists, that our problems are miles away.

"Stay at mine tonight," he says, watching my every movement as I step into my dress. "I'll bring you back in the morning before school. Stop," he demands abruptly when I move my hands to reach for the zip behind me. "Turn around. Let me."

Doing as I'm told, I pull my long hair over my shoulder a second before his heat at my back makes my skin prickle with awareness.

"Did I ever tell you that I love what you did with your hair," he whispers, his breath racing over my exposed neck. My nipples immediately pebble for him.

"N-no," I stutter.

"Well, I do. It's so fucking sexy."

His lips brush up the column of my neck before they come to rest just beneath my ear. His searing hot tongue laps at my skin a beat before he bites down lightly, his teeth grazing me in the most deliciously teasing way.

"Oh God," I moan, my head rolling farther to the other side to give him more space.

I jolt when his fingers brush down my spine painfully slowly. By the time he gets to the zip at the base of my spine, I'm aching for a whole new reason.

"I didn't think you wanted to be late," I groan as he continues planting wet kisses to my neck.

"Hmm..." he growls, nipping the patch of skin where my neck meets my shoulder.

Suddenly, my zip is pulled up and he takes a step back as if none of that ever happened and he hasn't left me burning up for him.

I turn around with a scowl on my face and meet his smirk.

"Not so funny when the shoe's on the other foot, hey Demon?"

"Dickhead," I mutter, throwing my hair back over my shoulder and going in search of a pair of shoes and a jacket.

"I'll take it. Just remember the deal."

"As if I'd be anything but a good girl at your parents' house."

"Stella's going to be there. I can only imagine the trouble she could get you into."

"I have no idea what you're talking about," I say innocently.

I might not know Stella's or any of Toby's friends—Nico aside— all that well yet, but one glance at his sister and I just knew she was my kind of girl. Even if the first time I met her I was running away from Toby with my heart in smithereens.

"Sure."

With my shoes on, I turn back toward him and take a step forward.

"Do I look okay?" I hold his eyes, but I can't deny the butterflies that are fluttering in my belly at the thought of an official meeting with his parents.

"Baby, you look incredible."

I smile at him, knowing that he's stretching the truth slightly. I don't think I've ever had to use so much concealer under my eyes. We might have had three days of doing nothing, but that doesn't mean I'm not still suffering the lingering effects of our nightmare.

A shy smile twitches at my lips as I reach for his hand. "Let's do this then."

I pull him from my bedroom before I give in to my nerves and tiredness. I need to do this. I need to get out of the house—other than going to see Sara, like I did this morning. I need to find some kind of normal life once again.

We say quick goodbyes to Mum, and I tell her that I'm going to spend the night with Toby and that I'll see her in the morning before we slip from the house.

"Wait," I say, turning back when reality smacks me upside the head. "I haven't packed a bag."

"You don't need anything."

"Toby, I need—"

"Nope," he interrupts, pressing me back against his car. "All you need is this sexy body," he says, trailing a finger up the centre of me until he hits my chin. "And this smart mouth." He traces my lips teasingly, but he never leans forward to kiss me like I want him to.

"But what about—"

"Do you trust me?" he implores bravely.

"I shouldn't."

"No, Demon. You probably shouldn't. But that doesn't mean you don't."

I bite down on my bottom lip as he stares down at me, waiting for my answer. An answer he already knows. He wouldn't be standing where he is, having spent the last few days attached to my side if I didn't trust him.

"I do," I confess.

"Then you have nothing else left to worry about."

"I'm about to officially meet your parents, I think I should have plenty to worry about."

"Mum already loves you," he says, pulling the passenger door open for me, but he quickly captures my chin in his grasp before I have a chance to slip inside. "Just like I do."

His eyes darken with his words. He's said similar things a few times over the past couple of days, but he's never said the actual words.

I know why. After I begged him not to say them before, he's afraid of scaring me off again. Of being the final thing that tips me over the edge into the dark pool of grief that's always waiting to pull me into its clutches.

But not this time.

The time we had apart was exactly what I needed, and to a point, I've managed to put things into their place in my mind. I'm finding even after the fire that I'm able to process everything a little easier.

If I hadn't had that time, that space, I have no idea how I would have coped with all this now.

It's like he knew, although unless he's a psychic then I think the probability of that being the case is thin. But he gave me exactly what I needed to be able to focus, to see what's really important. And right now, life is important. Living every moment to the fullest and grasping every opportunity by the balls is the most important thing.

"Me too," I confess for the first time.

All the air rushes from his lungs as his eyes blaze with fire.

"Fuck, Jodie. I—"

"We're going to be late," I say, ducking under his arm and dropping into the seat.

"Can't I just take you back to my place instead?" he mutters, sounding mostly serious.

"Absolutely not. Your mum is waiting."

"Fuck," he hisses, scrubbing his hand down his face.

His eyes are still smouldering when they meet mine once more.

"Demon," he breathes before closing my door and stalking around the front of the car.

He joins me and brings the engine to life before looking over at me.

"If I can't sink this boner before we step inside Mum and Galen's place and they notice, I just want to point out that it's entirely your fault," he states so seriously that I can't do anything but fall about laughing. "I'm glad one of us finds it funny," he mutters, tugging at his trousers before putting the car into drive and pulling out of his space.

6

TOBY

"Finally. What the hell made you two so late?" Stella barks the second Jodie and I walk into Galen's kitchen, her eyes alight with amusement as she pokes her tongue into her cheek.

"Getting ready takes a little longer when you're covered in bandages and bruises, Sis," I say. It's a low blow, I know but I can't help myself.

"Sure. That was totally the reason," she mutters, not looking even slightly embarrassed by her announcement.

"Please ignore my daughter, her mouth runs away with her more often than not."

"Really, Dad?" Stella snaps at Galen, who just smiles down at her.

"Jodie," he says, holding his hand out for my girl. "It's nice to finally meet the girl I've heard so much about." A wide smile lights up his face, but when I glance at Jodie, the blood seems to have drained from hers and her neck ripples with a harsh swallow.

"I-I'm... uh... not sure that's a good thing given the circumstances."

"Trust me, it's all good." He continues to smile before turning to me. "Son, it's good to see you looking better."

Galen, Damien and Evan had briefly stopped by the hospital to check in on us at some ungodly hour while Jodie was asleep. It was a relief to see the three of them standing and in one piece. I didn't expect Damien or Evan to jump into the middle of things in Lovell, but I was confident that Galen and Stefanos were probably involved.

"Is there any news on your friend, sweetie?" Mum asks, joining us with a fancy looking cocktail for both Jodie and Stella.

"Not yet. She's still critical but stable."

Mum sighs, unable to come up with anything useful to say. I get it, there is literally nothing to say that can make it any better.

"If you need anything—a lift up there or back to visit, anything—you just call us, okay?"

My heart swells at my mum's offer, at how easily she's accepted, no, embraced, Jodie into our lives despite the obvious. It means everything to me that the person she is hasn't been tainted by the blood that's running through her veins.

"So what's for dinner? I'm starving," Seb

announces, stealing Stella's glass and drinking some of her cocktail, much to her annoyance.

"Uh... roast dinner, obviously," she mutters.

"You know, we can have other things. Other British things," he points out with a smirk. I don't know why he bothers, we all know what she's going to say.

"Why would you when you can have a roast dinner? By far the best thing to come out of Britain... ever, if you ask me."

Seb's brows rise as Galen smothers a laugh.

"The best thing?" Seb snarls. "Then you must be forgetting what I did the other night with my—" Stella gasps and smacks her hand over Seb's mouth.

"Don't you dare say another word of that sentence, Papatonis."

"Jesus Christ, what time is the beef ready?" I ask, more than happy to change the subject.

"We're good to sit down in about twenty minutes."

"You told us all to be here an hour ago," I point out.

"I know my kids, Toby." She winks before turning her back on us and walking deeper into the kitchen, and Galen quickly follows.

"Oh my God, even your mum thinks we were late because we were having sex." Jodie whispers the final two words as her cheeks darken.

"Damn, you're cute when you blush," I tell her, dipping down to drop a kiss on her temple.

"You're gonna try to convince us that you weren't," Seb says with a laugh.

"Trust me, we weren't."

"Oh, bro. She's not holding out on you because of a little smoke inhalation, is she?" Seb teases, but the way he locks eyes with Jodie as he does lets her know that he's only saying it to rile me up.

"Don't you worry your little head over it, Sebastian. I know how to treat her right. Don't I, baby?"

"You taken a trip to Hades yet?" Jodie asks, giving as good as she gets. She knows full well they haven't, because Stella mentioned it again when she came to visit.

"What's wrong, bro? Worried you can't handle all the big boy toys?"

"Fuck off. I'm just waiting for the right moment."

"Pretty sure that was Valentine's Day, but whatever," Stella scoffs, reaching for Jodie's hand and pulling her from my side so they can go and talk about us in private.

"Don't wait too long, Sebastian, or I might just let someone who's more willing to rock my world," she warns.

"You wouldn't dare," he growls as the two of them disappear toward the dining room.

Seb's still shaking his head when I look back at him.

"You do know that you're never going to hear the end of this until you take her, right?"

"I'm gonna take her. You think I'd pass something like that up? Like I said, I'm just waiting for the right time."

"We should see if we can book the place out. Have a private party down there."

"With your sister?" Seb baulks.

"It's not just one big gang bang room. But having the entire place to ourselves is definitely appealing."

He nods, seeing where I'm going with this.

"Nico and Alex would be pissed if we took them there without girls."

"It would be worth it to see the look on their faces when they realise the only free and single girl is Calli."

"Surefire way to get Alex killed."

"You think he'd go for it?"

"Hell yeah. There's more to his flirting than he lets on. He's probably at home right now knocking one out over our innocent little princess as we speak."

"And there's a visual I never needed," I quip.

"Seriously though, bro. Haven't you wondered why he hasn't moved in yet?"

"Obviously. I just assumed he was banging his dad's new housekeeper or something."

"I mean, yeah. That's definitely a possibility. But I was more thinking that it's because Evan's house is closer to Stefanos' than our place. Would be easier to sneak around, get a little busy in the basement. Hell knows we all snuck down there unnoticed enough times while Nico was there."

My chin drops, because what he's saying makes a lot of sense, and it does sound like something Alex would do. But with Calli... nah, surely not?

"You know I'm right, bro," he says with a smug-as-shit grin.

"Nah, I don't think so. He might have a hard-on for her, but he's not that fucking stupid."

Seb's brow lifts as he stares at me. "This is the same Alex we're talking about who fell out of a tree in year ten after trying to look into Miss Hancock's bedroom."

"Okay, so maybe he is stupid enough," I concede. "I'm just not sure."

A buzzer rings out and Mum and Galen start crashing about in the kitchen.

"I'm gonna get us some beers. We should probably then go and see if Jodie needs protecting from Stella," I say lightly.

"That's your sister you're talking about."

"Exactly my point. Jodie doesn't need any more reasons to hate me."

"That girl is far from hating you, man. You've got her hooked."

He smirks at me as we head toward the door, their voices getting louder as we close in on them, and I can't help but smile as I think about her confession outside Joanne's house. My heart swells and my body burns to have her close. She might not have said the exact words, but she didn't need to. I already see it deep in her dark chocolate eyes.

Wednesday night might have been all kinds of hell, but I can't help feeling grateful that it brought us back together. She might have told me since that she was always going to come back to me, but I'll never know if that was how it would have played out. I remember all too well how I felt as our communication got less and less with every day that passed. The fear that we were over was real. I just have to believe that we always had a future ahead of us, even with everything that's happened.

The loud ring of Jodie's phone cuts through the conversation around the table as we eat, and she hops up as if her arse is on fire.

I know who it is before the words roll off her tongue. I remember all too well when she set that ringtone so that she wouldn't miss anything.

"It's Jesse," she explains to everyone else, her eyes landing on Mum's as an apologetic expression falls over her face.

"Go, sweetheart. We understand."

"Thank you," she says in the rush, damn near running from the room so she can take it in privacy. She just lifts the phone to her ear before she turns the corner and my heart lurches in my chest as she greets him, demanding to know if something has happened.

My skin prickles with everyone's attention on me.

"You should go," Mum says softly. "If he got..." she trails off. "She might need you."

I nod, already half out of my chair before she even said the words.

"Whatever happens," Stella says, stopping me before I can escape, "she'll be okay. She's stronger than you think."

"Of course she is. She's got Cirillo blood running through her body," I state proudly, although ignoring the obvious with that statement.

"Calli is busy at work on her Princess jacket," Stella quips as I walk out of the room.

I have a love–hate thing going on with those fucking Cirillo Pink Ladies jackets Calli made. They bring back memories I'd rather forget from Halloween, but also, I really kinda wanna see Jodie wearing one. Or even better, one of the dresses from Oxford. I can just picture her in one of those with my name and number on her back telling everyone that she's mine.

Hell yeah.

"Yeah?" she asks hopefully, as I breathe in and a sigh of relief falls from my lips. "Jesse, that's—" Her words are cut off as he speaks.

I stand at the end of the hallway, watching as she leans back against the wall and stares up at the ceiling as she absorbs everything he's saying.

"Yeah, I know. But it's the first step, Jesse."

They talk for a few more minutes before she says goodbye, instructing him to give her a kiss from her and hanging up.

She blows out a long breath as she clutches her phone to her chest.

"Baby," I whisper, not wanting to startle her. "What did he say?"

She turns to me with hope filling her eyes.

"She's responding to treatment. Her stats are improving."

The corners of my lips twitch up with the beginnings of a smile.

"That's great."

"It could all still go very wrong, but it's a start."

"It is. It's progress. She's fighting." I take her hands in mine and pull her close. "She wants to come back to you both."

Jodie sniffs as she blinks back the tears filling her eyes.

"You wanna head up to see her?" I ask, knowing full well it's exactly what she wants to do.

"Is that okay? I don't want to run off and ruin—"

"You're not ruining anything. Everyone understands. Come on." I tug her from the wall and tuck her into my side.

The second we re-enter the dining room, everyone looks at us with anticipation.

"She's started responding to treatment," I say when Jodie sucks in a shaky breath.

"Oh, that's fantastic," Mum gushes.

"It's still really early days, but it's a good sign."

"Did you want me to box up dessert for you so you can go and see her?" Mum asks before we have to say anything.

"That's really not necessary, Maria. You don't need—"

"Don't be silly, sweetheart. Plus, it's Toby's favourite. I'd hate for you both to miss out."

My stomach rumbles despite the huge roast dinner we've just eaten. It's no secret that while Stella might come here for the main course, my sights are always on what comes after.

"That's an offer I can't refuse," I say, and Mum rushes from the room. Finding Stella's eyes, I promise to call her later with an update, and after a quick goodbye and a detour via the kitchen for my New York cheesecake, we rush out of the house.

I place it in Jodie's lap after we've dropped into my car, and she looks down at the container before coyly glancing back up at me.

"*Déjà vu* much?" she mutters.

"Tonight will have a better ending," I tell her seriously.

"Is that a promise?"

"Hell yeah. I've got my favourite girl and my favourite dessert. What could be better?"

Silence falls between us as we drive through the gates of Galen's house and turn onto the road.

"You know, we still need to talk about what's

going to happen... with him," Jodie says, making my stomach knot.

"When you're ready. He's secure and being looked after... to a point."

Reaching over, I take her hand in mine and lock our fingers together.

"One problem at a time, yeah? Sara needs you right now more than he ever could."

She nods in agreement but carries on regardless.

"Mostly, I think it would be better for everyone if he didn't exist. Even down there, I know his presence is weighing on you. On everyone."

"All you've got to do is say the words. Just remember that a lifetime is a long time to live with regrets, so make sure you're certain before we do anything we can't take back," I warn.

I might have no issues with going down there and putting a bullet between his eyes and finally putting this behind us. But all of this—this world—it's new to Jodie, and I don't expect her to deal with something as final and life-changing as taking another's life from them as easily as we all can now.

7

JODIE

M y mood immediately darkens at the mention of *him*. And it's not because he lied to me, or because I'm still mourning my loss. It's purely because of the dark cloud his existence is hanging over all of our heads.

While he's still breathing, I know that Toby is never going to be able to let go of his past. Stella is never going to be able to forget the awful things that happened to her because of his need to control every aspect of the lives of those around him. And Mum... I let out a sigh, my stomach knotting that I haven't even told her he's still alive. Guilt assaults me as I think about the fact that I've been lying to her.

But it's for her own good... isn't it?

"You okay, baby?" Toby asks, glancing over as we race toward the hospital.

I know that nothing has really changed with Sara's condition. I'm not expecting to go racing into her room and find her staring back at me or anything —I know we're a long, long way from that. And I'm achingly aware that things could take a U-turn fast.

But I need to be there. I need to believe that she's aware we're all rooting for her. And I need to be there for Jesse.

He's barely holding onto his sanity right now, and if my presence helps in any way to keep him together, then I'll willingly do it.

He's scowled at me every time I've turned up to see her over the past few days. He was trying to pull his scary bad boy gangster act on me to force me home to rest. He needs to realise though, I'm not the same weak, naïve girl he first met. It might have only been weeks really since I met Toby and discovered the truth of my roots, but I feel like a different person.

I'm stronger, more resilient.

And it's empowering as fuck.

I might not be as bad-arse as Stella, but I've certainly found some strength and some pretty impenetrable armour throughout all of this.

Toby did that.

He may have hurt me in ways I never could have imagined, in ways I never want anyone else to hurt. But he also set me free when I didn't even know I was caged. He showed me a part of me that I never knew was missing, a way of life I never knew existed. And as terrifying as it might be, I think I'm ready to embrace it.

I might never claim my true father's name as my own, but that doesn't mean that I'm not one of them. And aside from the obvious, all they've done since the truth was revealed has been to open their family to me.

I want it.

I want it so fucking bad.

I think of each of them. Toby's caring, loving heart. Nico's... quirks. Stella's strength, and the love she has for Seb, for each of her boys. Emmie's resilience. Alex's humour and lightness compared to Daemon's darkness and rough edges. Theo's subtle but controlling demeanour that ensures everyone knows who's boss. And Calli's quiet confidence that I think the guys misinterpret for innocence.

I've never wanted to be a part of a group before, but damn if I don't want to be swallowed into the middle of their family, to become one of them.

A smile curls at my lips as Toby sits silently beside me with his hand still locked on mine in quiet support while I try to process my thoughts.

"Yeah," I finally say. "I'm good."

He glances over once more. "Good. Me too."

We share a smile before he's forced to look back at the road.

As expected, Sara's improvement was just in the stats. She looks as pale as she did this morning. But there was a little more hope in my veins this evening, and I'm sure when Jesse smiled at me, it was a little less forced.

He also had been convinced by Archer to head back to his place when Sara's parents arrived to shower and change, which is a small miracle, and he looked better than I've seen him since this whole ordeal began.

Everything was slowly beginning to move in the right direction, and for the first time in a long while, I was feeling good about where the future might take me.

"What the hell are you doing?" Toby barks when I make a show of pulling the lid off the container of his beloved cheesecake when we're only a few minutes from his building.

"Feeling a little hungry," I say as innocently as possible. In reality, I'm feeling antsy and more than a little horny, knowing that there's every chance he's going to shut the front door of his flat and follow through on all the dirty promises he's made me over the last few days.

His chin drops and struggles to keep his eyes on the road as I swipe my finger through the sweet, creamy topping.

"Jodie," he growls, his gaze dropping to my lips

when I part them before he's forced to look forward once more.

Lifting my finger to my mouth, I push it inside and make a show of sucking it while letting a low moan rumble in my chest.

"Mmm... that's so good."

His Adam's apple bobs as he swallows harshly, his grip on the wheel turning his knuckles white.

"Jesus," he mutters, shifting in his seat a little.

"Oh, did you want some?" I ask as if the thought hadn't occurred to me.

His jaw pops in frustration as he takes a corner, not noticing as I collect up some more cheesecake topping on my finger and move it toward him.

"Jodie, I—" he begins to growl, but his words are cut off when I brush my finger over his lips before pushing it inside, giving him little choice but to lick it clean, which he more than happily does.

His speed slows as he savours the sweetness.

"It tastes even better on you, Demon," he says, licking his lips hungrily.

"Well then, you'd better get us back fast," I tease.

"Wha—" he starts, but again, his words quickly vanish as I unbuckle my seat belt and lean over the centre console. I lick up the topping I've just painted his jaw with as he pulls into the car park outside his building and heads toward the underground garage. "Jesus, Demon."

"I wanted to see how it tastes on you. If I remember rightly, you had all the fun the last time."

I cast my mind back to the better part of *that* evening—of the tiramisu I barely got a taste of.

"You won't hear me complaining. I'll willingly be your plate any day," he says as I kiss my way down his neck, his pulse thundering beneath my lips.

Balancing on my knees, I place my hand on his chest and slowly move it south as the garage door opens before us.

Toby's hips lift off the seat in desperation for my touch long before I reach his waistband.

"Someone's a little impatient," I mumble against his throat as my fingers dip beneath the fabric of his shirt.

"You're telling me that those tiny knickers you teased me with earlier aren't soaking wet for me right now, Demon?"

My body burns with desire and my cheeks heat at his words, knowing they're more than true.

"Probably about as dry as you are soft," I confess, dropping my hand lower to palm his junk through the fabric of his trousers.

"Jesus," he grunts as I squeeze his rock-hard length.

Licking around the shell of his ear, I lean in close and whisper, "I wonder how sweet you'd taste covered in cheesecake?"

His cock jerks in my hand at my words.

"I-I think you should probably find out the answer to that question," he groans as I pull his belt loose and make quick work of popping his button open and lowering the zip. "Fucking love it when you're greedy for my cock, Demon." Another loud moan rips through the air as I push my hand inside his boxers and grasp him.

"Jesus. Fuck."

The car jolts to a halt, and not a second later, he helps me out by lifting his hips and pushing both his trousers and boxers down, letting his cock spring free.

His fingers thread into my hair, dragging me forward to where he needs me most.

"Wait," I cry, and he immediately lets up.

"Shit. Did I hurt you?" he asks, his brow pinching in concern.

"No, no. I'm fine." Nothing the last few days of my painkillers can't handle. "I just need..."

I scoop up a huge dollop of cheesecake and paint the end of his cock with it.

"Fuck, yeah," he moans before pushing me back down again, his need for control too much for him to deny, even in a situation where he knows I hold every ounce of power.

The second I'm hovering right above the head of his cock, I stick my tongue out and lick at the sweet topping.

"Mmm," I hum, continuing to lap at him, delighting in the sweetness of the cheesecake along with his unique addictive taste.

"Fuck, baby. Need more," he grunts, thrusting his

hips in his need to sink past my lips, but I lift up, not letting him take over.

"Nice try."

His grip on my hair tightens in punishment, heat blooming between my thighs. He knows it too, because he bunches the skirt of my dress around my waist and dips his fingers between my thighs.

"You're dripping, baby."

"It's been a while," I tease.

"Too fucking long."

This time when he pushes me lower, I part my lips and take him. Just as he hits the back of my throat, his fingers dip under the lace covering me and he pushes two thick fingers inside me.

I moan around his shaft as he stretches me open in the most delicious way and his precum coats my tongue as I pull off his length.

"That's it, Demon. Fuck, yeah," he barks, keeping control of my speed and movements with the hand that's twisted in my hair.

I can barely breathe as he works me dangerously close to orgasm in an embarrassingly short time. I don't let up, desperate to make him lose control.

But right as his cock swells ready to blow, he drags me off him, my scalp burning with the harsh movement.

"Toby," I complain as I mourn the loss of his fingers as well as his cock.

"I'm not blowing in your mouth, baby. It's been

too long. I need to be buried balls deep in your body and feeling you coming around me."

My squeal of shock echoes around the enclosed space as Toby's seat shoots back and he drags me over the console, straight onto his lap.

"You okay?" he asks, and my heart soars that he doesn't forget my comfort even while riding on the edge of his orgasm.

"I'll be better when I'm impaled on your cock."

"Jesus."

His large hands wrap around my waist and he positions me over him.

"Line us up then, baby."

Reaching between us, I tease my entrance with the head of his cock before he thrusts up and drops me down simultaneously.

"Toby," I scream in shock as my body fights to adjust to the invasion.

He waits for a beat, aware that I need a moment before his fingers twist in my hair once more and my lips slam against his as he begins thrusting up into me like a man possessed.

His tongue strokes mine before he bites down, sending a bolt of pleasure straight to my clit.

"Oh fuck, Toby," I cry, my back arching, allowing his cock to hit that sweet spot inside of me.

Releasing my hair, he drags my hands from his shoulders and tugs them behind my back, pinning them there with just one of his, forcing me to keep my angle.

"Fuck, Demon. Your pussy is so fucking good," he forces out between clenched teeth. "I've dreamed about being inside you every night since I let you walk away."

"Toby," I pant, quickly losing control.

My chest heaves, making my lungs ache, but I don't care.

I don't give a fuck about anything right now other than the guy between my thighs and watching him shatter beneath me.

"You're gonna make me come so fucking hard, baby. But you want that, don't you? You want me to fuck you so good that you feel it with every step up to my flat."

"Yes, yes," I cry, clenching down on him in my need to watch him break.

His jaw pops as he desperately tries to hold off, but we both know he's not going to be able to do so much longer. The last two weeks, especially the past few days, have been too much. The need, the desire that's only been growing between us with every glance, every touch is just too much.

"You're so fucking beautiful riding my cock, Jodie."

"Yes, please. Toby. Toby," I chant, my release edging ever closer—until his hand disappears under my skirt and his thumb presses on my clit, sending me tumbling over the cliff I'd been climbing.

"Tobyyyy!" I scream, my body convulsing and

twitching as my release slams into me with the force of an articulated lorry.

Every single one of my nerve endings tingles with electric sparks that shoot around my body as my orgasm goes on and on before I finally drag Toby's out of him.

His loud roar echoes around the confines of the car as his dark and hungry eyes bore into mine with such intensity that it makes emotion burn up the back of my throat until tears begin to form.

His cock jerks violently, releasing everything he has inside me.

A loud bang outside the car a beat later has my heart jumping into my throat. Our eyes collide before more thuds sound out and the car starts rocking.

"Fucking get in there, Tobias," a familiar booming voice shouts.

"Oh my God," I breathe, falling forward into Toby's body and hiding my face in the crook of his neck.

He doesn't seem to be anywhere near as mortified, because his body soon begins to rumble with laughter. With his softening cock still inside me, the movement sends delicious little aftershocks shooting out, allowing me to cling onto the pleasure a little longer.

The sound of the window being lowered makes me squeeze my eyes closed before Toby's chest rumbles beneath me as he speaks.

"Fuck off and go and find your own girl."

"Gonna fucking have to," a different voice says, and when I peek and take a look, I find Alex standing there with a shit-eating grin. "I'm hard as fuck right now."

Digging up some confidence from somewhere, I pull my head from its hiding spot.

"Too much information," I call.

"Says the girl who's still got our boy's cock inside her," Nico quips.

"At least it's bigger than yours," I deadpan.

The silence that follows is deafening before both Toby and Alex bark out laughs.

"Aw, it's okay, bro. There's not that much shame in a girl having to finish herself off afterward," Alex teases, their voices getting farther away.

"Fuck you. I've never left a girl high and dry."

"Sure. Because you've always been a sex god," Alex mutters before a door slams shut, followed by blissful silence.

8

___

TOBY

J odie's laughter makes every inch of my body light up. It also fucking helps that with every chuckle, she clenches down on my fast-swelling dick.

"Your friends are—"

"Friends?" I ask with a smirk. "I barely even know them."

Reaching out, she swipes her thumb across my bottom lip, keeping it just out of reach, stopping me from sucking it into my mouth.

"So, what now?" she asks, her eyes following the movement of her thumb. "You've had your wicked way with me. We've given your non-friends a show." She tilts her head to the side in a move that is too damn cute considering she's currently impaled on my dick as my cum leaks from her body.

"You think I'm done with you?" I ask, wrapping

TRACY LORRAINE

my fingers around her wrist and lifting her arm so I can finally capture her thumb.

Swirling my tongue around the tip, I gently bite down, loving the way her pupils dilate.

"Toby," she moans, her pussy flooding me at the almost innocent move.

"Fuck, baby. You totally fucking disarm me."

I watch her as her hips begin to roll and she starts to ride me once more.

"You like my cock inside you, don't you, Demon?"

"You know I do."

"Use me. Get yourself off again. But I'm not fucking you until we're upstairs. I'm going to take my time stripping you naked, teasing every inch of your body."

Her head falls back as her movements get more and more erratic and the fingers of her free hand curl around my shoulder.

It takes every ounce of my restraint not to just fuck her again. But watching her come apart, using me for her own pleasure? Fuck. It's mesmerising.

Pressing her hand that I'm still holding against my chest, I allow her to feel just how hard my heart is pounding.

"Toby," she sighs when her eyes find mine.

Hers are so full of heat and hunger, but there's so much more within their depths. I see everything. All the things she's too terrified to properly confess out loud.

But I don't need her words. Not when I have this.

"You feel that, baby?" she nods, and I have to wonder if she realises I mean my heart and not my cock.

"Y-yeah. Shit." Her body trembles with her impending release and her skin flushes the most beautiful shade of red as she prepares to fall.

"I'm yours," I tell her seriously. "I might have let you go, but I was never going to set you free."

"Yes, yes," she chants, her hips circling so that my cock continues to rub the exact spot she needs it in. "Yes. Fuck. TOBY," she cries, and despite telling her that I wasn't going to fuck her again, I find my hips thrusting upward before I unexpectedly shoot my load inside her again.

"What do you do to me, baby?"

"Make you feel good, hopefully," she forces out between her heavy breathing as she comes down from her high.

"Out of this fucking world."

Tucking my hands under her skirt, I wrap my fingers around the flimsy lace and tug until it rips and falls free of her body.

Jodie's gasp rips through the air as I drag it from beneath her and lift it to my nose.

"Oh my God," she whimpers.

"Can't wait to taste you, baby. To lick you clean before I dirty you up all over again."

Her teeth sink into her bottom lip as she watches me stuff them into my jacket pocket.

"Dirty dog."

"You love it," I point out, finally lifting her from my lap and depositing her back in her own seat. "Careful though, cum stains are a bitch to get out of this upholstery," I tease, fighting to keep my smirk at bay.

Her head snaps around to me, her lips parting in shock.

"Just how many girls have you fucked in here, Tobias?" she hisses.

"Aw, baby. Jealousy looks so damn good on you."

"Fuck off, I'm not jealous," she argues with a huff of annoyance.

"Sure. So you're not currently imagining a hundred and one ways you could hurt any girl who's ever touched me?"

"No, of course not. I'll leave you with thoughts of torture and murder, if it's all the same to you."

I throw my head back on a laugh at her words.

"Damn, I thought it might be some kind of couples bonding thing that we could do together."

"Killing your exes?" she asks, her eyes widening.

"Well... I wouldn't go as far as calling any of the girls I've spent time with before exes. You're the only girl who's ever meant anything to me," I confess, reaching out and cupping her cheek.

"Aw," she sighs, her expression softening. "And yet, you haven't actually asked me to be your girlfriend yet. Be careful, Tobias, or I'll start thinking you're not serious about me."

Before I even manage to form a response to that comment, she pushes her door open and jumps out.

Reaching for the container of cheesecake she'd placed safely on the dashboard, I follow her, tucking myself away as I go and catch up to her just before she reaches the door.

"Trying to run, baby?" I ask, finding the bottom of her skirt and dipping my hand beneath it.

Her thighs are a mess as my cum drips down them.

"Toby," she cries and tries to shoot forward.

"You can't run from me, baby. And even if you could, it's unlikely you'd forget who owns you anytime soon with all my cum leaking out of you."

"Jesus," she mutters, as I push two fingers inside her.

"Push the call button, Demon," I demand before pressing her against the wall beside the lift as I continue to fingerfuck her, pushing all my cum that's not already running down her thighs back inside her.

My mouth waters at the thought of laying her out on my bed in only a few minutes and eating her until she can't remember her own name.

"You'd better hope these doors don't open and reveal your sister," she says on a gasp.

"Trust me, she's seen and done worse."

Thankfully, though, when the doors do open, they reveal an empty car.

Pressing the length of my body against her back, I brush my lips against the shell of her ear.

"Last chance to try and run, Demon," I warn. "You told me a few minutes ago that I hadn't asked you to be mine. Well, I can assure you that by the time I'm done with you tonight, there's going to be no doubt in your mind exactly who you belong to."

A violent shudder rips through her body at my words.

"You want to be mine, Jodie?"

"Yes," she cries.

"You want to be one of us? Dark, depraved, and fucking deadly?"

"Yes," she shouts louder as I continue working her.

"Fuck," I breathe, dropping my lips to her neck. "I can't wait to see you with a gun in your hand," I groan. I remember all too well watching Stella and Calli out on the range. I can only imagine how fucking hot Jodie will look.

"Toby," she whimpers as her muscles begin clamping down on me tighter. "I need—"

Ripping my fingers from inside her, I wrap my arm around her and paint her lips with our combined juices.

"Lick," I demand, twisting her around so I can watch her. "Good?"

She nods, sucking her bottom lip into her mouth to savour the taste, and my willpower snaps. I plunge my fingers into my own mouth, letting our joint taste explode on my tongue.

"So fucking sweet, Demon."

Grabbing her by the throat, I push her back into the waiting lift, and I don't stop until a gasp of shock rips past her lips when her back slams against the back wall.

Reaching out, I press the button for our floor before slamming my lips down on hers and losing myself in her as we climb through the building.

"What the hell are you doing?" Jodie barks when I abandon her in the living room of my flat and march toward the kitchen.

"Getting a spoon," I say as if it should be obvious.

"You cannot be serious?" she sulks, her eyes following my every move.

"What's wrong, baby? Did you think you were the only thing I wanted to eat tonight?" I say, pulling a spoon from the drawer and holding it and the container up as I spin back toward her with a massive smile on my face.

"Fine," she hisses, taking off toward my bedroom. "I guess I'll just have to finish myself off. Dickhead," she throws over her shoulder as I take off behind her.

With my eyes locked on what I know is her bare

arse beneath her dress, I scoop out a spoonful of cheesecake and groan as the sweetness hits my tongue. That tease she gave me of it in the car was not enough.

I allow her to keep thinking that she's walking away from me until she's in the middle of my bedroom.

Leaning my shoulder against the door frame, I pull the spoon from my mouth and bark, "Stop."

She does immediately.

"Good girl," I say with a satisfied smile.

Her head dips, and I can only imagine her lips curling up as well.

"Turn around, Demon."

It takes her a few seconds, and just when I think she's going to defy me, she spins, but she does keep her eyes on the floor. Standing before me in just her pink dress and her black bra hiding beneath it.

"Eyes. On. Me," I demand, and slowly, so fucking slowly, she lifts them until her dark chocolate orbs meet mine.

My breath catches at the depth of them. I love it when she opens herself up like she is now. I can read all her vulnerabilities, her fears, her emotions. It makes me feel closer to her than I have anyone in my life. It's a fucking heady experience.

Pushing from the door frame, I close the space between us. Scooping another spoonful, I lift it to her mouth, but right before her lips part to accept it, I steal it back and push it into my mouth.

"Hey," she complains.

"I thought I warned you, baby," I taunt once I've swallowed my mouthful. "When we want something. We take it."

"Don't worry, I'm well aware of what happens when you want something."

Her eyes follow me as I move around her.

Placing what's left of the cheesecake on the bedside table, I pull my top drawer open and lift out what I've been hiding in here.

"W-what's that?" she asks as I stalk back over.

"A gift," I confess, my stomach knotting that she's not going to like it, or think it's stupid.

"Toby," she sighs. "I don't need—"

"Shh..." I press my fingers to her lips to stop her arguing. "This isn't about money, this is about us."

"O-okay," she mumbles around my fingers.

"Open it," I encourage, dropping my hand and tapping the top of the box.

She reaches out and pulls the lid off, revealing two smaller boxes inside, one black and one white.

Ripping her eyes from them, she glances up at me.

"Black one first," I encourage.

She nods and reaches for it, lifting it out of the larger box and pulling the lid free.

Her brow wrinkles when she sees what's hiding inside.

"Have you bought me a teeny tiny person house?" she muses, taking in the size of the key.

"Nope," I say, reaching for it and pulling the

leather cord it's hanging from free. "It's mine." I place it over my head, letting the small key hang down on my chest.

"You're giving me a gift that belongs to you?" she asks, one of her brows lifting in confusion after ripping her gaze from it.

"Something like that. Next one."

My pulse spikes with anticipation as she reaches for it. The second she has the white box out, I throw the larger one to the floor and close the space between us.

She gasps the second she opens it and reality hits her.

"Toby, it's—"

"You sure you still want to be mine?" I ask as my heart thunders in my chest.

Her dark eyes hold mine, and my head spins as I wait.

Her lips part, and I swear the time it takes for her to speak is the longest second of my life.

"Yes."

All the air rushes out of my lungs and relief floods me. Anyone would think she'd just agreed to be my wife or something, but to me, this is enough. For now.

"It's beautiful."

"That's a relief, because you're not going to be able to take it off."

She runs her finger over the padlock that hangs from the silver chain.

"Good. I don't want to. I want this, Toby. I want you. I know it's crazy, and fucked up, but I kinda think that's part of our charm."

A wide smile splits my face. "I totally agree."

Taking the necklace from her, I place it around her neck before attaching the chain to the padlock and securing it in place.

"Too late to go back now," I tease.

"For better or worse."

"Careful, or you'll have me thinking you were expecting a ring in there."

She smiles softly at me, making me think that she wouldn't have been as freaked out as she probably should have been if there was an engagement ring in one of those boxes.

"We've got all the time in the world for that. But as for right now... I believe you've got some promises to uphold, Tobias."

Snatching the box from her hand, I throw it behind us and it hits the wall at exactly the same time my lips collide with hers.

"I love coming good on promises," I murmur into her kiss.

"You just love coming."

"Nah, baby. I love watching you come."

9

JODIE

"You're making me late again," Toby growls into my neck as he lowers my feet back to the floor of the shower, both our chests heaving from our exertion.

"I didn't invite you in here," I say on a sigh as he grazes his teeth down my throat.

"I like to think I've got an open invitation whenever you're naked and wet," he quips.

"Is that right?"

"Sure is. Now turn around and let me do my thing—"

"Pretty sure you've already done that."

"Demon," he growls, slapping me teasingly on the arse when I move. "Be a good girl. I want to change your bandages before I leave."

A contented sigh falls from my lips as his fingers push into my hair a beat after the floral scent of the shampoo he bought for me. It's not the only new addition to the bathroom, and I suspect there's more throughout his flat.

I wanted to chastise him for it last night when I first stumbled in here and found it all, but I was too exhausted to say anything.

"I'm more than capable of doing them myself." How neither of us caused ourselves any further damage last night is beyond me. I'm pretty sure what we got up to exceeded the light exercise the doctors advised for us for a week or so while our wounds heal.

"I know, but I want to do it. I want to take care of you."

"You're a little bit cute, you know that, right?"

"Shh, don't tell the boss," he teases.

"Your secret is safe, bad boy."

As soon as he's happy that I'm fully clean, he gives himself a once-over and instructs me to sit on the closed toilet so he can deal with my dressings.

"I don't even think they really need them anymore."

"The doctor said a week, so we're following the rules."

"Is that what you did last night?" I quip.

"Some rules are made to be broken, baby."

After tucking a towel around his waist, he grabs a first aid box stashed in the cupboard and drops to his knees in front of me.

My hand automatically lifts to the new chain

hanging around my neck, my fingers toying with the little padlock.

Spotting the movement, Toby looks up from picking at the old sodden bandage that's barely sticking to my calf.

"Mine," he growls, sending goosebumps shooting all around my body.

"Yours."

He smiles up at me, and the love and adoration I see in the depths of his blue eyes makes my heart tumble in the best of ways.

That moment doesn't last nearly as long as I wish it would before he looks back down and continues tending to my almost healed cuts.

His touch is so gentle, it makes my eyes burn with emotion. The memories of how I got them slam into me. The scent of burning, the sound of destruction that I remember all too well from that night assaults my senses.

"It's okay, baby. You're safe now, and I fucking swear to you, I'll never let anyone hurt you again."

Reaching out, I thread my fingers through his wet hair, hoping he can feel how strongly I care for him in my touch.

I don't respond. I can't. There's no way he can make promises for me like that. Well, not unless he keeps me locked up in here. It's not out of the realm of possibilities. Thanks to Stella, Emmie, and Calli, I know that these boys are no strangers to turning to extreme measures to get what they want when it comes to their girls.

"Thank you," I breathe instead, hoping he knows how much I appreciate everything he's done for me, how he's helped bring me back to life after I was convinced I was going to drown in my grief.

He glances up at me again before shifting to the last wound on my shoulder. He leans close, his clean freshly-showered scent filling my nose and eradicating my memory of the burning building.

My heart rate picks up and the movement of my chest becomes more erratic as I replay everything we've done since he drove into the underground garage last night.

"Demon," he growls, making me shudder. "I can practically hear your thoughts. You're a dirty, dirty girl."

"Exactly as you like me."

He laughs, the deepness of the rumbles rushing through me and making everything south of my waist clench. My core aches and my muscles burn but in the best possible ways, and I'm more than happy to embrace the newest additions to my bruise collection on my hips from where he took me last night and this morning in the shower.

"Guilty," he confesses, running his fingertips over my shoulder and standing to his full height before me.

My teeth sink into my bottom lip as I take in his

sculpted chest, toned stomach, and then the tent in the towel.

"Again?"

"Always." He winks before slipping out of the room to get dressed. I make quick work of rummaging through his bathroom cabinet, finding everything I could need, and all of it way more luxurious than my normal products.

By the time I step back into Toby's bedroom, he's looking entirely too mouth-watering in his Knight's Ridge College uniform.

"No one should be allowed to look that hot to go to school," I say, leaning against the door frame and running my eyes over him.

"You should see all of us together," he teases.

"Oh, to be a girl at Knight's Ridge," I breathe, fanning myself dramatically.

I can only imagine how the six of them run that place and have the girls wrapped around their little fingers.

Jealousy grips me in its evil clutches as I imagine all those wealthy, posh girls pawing all over what's mine.

"Aw, baby. You have nothing to worry about. You're worth ten on any of the girls at school and then some."

"But don't they all have killer family connections? I'm sure they'd be more—"

"I couldn't give a shit if they were related to God himself. No one is more important to me than you."

My brow wrinkles as a concern I've had a few weeks tugs at me.

"What is it?" he asks.

"Does it matter that I'm only half Greek?" I ask quietly. "You've said before that the reason Mum would never be accepted was beca—"

"No," he interrupts. "That's an old-fashioned ideal, one that *he* was obsessed with. He wanted us to be this pure organisation, the bloodlines to be pure. But the reality is very different. You don't need to worry about any of that. You're mine, Demon. And if anyone has an issue with it, then they'll have me to answer to."

A shiver runs down my spine as he morphs into his scary soldier mode for a few seconds.

"Okay," I breathe, embarrassingly turned on by his bad boy side.

"Good. I promise you, you have nothing to worry about."

Other than what to do about the man in the basement.

Those unspoken words hang between us as Toby's hand slips around the back of my neck to pull me closer.

"If you need me today, call me, okay?"

"Okay," I agree, although I already know I won't. Nothing could happen that can't wait until he's finished.

"Good. Now, be a good girl while I'm gone. Give Jesse my love," he teases, knowing that's my first port of call this morning. Leaning forward, he steals a kiss before whispering, "I've left you some little gifts."

"Oh?" I ask breathlessly.

"But you need to find them first."

His tongue plunges into my mouth, cutting off my response. He kisses me until my knees are weak, and after dropping one final kiss to the tip of my nose, he leaves me standing there, barely holding up my own weight as he marches away from me, then quickly leaves the flat.

My eyes scan the room, wondering what he could have possibly left for me.

I don't realise I'm playing with my necklace once more until I spot a sticky note on the wardrobe and drop it as my curiosity gets the better of me.

Open me.

Doing as I'm told, I pull the wardrobe door open.

My gasp of shock rips through the air when I find rails and shelves full of what are obviously women's clothes.

Another pink note catches my eye, and when I pull on it, I find it's attached to a pair of jeans.

Wear me.

Shaking my head at the pure insanity of this, I pull the jeans out, finding that the hanger is attached to another with an oversized hoodie.

On the front of the hoodie is another note.

Top drawer. Which do you think are my favourite?

My heart thunders in my chest as a million

butterflies take flight in my belly at how much I love this little game.

Reaching for the drawer, I pull it open to find the most incredible selection of lingerie. They're arranged like a rainbow of silk and lace.

"You're in so much trouble, Tobias," I mutter to myself as I try to imagine just how much money he's spent on all of this.

Running my fingertip over the delicate fabric, I select a lacy set the exact same colour as my dress the night we first met and pull it free.

The tags have already been taken off, so I'm unable to find out how much it all cost. I pray that it fits, because it would pain me to see all this go to waste.

I'm not sure why I was worried, though. The second I slide the incredibly soft lace onto my body, I realise it fits me like a second skin. Hands down, it's the most comfortable underwear I have ever had the pleasure of wearing.

A smile plays on my lips as I shake my head.

Walking toward where my bag sits on the bedside table, I pull my phone out and snap a photo before I chicken out.

Jodie: Did I choose right?

I hit send and try to forget that I've just sent a photo of my almost naked body to a boy. I have never,

ever done something like that before. But Toby makes me reckless in all the best kinds of ways.

His reply comes faster than I was expecting, and it makes my heart jump into my throat as I unlock my phone to read his response.

Toby: I'm coming back. DO NOT MOVE.

A laugh falls from my lips.

Jodie: Don't you dare, schoolboy. Be a good boy and don't get detention, and I might let you take it off me later... with your teeth.

Toby: Damn it, Demon. I'm so fucking hard for you.

Jodie: I'll take care of you later, bad boy. *winky emoji*

Toby: I'll hold you to that.

Jodie: *devil emoji*

Jodie: And thank you, everything is incredible.

Toby: It's the least of what you deserve. *heart emoji*

My heart beats wildly as I stare at his words.

Throwing my phone to the bed, I force myself to stop messaging him when I assume he's driving. Pulling on the rest of my clothes, I discover an entire shelf of shoes and boots and even a selection of designer handbags.

I want to be mad at him for spending so much on me. But I love it all so much that I can't even find the energy to be annoyed. I guess I'll just have to repay him in blowjobs, because it's not like I have an actual job to pay for much of it myself right now.

Switching my things to one of the new bags, I grab a tan leather jacket from the wardrobe and head out to the kitchen in the hope of mastering his coffee machine.

A laugh falls from my lips when I find the appliance in question with sticky notes all over it.

When the hell he had time to do all this, God only knows.

Start here.

Place mug here.

Insert pod here.

Press here.

And when I pull open the cupboard which has a note with *open me* stuck to it, I find a mug with 'Princess Jodie' printed around the outside and a sticky note inside with *fill me* inside.

With my new mug full, I carry it and my phone to the sofa to call Mum and send a message to Bri and another to Jesse to find out if anything has changed overnight.

I have no idea what it is about Toby's flat, but even when he's absent, I feel completely at home. It's probably his presence.

It might be early days, but I can actually see myself living here, being happy here.

The thought should freak me out, but it doesn't. Just like I didn't feel anything but wild excitement and recklessness when I thought for the briefest moment that there was an engagement ring inside one of those boxes last night.

Once again, I find myself toying with my necklace. My little piece of Toby that's going to be permanently locked onto my body.

If I wasn't aware that he owned my heart before last night, then I sure do now. He literally has it under lock and key, and I couldn't be happier.

Once I'm ready, I head toward the front door, ready to call for an Uber to pick me up from downstairs.

I stop when I find another sticky note attached to a gift box that's identical to the one last night on the dresser.

Open me.

Nervously, I pull the lid off. I have no idea why, but deep down, I know this is going to knock me on my arse.

Inside is another box and another note.

Please don't be mad.

"Okay," I whisper, pulling the lid off that box too, only to find another.

It's purely for selfish reasons...

My brows pinch as I find another, smaller box.

I want you to always be able to get to me.

"Oh shit. Toby, what have you done?"

My heart jumps into my throat when I pull that lid off and I find exactly what I was fearing I would.

A black key.

My hand trembles as I reach for it, plucking it from the velvet cushion it's resting on.

Turning it over, a bubble of excitement falls from my lips as a smile curls up.

We've never talked about cars or what I'd buy if I had enough money or a reason to do so. But it seems we're on the same wavelength, because although I'm sure this is way fancier than I'd ever have purchased myself, it's exactly what I'd have picked.

Pulling my phone from my pocket, I quickly tap out a message despite the fact that he's now in class.

Jodie: YOU ARE IN SO MUCH TROUBLE, TOBIAS DOUKAS!!!

Once again, his reply comes not a minute later.

Toby: You're welcome. I've checked how far the seat slides back, and I can confirm there's plenty of space for more than just driving. *winky emoji*

My cheeks burn at the image as my fingers curl around the key and I rush toward the door to find out exactly what's waiting for me in the garage.

There's a huge part of me that wants me to put the key back in the box and refuse the gift. I've done nothing to deserve having so much money spent on me. But then our time together flickers through my mind, the good and the bad, and I reason that he's just doing anything in his power to continue to prove to me that he's sorry about what went down. And I'm confident he's more than aware that I'm not here because of his money. I couldn't care less if he were skint. It's him I've fallen for. His heart, his compassion. His... everything. Even his bad parts.

The lift ride down to the garage is the slowest journey of my freaking life, but as the doors open, I find that I don't get out. I might be desperate to see what's parked down here for me. But I also can't ignore the burning need to go and explore the basement.

The B on the control panel taunts me, and before I realise I've even made a decision, I've pressed the button and I'm descending deeper into the building.

My heart beats wildly in my chest. I have no idea

what I'm going to find down here, but I guess I'd be naïve to think that I'm just going to walk into some kind of jail cell and find the man I've called Dad all my life sitting behind bars.

They're cleverer than that. But even knowing that, it doesn't stop me stepping out of the lift the second the doors open.

A solid set of wooden double doors greet me. The biometric pad beside it shows a red locked light and I almost give up on this little exploration mission before it's started.

Toby might have given me access to the main entrance and his flat, but I can't imagine that luxury extends to the rest of the building, especially when I know what—or who—they're hiding down here.

Deciding it's worth a shot now I'm here, I walk over and press my hand to the pad.

To my utter disbelief, the little light turns green and the doors before me unlock.

"Wow," I breathe, rolling my shoulders in an attempt to prepare myself for what I might be about to walk into.

My hand trembles violently, and I lift it and push the door open.

It takes a second for the lights to flicker on as I enter, but once they do, all I can do is blink in surprise. The massive room opens up before me and I struggle to take it all in.

It is by far the most impressive home gym I have ever laid my eyes on. It's even better than some of those I've seen on the fancy houses that Mum loves to drool over when they're on the TV. They've even got a full-sized fucking boxing ring.

Unable to do anything but step deeper into the room, I take in all the equipment, most of which I've never seen before let alone ever tried to use.

I guess this helps explain the shape all the guys'—and the girls'—bodies are in.

I feel fat and out of shape just looking at it all.

The pink boxing gloves that sit with all the other red and black ones on a shelf behind the ring make me smile. It's the perfect reminder to the guys as they beat the shit out of each other down here who is really in charge.

After a thorough investigation and discovering absolutely nothing suspicious, I make my way back to the lift, still hoping I might find a secret passage or something crazy.

Clearly, there has to be something. Toby wouldn't have told me that they have people—or at least one person—locked in their basement if it's not true.

Not finding anything, I head back up to the garage level, more than ready to discover what's waiting for me.

10

TOBY

I fucking love driving into our garage after school and finding Jodie's little black Abarth parked in the space next to mine. I can't fight my smile, knowing that she's upstairs waiting for me.

We got called into work this evening for the first time since the Lovell shitshow. It was the last thing I wanted after Jodie messaged to tell me that she was back at mine after visiting Sara, but I had little choice.

I've already tempted fate enough when it comes to ignoring the boss's orders in favour of my girl. He might have given me a free pass given the situation, but I doubt I'll ever get it again.

I'm just glad I've managed to secure the weekend off.

I can't wipe the smile off my face as I push my door open and climb out, Nico, Alex, Seb, and Theo right behind me.

Nico and Alex are too busy taking the piss out of each other to notice my excitement about being home. It's not something Theo and Seb miss, however. Probably because it's a feeling they're experiencing right alongside me as we head up to our flats.

The second the lift dings on our floor, Seb and I spill out.

"You going to play with Nico?" Seb asks Alex when he fails to follow us.

"Better than listening to you four fuck the night away through the walls," he quips.

"Fuck off, bro. You can't hear shit and you know it."

"I dunno," Seb mutters. "Didn't you hear that screamer he brought home the other night? Sounded like a dying fucking cat."

Alex's chest puffs out with pride.

"I was just that good."

"Pretty sure I heard, 'Get the fuck off me, you monster,' at one point."

"Nah, mate. You must be mistaken. That was probably Stella."

"Un-fucking-likely," Seb scoffs. "We all know how much Stella loves my cock."

"Jesus. I'm out," I say, pressing my hand to the pad beside my door, more than ready to leave these idiots behind in favour of my girl. "Enjoy your evening," I call over my shoulder a second before their bickering is cut off and the incredible scent of something my girl is up to hits my nose.

My stomach growls loudly as I kick my shoes off.

My heart pounds harder with every step I take, and my mouth waters—both for the food she promised she'd have ready for me when I was finished and for her.

What I'm not prepared for is the sight that greets me as I round the corner and find her standing in my kitchen with a spatula in hand.

"Hey," she breathes, a wide smile spreading across her face and her eyes twinkling in excitement.

"Hey. This smells—"

Behind her, something bubbles over, the hiss of the water against the electric hob filling the space around us.

"Shit. Shit. Shit."

Twisting around, she pulls the pan away from the heat and attempts to mop up the mess with a tea towel.

"I'm so sorry. I've been trying so hard to—"

"Whoa, baby," I soothe, placing my hands on her waist and pressing the length of my body against her back. "You're welcome to make as much mess as you want to," I tease, my lips brushing the shell of her ear.

"B-but your kitchen is—"

"A kitchen. It's a place to make a mess," I assure her.

Taking the tea towel from her hand, I throw it in

the direction of my washing machine and move the pan back to the hob, ensuring the temperature is down.

"I fucking love having you here, Demon," I growl, nibbling around the shell of her ear.

"Dinner is going to be ruined if you keep this up, Tobias."

"I'm happy eating you instead," I confess, working my way down her throat until my lips collide with the neck of the jumper she's wearing.

"Yeah, well," she mutters, twisting out of my hold. "I'd rather eat, if it's all the same to you." Her stomach growls loudly in agreement, and when my eyes find her face, her cheeks are burning red.

"Go and take a seat, baby. I can finish up here."

Stepping forward, she takes my cheeks in her hands.

"No," she says firmly. "I told you that I'd cook and have dinner ready for you, so that's what I'm going to do. Go change. It'll be five minutes."

"But I thought you liked me in the suit," I tease, wrapping my fingers around her wrists and dragging them down over the lapels of my black jacket.

Her throat ripples with a swallow.

"Trust me, I do. But right now, I want you in sweats."

She gasps as I force her hand lower until she's grasping my length through my trousers.

"You just want to see exactly what you do to me, don't you, Demon?"

The most wicked smile curls at her lips.

"Guilty."

I shake my head at her, desperate to twist my fingers in her dark locks and force her to her knees, but I hold myself back. For now.

"Later," she promises. "I'm gonna need dessert after all."

"You, Jodie Walker, are fucking perfect."

I leave her hand exactly where it is as I crush her to my chest and kiss her as if I'm not going to get another chance.

"I feel like a grown-up," Jodie says lightly as she takes her seat opposite me at the dining table and reaches for her wine.

She's stayed with me here all week, so this isn't the first meal we've eaten together. But the others were takeaway and sitting with tubs around us didn't feel quite so... real, I guess.

"I like it," I confess, running my bare foot up her calf.

"I didn't say I didn't. It's just—"

"I know I'm a lot, Jodie. I know all of this is a lot," I say, gesturing to the building surrounding us and the people who are living inside it.

"I love being here. Doing this, it makes me happy," she admits.

"Yeah?"

A coy smile plays on her lips.

"So you wouldn't hate the idea of living here with me then?"

"Whoa," she says with a laugh. "I wouldn't go that far yet. I still haven't worked out what annoying traits you have that will drive me to the edge of insanity."

"You've seen my worse, baby, and you're still here. I'm not sure leaving dirty socks around will come anywhere close to all of that."

She might be smiling at me, but I don't miss the flicker of... guilt that flickers through her eyes.

Picking up my fork, I twist some of her spaghetti around it in the hope she'll confess to what's bothering her without me pushing.

"You've got an impressive gym downstairs," she blurts after a few seconds.

"Been snooping, baby?" I tease, despite the way the words make my stomach knot. Even still, I force myself to eat.

The second the food hits my tongue, I can barely contain my moan of approval.

"Oh my God, this is good."

She beams at my praise—or at least, I think it's that and not the fact that I've just given her a potential out of our previous conversation.

It's clearly not because she willingly picks it back up.

"I went down to the basement on Monday after I found the car key," she admits.

"Did you find what you were looking for?" I ask, not wanting to even think about the real reason she'd have been hunting down there.

She shakes her head, dropping her eyes from mine in favour of her dinner.

"You only have to ask me if you want to go down there, baby. I told you, I won't hide anything from you."

"I-I know. I just... I'm... scared, I guess. I'm scared that if I see him it'll change everything again."

"Or it could confirm everything you already know," I counter.

She nods, before she silently begins eating.

I let her lose herself in her thoughts, her fears for a few minutes before I finally say what I was desperate to when I first came in.

"I know things are... up in the air right now with Sara and that this probably isn't the best time but..." She looks up, her eyes softening at my nervous rambling.

"What is it?" she asks softly.

"I want to take you away this weekend. I've got a place for us. It's not far, we can come back immediately if anything happens and—"

"Yes," she says with a wide smile.

"Yeah?"

"As long as there's a phone signal and we can get back to the city."

"There is. I swear."

"Then yeah. I could do with a little... space."

"Space with me?" I ask.

"Obviously."

I stare at her for a beat, wondering just how I managed to end up here with her.

There are times, so many fucking times, where I wonder if it's all a game. If she's playing me for some reason like I was her to begin with. It'd fucking wreck me.

But then she looks at me with her huge, dark eyes, and all I see is love. She touches me, and it's as if she's just struck me with a million volts, and I remember that there's no chance of this being fake. It's too real.

Everything I feel for her, I see reflected back at me every single time we're together.

This is it. I have no doubt.

My eyes drop to the small padlock that's hanging around her neck. The little key that rests against my chest burns as if it's red hot, knowing that I hold the only way for her to remove it, and my dick hardens once more.

Noticing where my attention has gone, she places her knife and fork down on her now empty plate and slides the whole thing back. She reaches for her necklace, twisting the little lock between her fingers as she looks at me from beneath her lashes.

Heat surges through my body, need tugging at my muscles, but nowhere is more insistent than my aching cock.

"Tell me what you need," she says, her voice low and sending a shockwave of desire right through me.

It takes me a second to fight my way through the

fog of desire that clouds my brain before I can force some words out.

"Get on your hands and knees and crawl under the table. I need your lips wrapped around my cock."

Her pupils dilate at my words as her hand drops from the padlock.

"Yes, Boss," she purrs, pushing her chair out behind her and sinking to her knees, disappearing from my sight.

Fuck, yes.

The anticipation only grows as the table becomes a barrier between us. My heart pounds, knowing she could be about to touch me at any moment, and the heavy beat of it soon becomes the only thing I can hear as I wait.

My skin prickles with awareness, my cock twitching with need.

I know she's teasing me, and it fucking kills me.

My fingers wrap around the base of the chair until they begin to hurt.

"Demon," I growl, my desperation evident in my tone.

A soft chuckle comes from beneath the table, and my teeth grind with the need to reach out and find her.

But I don't.

I force myself to wait and see what she's going to do.

It feels like a fucking eternity, but when she

finally does touch me, I damn near jump out of my chair.

The graze of her finger against the top of my foot is innocent, but fuck if it doesn't have precum leaking from my cock.

"Jodie," I grit out as her fingers begin walking up my leg.

"Patience," she breathes, turning up my inner thigh, making every single muscle in my body lock up.

"Holy shit," I gasp when her fingers gently brush my dick.

It's pathetic. It's like I'm a twelve-year-old pre-teen who's never had his cock touched before.

Her amused chuckle hits my ears again, and my grip on the chair only tightens.

She shuffles between my legs, letting me know that she's close enough to reach out and touch, to control. That knowledge does little for my quest to hold myself back.

I flinch again when she trails her fingers along the skin just above the waistband of my sweats.

"Jesus," I hiss between clenched teeth, but my torture only gets worse a few seconds later when something, her nose, maybe, runs up the length of my cock.

"So hard for me, bad boy," she groans as if her teasing is as painful for her as it is for me.

"I'm always fucking hard for you, baby."

My breath catches as the heat of her mouth sears me through the fabric of my trousers.

"Fuck. Did you just bite me?"

"I thought you liked a bit of pain, Tobias."

"Fucking demon," I groan, sliding lower in the chair and spreading my thighs wider, fully giving myself over to her.

She continues toying with me through the fabric, driving me fucking crazy with the need to just sink into the heat of her mouth.

"Baby, don't make me come in my pants like a damn schoolboy," I force out between heaving breaths.

She laughs. "But that's exactly what you are," she quips.

"I'm fucking nineteen, Demon. I'm all man, and you damn well know it."

"So what are you saying?" she teases.

"I'm saying get your goddamn lips around my cock and let me come down your throat."

My head falls back as a loud, relieved sigh falls from my lips as she follows my demand, tucking her fingers beneath my waistband and begins tugging them free from my hips.

Not needing to prolong this torture any longer, I lift my arse from the seat and allow her to pull the fabric right down my legs. But she doesn't stop there —instead of leaving them hanging around my ankles, she tugs them off and discards them as if they've personally offended her.

"Better," she whispers a beat before the heat of her lips lands on my thigh.

"Demon," I grunt, much to her amusement. "Oh shit," I bark when she sinks her teeth into my skin, hard enough to draw blood, I'm sure.

"Mine," she purrs, tracing over the bite mark with the tip of her tongue.

"You marking me down there, baby?" I ask, the realisation making my cock jerk violently.

"Wouldn't want any of those girls at your school thinking you're available, would we?" Her tone is meant to be all teasing, I'm sure, but I still hear a tinge of jealousy in there. And I fucking love it.

"None of them are getting anywhere close to my thigh, Demon. Don't you worry."

"Huh, maybe I should leave my mark somewhere a little more obvious then. Ward off the predators."

"Mark me anywhere you want, baby. I am all fucking yours."

She kisses and bites right the way up my thigh, leaving me wondering just how it might look with her teeth marks and bruises marring it.

Just before I think about moving so I can see, all the thoughts fall from my head as the heat of her tongue connects with the head of my cock.

"Yes," I cry as she laps at my precum as if she hasn't eaten for a week. "Do I taste good, baby?"

"Like reckless decisions."

A smile curls at my lips as she continues to tease me, building me up to what I've no doubt will be an earth-shattering release when she finally lets me have it.

The second she sinks down on my length, taking me right the way to the back of her throat, I damn near shatter. It takes every bit of strength and willpower I possess to hold off and allow myself to enjoy this for just a few minutes at least.

I just told her I'm all man, so now I need to prove it.

"Fuck, Jodie. Fuck. I fucking love your mouth."

11

JODIE

I work Toby in my mouth as if my life depends on it.

Today has been long. There's been no more change with Sara since the good news on Sunday. I spent all afternoon finalising plans for my future, plans that I haven't discussed with Toby yet, and I was desperate for him to come home and distract me from all the seriousness of life. Sadly, that wasn't how our evening was destined to go, because no sooner than he walked in the door, he was telling me that he had to go straight back out again once he'd got changed.

Dread settled heavy in my stomach at the thought of him being sent into some dangerous situation like that night in Lovell, but he quickly reassured me that he was just heading to the hotel for a meeting with the boss and a shift on security.

So I spent the night cooking up a storm—the *pièce de résistance* of my culinary experimentation is still hiding in the fridge. I'm hoping it will be the second thing that blows his mind tonight.

"Jodie," he groans from above the table, his salty precum coating my tongue as I pull back and tease his head.

I just sink back down when there's a bang of a door closing somewhere behind me.

My heart jumps into my throat—not that there's much space with Toby's cock filling most of it—as footsteps get closer.

I pull back, ready to scramble out from beneath the table, but Toby is quicker. He finally releases the chair he's been holding onto for dear life in favour of twisting his fingers in my hair and giving me little choice but to stay exactly where I am.

"This is your first and only warning, I'm about to walk into the room."

I try to lift my head at the sound of his sister's voice, but his grip tightens, making my scalp burn.

I sense the moment she joins us in the room, despite the fact that I can't see anything but Toby's crotch as he feeds me his cock once more.

"Where's Jodie?" she asks, obviously able to see the evidence that I should have been sitting at the table eating with him.

Despite her standing there staring at him, he never stops the movement of his arm, forcing me to continue bobbing up and down on his unwavering hard-on.

"She's... uh... in the bathroom," he grits out. To me, it's so fucking obvious just from his voice alone as to what's going on, but either Stella is far stupider than I've given her credit for, or she's just more than happy playing this sick and twisted game they seem to have going on, because she doesn't move, and instead of excusing herself, her only response is, "No worries, I can wait."

If I weren't already damn near choking on Toby's dick, I would be at her knowing comment.

"What do you want, Stel?" Toby barks.

"Oh sorry, didn't I make it clear enough when I walked in and asked where Jodie is?"

I can picture her rolling her eyes in frustration while a knowing smirk plays on her lips.

"I'll pass on that you were here."

"Aw, that's so kind of you, Bro. But I'd really like to see her myself."

I can almost hear the amusement in her tone, and it makes me want to die a million deaths. I'm pretty sure it would have been less mortifying if she'd have walked in and we were doing this out in the open. At least I'd have stood a chance of Toby letting me up.

Toby forces me deeper on his cock, and I have to fight not to gag on him, giving myself away.

Sadly, though, he doesn't manage to restrain himself, and a low moan rumbles in his throat. It's not overly loud, but it's more than enough to alert Stella to what's happening—assuming she didn't suss us out the moment she walked in, of course.

"Fuck off, Stel," he grunts.

Silence follows as Toby slows his movements, holding me down on his dick. He twitches, his length swelling with his impending release.

"Fine," Stella huffs, "but only because I love you. Tell Jodie not to make any plans for tomorrow. She's mine. That's assuming she can't actually hear me right now."

Fucking thankfully, her footsteps quickly get quieter and I wait for the slam of the front door so I can finally push him over the edge.

"Oh, Tobes?" she calls from down the hall.

His response is nothing more than a pained groan.

"You can let go now. See you tomorrow, Jodie. Try not to drown." Her laughter is quickly cut off by the front door finally slamming and Toby's loud growl as he pushes me deeper, cutting off my airway as he comes violently down my throat.

The second he's done, he shoves his chair back with such force it tumbles to the floor with a crash, and he drags me out from beneath the table by my hair.

It hurts, but in only the best way.

The second I'm up, his lips crash down on mine and he groans as he no doubt tastes himself on my tongue.

Without breaking our dirty kiss, Toby

manages to shed me of my jeans and knickers, and before I know he's even dragging it up, he rips his lips from mine and pulls my jumper from my body.

The second my bra is gone, my feet leave the floor and my back crashes down on the table.

"Toby," I cry as his hands press against my inner thighs, exposing me to him.

"Sucking my cock gets you so wet," he drawls, staring down at me as if he's hungrier for me than he was the dinner he just devoured.

"Please," I whimper, more than a little desperate to feel him against me.

"Fucking love it when you beg me, Demon."

"Yes," I cry when he drops to his knees and immediately sucks my clit into his mouth.

"You're not being serious," I groan when I roll over and find Toby walking back into the bedroom. He's wearing nothing but a smile and carrying two mugs and the special treat I made for him last night that we never quite got around to.

After he brought me to ruin on the table, he swiftly bent me over it and started all over again.

By the time we were done, my knees were weak and I could barely hold my own weight up. Something that, thankfully, wasn't an issue, seeing as he insisted on carrying me to the shower so we could resume.

We spent the rest of the night watching TV, curled up in his bed and locked in each other's arms. It was perfect. I was easily falling into a content routine with Toby, and as exhilarating as that was, it was also terrifying, because my life wasn't always going to be this... free and easy. I can't remain having nothing to do but visit Sara and cook dinner for Toby every night. It's not me.

I need... something. A job, a focus.

I just need to figure out what that looks like for the next few months before everything changes again and I finally embark on life as a student at last.

"I can't believe you distracted me with your pussy," he mutters, placing the mugs on the bedside table and climbing back into bed with the plateful of cheesecake and two spoons.

"We can't have this for breakfast," I gasp, my smile threatening to give me away.

"Says who? There are no rules, baby. You want cheesecake for breakfast and porridge for dinner, be my guest."

He holds the plate between us in one hand while he dives for the dessert with his spoon, scooping up an obscene amount before stuffing it all in his mouth.

"You're a pig," I scoff. Reaching out, I swipe my thumb across the corner of his mouth, collecting up everything he couldn't fit inside before helping myself to it.

"Hmm, maybe I should just smear it all over my body and have you lick it off me again."

"Maybe another time, bad boy. You've got school."

"Goddamn it. Only a few weeks until the holidays. Then we don't have to get up for a whole two weeks." Ignoring the spoon I'm holding, he loads his again and offers it to me. "I might take you somewhere. A private island with our own infinity pool. We can be naked the entire time and I can fuck you outside where only the dolphins can see."

My mind wanders, conjuring up my own little fantasy from his words.

It sounds like heaven, and something I never thought would even be a possibility in my life.

But I guess all of that has changed now I'm here in the middle of all this... insanity.

"I don't need all that, Toby. As long we're together, we could be camping in the middle of a muddy field with only the cows watching us."

"As... wonderful," he says, screwing up his nose and showing me just a flash of the little boy he used to be, "as that sounds, we can do better than getting cold and wet in the middle of a smelly field."

"Maybe so, but I need you to know that I would be just as happy as long as I was with you."

He smiles at me. The sight of his pure happiness at my words makes my chest feel too small.

"Are you still up for this weekend?" he asks, steering the conversation back to the here and now.

"As long as nothing changes with Sara, yeah. I'm ready for a few days of forgetting about real life."

Toby's phone vibrates on the bedside table and he spins around.

"Shit, I'm going to be late again."

"Nico?" I ask.

"Yeah. I never thought I'd see the day when he was the one waiting for me.

He has one last spoonful before he leaves me with the plate and quickly rummages around his room and drags on his uniform.

"Shouldn't Stella be at school today?" I ask, my eyes trailing him around the room and in and out of the bathroom.

"Yeah, but I told her about this weekend and she clearly has plans."

"Christ, she's going to take me for another waxing session, isn't she?" I ask, squeezing my thighs together as I think about my last experience in that salon in Lovell before my disaster shift at Foxes that I never want to think about ever again.

His eyes roll down my body as if he's imagining me laid out naked before some unforgiving woman rips all my hair from my skin.

"Maybe, but I guess you don't have long to wait to find out."

I glance at my own phone and realise just how late it is.

Abandoning the cheesecake in the middle of the

bed, I walk shamelessly naked toward Toby as his eyes eat up every inch of me.

"Have a good day, schoolboy," I breathe, reaching up on my toes, my breasts brushing his jacket and sending a shiver racing down my spine. "I'll be here waiting to see what you've got up your sleeve for me this time."

"Tonight can't come soon enough, Demon. Try not to get into too much trouble with my sister."

"I can't make any promises."

I brush my lips across his in the most teasing of kisses before I dart away and out of his grasp before he can deepen it.

"Later, bad boy," I purr, kicking the bathroom door closed behind me.

"Tease," he shouts.

"You love it."

"I love you." I still in the middle of the bathroom as his words rock the ground I'm standing on.

He hasn't said those words since that night I begged him not to and they slipped out anyway. I might not have been ready to hear them back then. But my reaction right now is the proof I needed to remind myself of just how much I've grown in the past few weeks. I've been to hell and back, and I feel like an entirely different person.

I've shed my naïve skin, I've stopped viewing the world through rose-tinted glasses, and I couldn't be happier with my new life, even if it is full of blood, pain, and destruction. Everything about it just seems right.

A door slams somewhere in the flat, and I quickly realise that I never said anything in response.

I let out a sigh, trying to imagine how he left feeling. I guess I'll just have to make it up to him this weekend.

To my amazement, Stella decided against letting herself in this morning to find me, and once I'm dressed, I head across the hallway and knock on her door.

Part of me wonders if yesterday had all been a bit of a joke and that she's actually gone to school with the others.

But not two seconds later does the door open and a very happy-looking Stella is standing there.

The scent of bacon hits me immediately and my stomach growls in delight, my cheesecake breakfast already long forgotten.

"Ah good, you came up for air," she deadpans.

My chin drops as she holds her expression steady for a beat before she cracks and falls about laughing.

"You know, there's something really wrong with all of you," I mutter, slipping past her and deeper into her flat.

It's the first time I've actually been inside, and I

must admit that I feel almost as at home here as I do in Toby's.

"And yet you're willingly standing in the middle of us. What does that say about you?" she quips. "Anyway, you seemed to be enjoying yourself. I must admit, if the situation were reversed, I'd have stayed down there worshipping Seb's cock too."

I stare at her, feeling more at home listening to her filth than I probably should. But she reminds me of Bri and her lack of filter when it comes to... well... anything.

"You should have seen his face. It was priceless. He was so pissed."

"He wasn't the only one," I mutter, helping myself to a stool at their breakfast bar. "So what's going on? Shouldn't you be at school?"

"Meh," she waves me off. "I'm taking a personal day."

My brows lift in curiosity. "I only went to a normal school. But if that's a thing at your posh one then I guess—"

"Oh, it's totally not. I've just called in sick in favour of spending the day with my sister." She winks, continuing before I manage to get a word in. "So, we can go and see Sara this morning. Then I thought we could go and do a little shopping, get you something sexy for the weekend, get our nails done. You know, just... hang."

"Will there be cocktails involved?" I ask,

remembering all too well how many we drank our way through the day we went to the spa.

"Oh, hell yeah. And actually, now you mention it..."

She spins around and pulls her fridge open, revealing a bottle of prosecco and a carton of orange juice.

"Let's start the day as we mean to go on."

"Don't get me wasted. I want to enjoy my weekend with Toby, not be hanging out of my arse."

"I take zero control over the decisions you make, Jodie Walker. You are your own woman who can make her own bad choices, present company evidence of that fact."

"You're something else," I mutter, watching as she mixes us, thankfully, fairly weak drinks.

"I went American-style," she says a few seconds later once I've got my drink and she pulls a plate of freshly made pancakes from the oven.

"Oh my God, yes. Gimme." I reach out with little grabby hands, more than ready for the mouth-watering mix of the sweet and fluffy against the crisp and salty bacon."You know how to make a girl happy."

"And you know how to make my brother smile like I've never seen before, so I'm happy too."

"You're never going to let me live down last night, are you?"

"Uh..." She pretends to think for a second. "Nope. Seriously though, none of us care about that shit. Enjoy yourself, have fun, and as long as you don't break his heart, we're never going to have a problem."

Her thinly veiled threat lingers in the air as she slides a plate closer to me.

"Don't look so worried. Hang around long enough and I'll train you up so that you can at least try and take me in the ring."

"Jesus," I mutter, although the tension quickly disappears when I have a mouthful of her breakfast. "Have you made these for Toby?"

"Yep. Why do you think he lets me get away with all my shit so easily? I supply him with his sugar hit regularly."

"So you've bought them all with pancakes?" I joke.

"Nah, mostly just Toby. I hooked Seb with my pussy; the others just love my glowing personality and warm heart."

I stare at her, unable to decide how to act.

"I'm joking," she says with a smile. "Mostly. When I beat them all in the ring, they had little choice but to admit who really held all the power around here."

"I envy you," I admit quietly.

"Me? Why? You're pretty fucking awesome, Jodie."

I shrug. "You're so headstrong. You seem to know exactly what you want in life and take it by the balls. Quite possibly literally, in Seb's case."

"Want me to let you in on a little secret?" She leans over the counter as if she's about to whisper something life changing.

"Sure."

"I don't have a fucking clue what I'm doing. I make shit up as I go along. It's all perception, Jodie."

"Well, consider me convinced."

"Seriously though, when you've moved about as much as I have, when your world seems to be changing almost on a weekly basis, then you have little choice but to learn to roll with the punches.

"This place? It's really only the second place I've ever called home."

"Where was the first?" I ask, desperate to know more about her unconventional upbringing.

"A place in Florida called Rosewood. It was my home before we moved here. The friends I made there were... incredible."

"You miss them?" I ask when her sadness becomes palpable.

"Yeah," she breathes. "But we talk a lot. And I'm hoping they'll come to visit once they graduate this summer. They've met Seb, know all about my life here. But I really want them to meet the rest of the guys, see this place, you know?"

I nod. "I'm glad all your moving about wasn't all bad," I say with a smile.

"It taught me a lot. And it made me appreciate just how good things can be when they're right, even if to everyone else they look completely wrong."

Her words hit me right in the chest as if she's talking about my life, about my relationship with Toby.

"Fuck what the rest of the world thinks, Jodie. All that matters is what's in your heart. Everyone else can go fuck themselves."

12

TOBY

"**D**id we have a date I forgot about or something?" I ask as I stroll out of my class to find Seb leaning back against the opposite wall with one foot propped up and his phone in his hand.

A wicked smile curls at his lips when he realises I've found him.

"Oh bro, we're about to have the date of all motherfucking dates. I hope you lubed up."

I glare at him.

"What the actual fuck are you talking about?"

"You remember how I never got you a birthday present?"

"Uh... yeah. But you're tighter than a duck's arsehole when it comes to presents, so I wasn't exactly expecting much," I mutter.

"Pfft, that's bullshit. Have you seen the number of diamonds in that necklace around my girl's neck?"

"Stella doesn't count."

"Well, whatever." He wraps an arm around my shoulders and steers me toward the main exit. "I'm about to make it up to you tenfold."

Curious, I allow him to walk me out to the car park.

"You could have just fed me. I'm fucking starving," I complain when it becomes more than obvious we're about to leave campus for whatever this little surprise is.

Turns out that Jodie was right to question my choice of breakfast this morning. Cheesecake isn't all that filling. I was only halfway through my first lesson of the day before my stomach was growling so loudly I was sure even the teacher could hear it over his overly eager explanation.

Okay, so maybe it was pure boredom that was making me hungry.

"I promise, I'll get you something to eat," he says as he brings the engine to life and backs out of his space. "So I hear you had quite the treat after your dinner last night."

"Jesus," I mutter, scrubbing my hand down my face.

"Is there nothing you and Stella don't share?"

"Secrets, bodily fluids, murder... nope. We're almost one person at this point. Fucking glad she walked in on you though, man. She came back horny as—"

"Stop. Please, just stop," I beg.

His laughter rips through the car. "You're too fucking easy to get to these days, Tobes."

"Yeah well, how would you feel if I were banging one of your sisters and telling you all about it?"

He winces.

"Exactly."

"You'll forgive me in about ten minutes."

"We'll see," I mutter, folding my arms over my chest as I stare out of the window, trying to guess where we're going.

Only a few minutes later, we pull up into a car park I've never been to before and Seb instructs me to follow him.

"If you've brought me to help choose Stella's lingerie, then I gotta tell you, you dragged the wrong person along for this little trip. I don't even care what food you bribe me with, I can already tell you it won't be—"

"Stop fucking complaining. I don't want you to choose Stella's underwear. Sex toys, on the other hand..." I turn on my heel, but Seb's expecting it and his fingers grip onto my upper arm before I get a chance to move. "I'm joking, obviously. Although something tells me that your expertise in that area could come in handy."

"I'm not a fucking expert. I just like—"

"A bit of kink. Who knew? Nice little Toby likes tying his girl up and spanking her until she's glowing."

"Don't knock it until you try it," I scoff, my mind going back to our first night in Hades.

"Oh, I have every intention of fucking trying it."

"Funny, because I thought you were being a pussy about taking Stella."

"Nah." He rubs his hands together hungrily. "It's gonna happen."

"Why are we here?" I ask as he drags me into a department store and immediately heads for the escalator.

He looks over at me and winks.

Deep down, I already know. I did from the moment he steered me out of school, but I desperately didn't want to be disappointed so I kept any kind of hope that wanted to bubble up firmly locked down.

"You can tell me how much you love me later, bro."

"You're a dirty motherfucker," I tell him as we walk through the rails of ladies' clothing in the direction where the signs are pointing toward the fitting rooms.

"Oh, because you're a fucking angel," he deadpans.

Tapping out a quick message on his phone, he tucks it back in his pocket.

Suspiciously, there are no members of staff anywhere near. Their little station at the entrance is completely abandoned as we enter.

"At the end on the left. We've got ten minutes.

Whoever makes them scream loudest gets out of buying lunch."

"You're a dickhead."

"Meh, couldn't give a fuck."

Pulling the curtain back of the cubicle opposite the one he directed me to, he slips inside a beat before Stella starts giggling.

Well, when in Rome...

Reaching out, I copy his move, finding my girl standing in just a lacy red thong I ordered online for her when she was sleeping last week.

The sight of her makes my mouth water, which isn't exactly how I'd describe her reaction as she screams in fright, her arms wrapping around her exposed tits in an attempt to cover up.

"Get the hel— Toby?" she gasps once her brain has caught up with her shock.

I don't respond. There isn't time for small talk.

Instead, I surge toward her, spin her around and push her against the mirror. She cries out in surprise as the cold glass collides with her heated skin.

Another yelp passes her lips when my palm collides with her bare arse cheek.

"Shit, Toby," she pants, already desperate from just that one touch.

Sinking to my knees, I twist the thin sides of her thong in my hands until it falls away from her body, allowing me to stuff my prize into my pocket.

I might own her now, but I'm not sure stealing her underwear will ever get old.

"Open your legs, Demon. I want your cunt."

She does exactly as she's told and in only seconds, I'm between her thighs with my back to the mirror.

Our eyes collide as she stares down at me before I sweep my tongue up the length of her, letting her taste fill my mouth.

"Fuck, baby," I groan at how wet she is. "Were you in here thinking about me?"

I push two fingers deep inside her, curling them in a way I know she loves.

"Toby," she cries, as very similar noises come from the cubicle opposite us.

Pushing the thought of them aside, I focus on my girl, sucking her clit into my mouth and grazing her with my teeth.

I have every intention of using my ten minutes in here with her to the max. And that means she's coming at least twice. Once on my face, and then again as she takes my cock.

Reaching down with my free hand, I flick my trousers open and somewhat awkwardly shove them down to expose my length. Wrapping my fingers around it, I slowly work myself as I go to town on my girl.

Her eyes get heavier and heavier as she stares down at me, but she never closes them, too desperate to experience every second of this with me.

"You're so fucking beautiful, Demon," I growl, letting the vibrations of my deep voice flow through her.

"Fuck. Toby," she moans as her muscles start clamping down on my fingers.

"Does it get you hot, knowing anyone could be out there listening to you cry my name like a dirty whore?"

Her eyes flash with heat at my crass words.

"Yes," she breathes. "And I fucking love this side of you."

"You like me bad, huh?" I growl.

"You know I do."

Dragging my fingers from inside her, I tease her entrance.

"Just how dirty do you feel like being, baby?"

I move them behind her, teasing her arse.

Her entire body tenses at the sensation. We haven't gone there yet, although she's never told me she's against it, so I'm gonna take my chances.

She hisses as I press against the tight ring of muscle, my fingers more than slick enough from her cunt.

"Holy fuck," she gasps as I push deeper.

"Come for me, Demon. Show me how good this feels."

My tongue continues working her clit, and with my finger slowly fucking her arse, it only takes a few more seconds before she falls into her first blissful release.

"Good girl. Don't move," I bark, pulling my finger from inside her and standing back up.

My heart pounds and my cock aches with need as I stand behind her.

Wrapping my fist in her long ponytail, I drag her back against me, her arse teasing my cock in the most incredible way.

My teeth graze the shell of her ear as she fights to get her breathing back under control.

Finding her eyes in the mirror, I whisper, "I'm going to fuck you hard and fast, and I want you screaming my name so fucking loud that every motherfucker in this place knows you belong to me. You got that, Demon?"

A smirk twitches at her lips. "Yes, Boss."

Pride for my girl surges through me a beat before I force her to bend over.

"Hands on the mirror, and don't fucking move them."

Sucking in a breath through my teeth, I take in the sight of her bent over before me.

Wrapping my hand around my length again, I trail a fingertip down the ridges of her spine, loving the way she shudders at my touch.

"Toby," she moans, wiggling her hips.

"Desperate little whore," I mutter. "You like being my toy, don't you?" I ask, running the head of my cock through her pussy, covering it in her juices.

"Yes," she cries when I push inside just enough to tease her. "Toby, please. I need—"

I thrust forward, knowing exactly what she needs.

Her arms give out with my force, and I just manage to catch her before her face collides with the mirror.

"Hold steady. This isn't going to be gentle," I warn, releasing her shoulders and wrapping my fingers around her hips instead.

"Eyes on me," I demand. "I want you to watch me own you."

Her dark chocolate orbs find mine in the mirror, and this time when I thrust into her body, she's ready for me and takes it like the demon she is.

Aware that time is slipping away from me, I fuck her like a savage as sweat starts to run down my spine.

"Come for me, baby. I'd hate to have to leave you here wanting."

"You wouldn't," she moans, letting me know that she's just as close as I am.

"I wouldn't test me if I were you."

My grip on her tightens as I ride the edge of my release.

Sliding one of my hands lower, I pinch her clit between my fingers and she almost immediately goes off like a rocket, screaming my name loudly exactly as I demanded.

I follow not a second later, growling as my cock jerks deep inside her, filling her up.

The moment I'm done, I pull out and spin her around, slamming her back against the mirror once more and crashing my lips to hers.

She kisses me almost as hungrily as I do her. Her fingers twist in my hair, holding me against her as if she never wants to let go.

Dropping my hand between her thighs, I run my fingers through her cunt, my chest swelling as I feel my cum slipping out of her.

"You're wasting it, baby," I growl, pushing it back inside and making her moan once more.

"Tobias, your time is up, man," Seb's amused voice booms through the curtain.

"As if you were keeping fucking track of the time," I shout back, capturing Jodie by the throat to hold her in place.

I hold her eyes for a beat, letting her see everything I feel for her in my blue depths.

"I'll be home after practice," I tell her, contentment washing through me as I think about the flat that used to be mine as ours. "Be ready for the weekend."

"What do I need to pack?"

"Normal shit. And a bikini. Smallest you can find."

"Tobes," Seb barks.

"All fucking right," I snap back, releasing Jodie and tucking myself away while she stands against the mirror with her chest heaving and her skin flushed with desire.

"Until later, baby." I wink, lifting my fingers to my mouth and licking her taste off them.

Her chin drops and her eyes darken before I

regretfully back out of the curtain and leave her alone to put herself back together again.

"Fucking told you it would be the best present of your life," Seb says happily as I walk toward him. "Oh, you've got a little..." He taps the corner of his mouth before nodding down to mine.

Unable to stop myself, I wipe my lips, much to his fucking amusement.

"You're a cunt," I mutter.

"You wouldn't have me any other fucking way. Come on, let's go finish our day before we can do our girls all weekend."

"Addict."

"And fucking proud, man."

13

JODIE

I was nervous about leaving town for the weekend, there was no denying that. But there was no change in Sara's condition this morning, and her doctor wasn't really expecting that to change any time soon. For now, she's stable and we just have to continue praying.

But even knowing there's nothing I can do for her, guilt claws at my insides that I'm not there for Jesse. He's barely holding it together. He scarcely even resembles the man I'm used to with his dark eyes and wrecked expression. It pains me to look at him and know that the only thing I can do is to be there. To deliver him coffee and food and try to say all the right things, which at the time always feel like the wrong things.

It's hard.

So fucking hard.

And I have a fear that it's only going to get worse before it's going to get better.

Jesse sits there day in and day out, like she might wake up at any moment. I get it, I really fucking do. If it were Toby, then I'd be right there egging him on, giving him all of my support. But I can't help but feel like he's losing himself right alongside her.

Even if she does pull through this, it's going to be a long, slow road to recovery.

She gave up everything to chase her dreams, and then, even more, to have a life with Jesse. What happens when that is stripped away?

Her parents have already declared their wishes for her future care. I think if it weren't for Toby securing the best treatment in the Cirillo ward of the hospital, then they'd have already moved her closer to their home and taken away Jesse's ability to see her.

The thought of that happening makes my heart ache. Sara is his entire life. I have no idea how he'd cope if he lost that contact now.

"We can turn around or go back whenever you need," Toby assures me, predicting where my head is at. His hand tightens on mine as we head toward wherever we're going.

The only thing I know about this trip is that it's been organised through Galen and that it's not Evan's cabin. So really, knowing Toby and the people he's connected to, it could literally be anything.

"I know," I say softly. "I just got lost in my own head. I wish there was more I could do."

"Same, baby."

"I'm worried about Jesse. He's not coping."

"The boys are keeping a close eye on him," he assures me. And I know they are. Archer, Dax, and Jace have been up there every day, ensuring Jesse has everything he needs and forcing him to take care of himself.

I nod, knowing that even their friendship isn't going to help much right now.

"How are things in Lovell now?" I ask, needing to divert the conversation away from that depressing hospital room.

"Yeah, as far as I know, it's all settled down, and Archer has control back over the estate."

"Did you..." I hesitate, hardly able to believe I'm about to ask this question seriously. "Did you... get rid of the members who were causing issues?"

"Get rid of?" Toby asks with a smirk.

"Did you kill them?" I laugh.

How exactly does my life involve asking if my boyfriend killed the bad guys?

"Well, not personally, but they got most of the main players in the takeover attempts."

"And what about the ones they didn't?"

"Fled with their tails between their legs."

"That sounds... dangerous."

"Nah. They're not stupid enough to try anything now. They lost. They'll most likely start over somewhere else. Weasel their way into some other gang in another city and start the process over."

"I thought gangs are all about loyalty," I say with a frown.

"They are. But shit gets fucked up when you find your loyalties are in the wrong place. They made a mistake backing Luis, and now they have to pay the price.

"If they hang around, they'll be dead. So the only option really is to start over. And gang life is all they've ever known. They're hardly going to find a job somewhere and become an upstanding citizen."

"I guess."

"Things are going to be okay there now. And with us and the Reapers behind them, Archer has everything he could need to make a new start."

Silence falls between us as I pull my eyes away from Toby and look out of the window. My eyes widen when I realise we've left the main road behind and are currently surrounded by perfectly kept bushes.

"What the hell is this place? One of the Queen's holiday residences?" I ask when the biggest set of gates I've ever seen appears over the small hill before us.

"I'm not sure. That wasn't one of the questions I asked," Toby quips as he brings the car to a stop in front of them before he lowers the window and taps a code into the little keypad.

"Bingo," he announces as the light turns green and the gates before us begin to swing open smoothly.

"Ho-ly shit, Toby," I gasp as he pulls forward and the most insane house comes into view. "It's—"

"Fucking massive," he breathes, sounding almost as shocked as I am.

The white building before us is so modern it's damn near futuristic.

The orange hue of the setting sun behind us reflects in the huge windows that cover a massive part of both the ground and first floor of the building.

Huge double doors sit smack bang in the middle. The whole thing is perfectly symmetrical, right down to the flower pots that line the path toward the huge porch.

"It's insane."

"Galen said it was a nice place, but shit. This is—"

"We can't stay here. It's too much."

"It's ours for the whole weekend. The owners are happy for us to make use of it."

"Toby, we'll get fucking lost in there."

He turns to me, a salacious smile curling at his lips. "You fancy a game of hide and seek?"

My eyes drop to his lips as his tongue runs along the bottom one.

"I guess that all depends on what the winner gets," I whisper, my voice barely above a breathy moan as his teeth replace his tongue, sinking into the soft pillow of his lip.

"Head," he growls. "Whoever loses has to make the other scream."

I study him, my heart thumping almost as hard as the pulsating between my legs.

"Sounds like a game I could get behind," I mutter. "I guess we should maybe go and check it out then. I need to find some good hiding spots."

"And to think, this was meant to be a relaxing weekend. Come on," he says, shouldering the door before I get a chance to respond.

I sit there for a couple of seconds, just taking in the insane design of the building in front of me until Toby slams the boot closed and walks around to my side, pulling my door open for me.

"My lady," he murmurs, gesturing for me to exit.

"Thank you, kind sir."

We walk to the front door in silence. Toby might be used to wealth and luxury, but something tells me that this place has even shocked him.

My chin drops as he pushes the door open. We step into a perfectly white huge hallway with an elaborate staircase rising from the centre before it splits around both sides of the vast space, toward what I assume are bedrooms.

My shoes tap against marble flooring that I'm sure cost more than I'm likely to make in my lifetime alone.

I feel like a total fraud even standing in here.

"You remember me telling you that your money didn't impress me, right?" I say, staring at a painting that I'm sure I should probably recognise as one of the greats. But as I study it, I realise that I don't even really like it. To me, it says nothing. It means nothing, and quite honestly, it's not even that attractive. It's just for show, and that alone turns me off.

"Well, lucky for us, this isn't my money. It belongs to someone who clearly has way too much. And after all the shit we've been through, I think we more than deserve a couple of days pretending to live the luxury of their life."

"Do you even know who the place belongs to?" I ask, watching as he kicks his shoes off and places the cases we packed against the pristine walls.

"Nope. And right now, I couldn't give a fuck."

The second I follow his lead and abandon my shoes, he takes my hand and drags me down the hallway toward the first door.

I squeal as my legs struggle to keep up with him, and a wide smile spreads across my face at his playfulness.

"This is a chef's wet dream," I announce as we stumble into a kitchen that is beyond anything I've ever seen before.

"Fuck the chef, the only thing I want to eat in here is you on top of that granite counter."

"Toby," I gasp as his large hands wrap around my waist, ready to put me in position. "No," I cry, darting away from him before he can lift me from my feet.

"Demon," he growls as I fly from the room, quickly finding myself in another full of sleek black furniture. But in the corner, there's a pink dollhouse which looks totally out of place. The sight of it makes another laugh tumble from my lips. I guess this is what the mega wealthy call a family room.

Heavy footsteps pound behind me as I continue forward and emerge back into the hallway we started in. Or at least, I think it is. I move too fast to take notice of the details of the room as I race for the stairs.

The thick pile of the carpet beneath my feet softens my footsteps, and I smile to myself that I might just be able to put some distance between us to prolong this little game of cat and mouse.

My heart pounds as adrenaline races through my veins. I pause at the corner and listen. A laugh bubbles up when all that greets me is the sound of my heavy breathing.

Pulling my cardigan off, I throw it at the stairs and run once more, nothing but joy and recklessness filling my body.

As I move, I unbutton my blouse, finally letting it fall from my arms and abandoning it in the hallway.

I rush around another corner as footsteps thunder up the stairs behind me.

"You can't outrun me, Demon. I will find you and I'll even graciously claim my winnings."

My stomach tumbles with excitement as I push forward.

Tugging my jeans undone, I awkwardly shove them down over my hips as I discover another set of stairs.

I leave my trousers behind on them, quickly followed by my socks.

My bra hits the carpet in the hallway before I push through the first door I find and rush inside.

I'm already deep in the room before I actually look up and take in my surroundings.

"Holy crap," I gasp as I take in the sheer size of the bedroom. But as stunning as the room is, it's the windows, or more so the sunset beyond that steals my attention.

The sky is beautiful shades of orange and red as the sun makes its final descent toward the horizon, reflecting in the still water of what I can only think is a lake in their freaking garden.

This place is like heaven on earth.

It's a shocking reminder of just how much my life has changed. My weekends away are no longer at an old holiday park with Bri, getting as wasted as we possibly can and riding high on life. Instead, I'm in the middle of a millionaire's mansion, playing hide and seek. Well, I guess we never really grow up, do we?

"Come out, come out, wherever you are," Toby's voice calls from beyond the door.

In a rush, I shimmy my knickers over my hips and let them drop to my feet.

I quickly snatch them up and throw them toward the door I left slightly ajar. This might be a game, but we both know the thrill is really in the capture.

Forgetting the fact that I'm currently standing in

what I assume is someone's master bedroom butt naked, I quickly look around. Not finding a location that does it for me, I stalk toward the huge bed. I swear it's big enough for at least four people. That thought only stirs up more questions about the owners of this place.

Lowering my arse to the edge, my pulse thunders in time with Toby's approaching steps, and the riot of butterflies continues to multiply in my belly.

My gasp rips through the air when he comes to a stop outside the door, his shadow filling the few inches I left it apart a beat before the small heap of lace I threw over there is stolen.

"Mmm, smells like my girl could be close," he murmurs. "I can almost taste my sweet, sweet vict—" He swings the door open and his words cut off when he finds me resting back on my palms with my legs spread and my chest heaving.

"Shit, Demon."

In seconds, his hoodie is on the floor, his shoes and socks are off, and his fly is ripped open.

The way he moves toward me can't be described in any way but a prowl, his eyes drinking me in and eating me up all at the same time.

My breathing only becomes more erratic as his scent hits me, and my core only gets slicker with need.

"Well, well, well, look what I have here. A little mouse in my trap, ready to be destroyed."

He drops to his knees, his eyes impossibly dark as

his tongue sweeps along his bottom lip as if he can already taste me there.

"But you won, I thought—"

"Oh, baby. I have fucking won." His hands grip my hips and he lifts my arse from the bed as he latches onto me, his tongue plunging inside me as my head falls back on a scream of pleasure.

14

TOBY

I have no idea who this place belongs to, but it doesn't matter, because their master bedroom may as well be ours now. The memories I have from last night of finding her, devouring her, making her come in every which fucking way will be ingrained in my mind forever. Watching her writhe about on the huge bed is something that I'm probably going to think about for the rest of my life. The gorgeous soft glow of the setting sun and the moonlight left on her skin as I ruined her in all the best ways is etched onto my eyelids. She was a demon, but really, she's my angel.

She saved me in so many ways. Ways I'm sure she'll never really truly understand. Hell, I'm not even sure I really understand. All I know is that I was on a one-way trip to self-destruction, and if I didn't drag her along for the ride to hell with me then I have no idea where I'd have ended up.

I thought she was put on this earth to help get me the vengeance I craved, but really, she was put here for me.

The one and only good thing that cunt has ever done in his life is lead me to her. My solace. My saviour. And while my hate for him might still poison every ounce of my blood, I can't say that it's not lessened a little. He gave me a gift. One he tried to keep hidden, but one I discovered and made my own despite his wishes.

"What are you thinking about?" Jodie asks, placing a drink down in front of me and stepping between my legs where I was sitting, watching her in the kitchen.

Dread settles in my belly, but I don't shy away from the truth.

Jodie has shown me time and time again that she's more than strong enough to handle the reality of my life, and I'm fully prepared to share everything I can about it with her.

"About *him*," I confess. "About you." I shrug as a soft smile plays on her lips.

Our time here has been nothing short of amazing. We'd spent the day down in the cinema room we found in the basement. After we made good use of the master bedroom, we finally went on a mission to discover every single room this place has to offer, and we both agreed that what we found beneath the ground was by far the best.

I didn't want to let her see it, but I was hesitant to

go down those stairs. The only experience I've had with basements in my life has been less than pleasant, but with my hand in hers, I stepped down and left my demons well behind. Thank fuck I did, because the room that appeared before us was as breathtaking as the rest of the building.

Jodie is about to reply when a car horn sounds out.

"What the hell?" I bark, standing and marching toward the window when headlights illuminate the whole kitchen. "Galen said this place was going to be em—" My words falter as two cars come to a stop beside mine. "Motherfuckers," I grunt.

"What is— oh," Jodie says with a laugh as everyone spills from the vehicles.

"Yeah, oh. I hope you weren't planning on a nice quiet night in," I say, knowing full well that we were. I've already got the firepit outside loaded, ready for us to spend the night sitting around as we just do, well... nothing.

"Yeah, but this could be fun too. Oh my God," she squeals, spotting something, or someone I hadn't previously before she bolts toward the front door.

I take off behind her, half cussing them all out and half glad to see them.

By the time I get to the door, Jodie is running down the path shouting, "Brianna," before she jumps into her arms.

"What the actual fuck is this?" I bark, folding my arms over my chest as I glare at Stella and Seb. I may have zero evidence, but I know for a fact that they are behind this little ambush.

"So..." Stella starts. "Dad might have accidentally let slip about where you were and we thought that maybe it might be fun to—"

"Gatecrash?"

"I was gonna say party, but sure, if you wanna call it that, go right ahead, Bro." She taps me on the chest patronisingly before slipping past me and into the house. "Fuck. This place is insane," she mutters before her footsteps fade away and Nico storms toward me, his face like fucking thunder.

"I didn't agree to this," he says, pointing behind him where Jodie and Brianna are still talking. "She's infuriating."

"Aw, didn't she let you fuck her in the back of the car? Poor little Nico," I mock.

"Fuck you. We both know I could have her bent over for me in three seconds flat if I tried." I can't help but smirk at his arrogance.

"So what you're not saying is that since you left her tied up and at the mercy of whoever walked into that hotel room on Valentine's Day, she isn't talking to you?"

"It was just a joke," he scoffs, pulling his bag higher up on his shoulder and taking off into the house. Alex, Theo, Emmie, and Calli quickly trailing behind him.

"Hey, Brianna," I greet, walking toward the two of them.

"Hey, Toby. I hope you don't mind me joining. Not that Stella really gave me a choice. Your sister is fierce, man."

"Anything that makes my girl squeal like that is good with me," I quip.

"Oh hell, yes. I hope you've been treating her right, Tobias." Brianna winks before grabbing Jodie's hand and tugging her toward the house. "Didn't I always tell you that you should bang the ones with money?"

"You're a nightmare," Jodie laughs, shooting a look back at me. My heart melts at the genuine happiness radiating from her, and I quickly forget about any irritation I had with the guys for turning up and ruining our peace like this.

Their voices and laughter fill the entire downstairs as I close the front door behind us all and return to the kitchen.

Stella and Brianna are busy making jugs of cocktails, and Alex and Nico are filling the fridge with beer, vodka and a few other bottles I can't make out.

Theo and Seb are nowhere to be seen, but I can hear them.

"They're starting the firepit for you," Jodie says, noticing who I'm looking for as she steps up to me. "You okay with this?"

I smile down at her as she brushes her hands over my chest before resting her arms over my shoulders.

"Are you happy?" I ask, lowering my brow to hers and cutting everyone else off from my vision.

"I am. I love your family."

"Shh, don't let them hear you say that. It'll go to their heads."

Her laugh lights me up from the inside.

"We ordered Chinese on the drive here. It should arrive in about ten minutes."

I drop a kiss on the end of Jodie's nose before turning to look at my sister.

"That was very presumptuous of you. We could have refused to open the door."

"Maybe. But you didn't, did you?" She grins at me, and all I can do is laugh. "Come on, kids. Let's go get drunk and reckless."

"Oh God," I groan, more than aware of the kind of reckless shit she can get up to when she's drunk. "Just keep your fucking clothes on," I call after her as she carries a jug of something out to the patio where the others have disappeared to.

"I can make no such promises, big brother. I suggest you just get good and drunk with the rest of us."

Jodie laughs, pulling me tighter into her tempting body.

"Tonight is going to be wild isn't it?"

"I think you might be right, Demon."

She gasps when I suddenly wrap my fingers around her throat and give her little choice but to walk backward until she collides with a wall beside the open French doors.

"Can't beat 'em, join 'em," I mutter before slamming my lips down on hers.

It doesn't take long for someone to look back and find me grinding up against my girl, and the predictable whoops and hollers follow.

***

"Let's play a game," Alex slurs from his place on the end of the corner sofa. He's sitting sideways with his legs resting over Calli's thighs, not that she's complaining at using him like her own personal blanket.

It's cool out, it's barely even spring after all, but with the firepit roaring and the heaters we all dragged over and put up high, it's nice sitting out under the stars with my family.

Jodie is curled on my lap under a thick blanket on the huge round outdoor sofa thing we claimed for ourselves when Nico vacated it an hour or so ago in favour of relieving himself in the lake. Fucking animal.

"That sounds ominous," Jodie mutters. She sounds almost as wasted as Alex from the number of Stella's cocktails she consumed.

"Shoot, man. I'm more than ready for some excitement," Nico barks, pushing his hand through his hair and flexing his muscles in a way I'm sure he thinks none of us notice. I mean, one of us doesn't, or at least she does a good job of pretending despite the fact that the show he's putting on is clearly for her benefit.

"Truth or dare," Alex announces happily as the rest of us groan.

"We're not twelve, man," Theo mutters.

"I'm more than aware. I wasn't going to suggest you go and egg one of the neighbours." Alex rolls his eyes. "We can come up with much better shit than that."

"I'm in," Stella says happily, quickly followed by Brianna, who is probably just hoping she gets the chance to torture Nico.

"Fine, fuck it. I'm in," Emmie announces. "Boss?" she purrs, looking up at Theo through her lashes.

"Fine," he mutters, sounding anything but happy about it.

"How do we pick who goes first?" Calli asks, sounding more excited by this than I expected her to.

"Easy," Brianna says, pushing from her seat on the sofa and walking around the table in the middle of us all. A smile twitches at my lips when she bends over in front of Nico, giving him a right eyeful of whatever she might—or knowing Bri, or might not—be wearing beneath her short skirt.

Jodie snorts a laugh as we watch Nico's eyes almost pop out of his head.

"He's aware he's started a battle with her that he'll never win, right?" she whispers in my ear.

"Nico believes he never loses anything."

"Well, that's bullshit, right there," she barks.

"You don't need to tell me that, baby."

She finally stands back up and places his empty beer bottle in the middle of the table and spins.

"And we thought truth or dare was childish. Spin the bottle, really?" Nico taunts.

"What? So you'd refuse to kiss me if the bottle decided that was your fate?"

Brianna's voice is pure sex as she stands before him and drags her hand down her body seductively.

"She's good," I confess to Jodie.

"He doesn't stand a fucking chance. She'll take what she wants and spit him right back out again."

"Literally?" I ask with a laugh and earn myself a gentle slap around the head.

"You're such a boy."

I shrug, not really giving a shit. "Maybe. I prefer it when you swallow though, Demon."

She squirms on my lap, and my cock swells as her arse grinds against it.

Brianna drops back into her seat as the bottle comes to a stop on Alex.

"Ah good, we get to torture the instigator of this bullshit first," Theo mutters.

"Truth or dare?" Brianna asks with a shit-eating grin on her face.

"Truth."

"Pussy," Nico scoffs behind his fist.

"Okay... who around this table have you fantasised about while getting off?" Bri asks happily.

Alex's eyes hop from each of our girl's to the next. "What's this, starting easy?" he asks, taking a pull on his beer.

"I guess that all depends on your answer."

"True. Well, I'm sorry to disappoint, boys, but you're all far, far away from my wank bank material. Stella and Calli, however..."

"Alex," Calli squeals in horror as Nico launches an empty can at his head, which he catches with ease.

"What, bro? Would you rather I was thinking about you?" Alex makes a show of checking Nico's body out while he wraps his arm around Calli's shoulders when she tries to escape.

Nico scoffs, because Alex announces loudly, "Don't worry, baby C. You're always the best I've ever had."

"Well, obviously," Calli huffs.

"Isn't she a virgin?" Jodie whispers in my ear.

"As far as I know. Pretty sure someone is going to steal that soon, though. Alex is like a dog in heat."

"He wouldn't... would he?"

"With this much alcohol involved, I wouldn't like to say."

"Right, my turn." Alex rubs his hands together and reaches forward to spin the bottle for his victim.

It comes to a stop in front of Theo and Emmie,

and with her tucked right into his side it could easily be either of them.

"Emmie," Alex announces.

"How'd you figure that?" she argues. "It could just as easily be Theo."

"Because, Hellcat," Alex winks as Theo rolls his eyes at him, "our pussy of a boss here will choose truth, and I've got something much more fun up my sleeve."

"Great," she mutters. "Do your worst then, Deimos." Emmie grabs her abandoned cocktail and throws it back in one. "Dare."

The smile that curls at Alex's lips is pure fucking evil.

"This is about to get messy, isn't it?" Jodie whispers as apprehension crackles around us.

"Did you ever think it wouldn't?"

"Fair point," she mutters as Alex turns his attention toward Stella, and I groan, knowing exactly what's coming. I can read his dirty thoughts like a fucking book.

"Emmie, I dare you to kiss Stella."

Without missing a beat, Emmie stands and throws her long, dark hair over her shoulder.

"Is that it?" she asks. "I thought you were going to give me a challenge."

Alex's chin drops while Theo and Seb watch with more than a little interest darkening their eyes.

Not as invested in the outcome as them, I slide

my arm under Jodie's bare legs and pull her further onto my lap.

She was only wearing my shirt when everyone turned up, and much to my delight, she hasn't changed since.

"Toby," she gasps as I run my hand up her inner thigh to find out if she's snuck on a pair of knickers recently. I know for a fact she wasn't wearing any earlier.

"What?" I ask innocently. "I just need to check something."

"Sure you—" Her gasp cuts off her words.

"You're a dirty girl, Demon. Sitting here getting all nice and wet for me without any underwear on."

I slide my fingers through her folds, painting her skin with her own juices.

"Y-you can't," she argues, wrapping her hand around my arm and trying to tug me away.

"Look," I command, "everyone is watching them. No one will even know."

She gushes at my words.

"Watch the show, Demon."

She swallows nervously and I push my fingers lower, teasing her entrance.

Ripping my eyes from her, I watch Emmie as she prowls toward Stella.

Nico sits forward on his elbows as if it'll help him get a better view.

"Hey girl," Emmie purrs, putting on the seductive voice she uses on Theo when she wants to get him to agree with whatever she's saying. "I hope you're drunk enough to handle this. I'd hate to turn you with one kiss."

Seb scoffs. "Hardly. She's addicted to my cock."

"We'll see," Emmie mutters, pressing her knee to the seat beside Stella and straddling her lap.

"Oh God," Jodie moans in encouragement.

Thankfully, Emmie's back blocks my view from what's happening, but I get a good fucking clue when Alex shouts, "Oh hell yeah," and Seb tugs at his jeans in a way that actually makes me feel a little sorry for him. That shit's gotta be uncomfortable.

Seb and Theo share a look, silent promises crackling between them that I can predict but can't read.

"So what do you say?" Emmie asks, sitting back. "You gonna change teams and run into the sunset with me, Princess?"

"Sorry, baby," Stella purrs. "You've just not got enough cock for me."

Reaching over, Stella runs her hand up Seb's thigh, and he groans loudly as she grasps him through his jeans.

"Damn. I guess I'd better try harder next time," Emmie teases before returning to Theo and mimicking the move she just pulled on Stella. She sinks down onto his lap, twists his hair in her fingers, and drags his head back to exactly where she wants him. "You enjoy that, Boss?" she teases, grinding down on him.

No one to sit back and take it, he wraps his arms around her, crushes her body to his, and claims her lips. Wiping away any memory of Stella's kiss, I'm sure.

"Emmie, it's your turn to spin," Alex shouts, but all she does is lift her hand and flip him off.

"Lovely," he mutters lightly.

"I'll spin it," Stella says, leaning forward and twisting it.

Alex uses the table for a drum roll, and I take the opportunity to push my fingers deeper inside my girl and curl them until she moans.

15

JODIE

My body burns as Toby continues to tease me mercilessly. He knows exactly how to play me, to get me right to the edge and then bring me back without me even getting a toe over the cliff.

My chest heaves and my teeth grind as I desperately try to keep my reaction to what he's doing off my face.

The bottle begins to slow, and I pray that it's not about to land on me. I swear the second anyone looks, they'll know what's happening, and our dare will involve everyone around me getting to experience more than I'm sure they need to.

"You hot, baby?" Toby asks, paying zero attention to the bottle as he holds my drink up in front of me with his free hand. "You really should drink."

"You're an arsehole," I breathe.

"Just having fun, Demon. And from the way

you're dripping down my hand, I think you might be having the time of your life too."

"I hate you," I hiss, throwing back the remains of what is arguably the strongest cocktail I've ever drank. It burns all the way down to my stomach and almost instantly adds to the buzz I'd already got going on.

Toby chuckles in my ear as the bottle comes to a stop, thankfully not on us.

"Yes," Brianna shouts, and when I focus once more, I find the bottle pointing straight at Nico.

"Go on then, Princess. Let's see what you can come up with," Nico says, a wide, boisterous smile splitting his face.

"Oh no," Stella says, shooting my best friend a conspiratorial look. "I think it's fair that Bri gets to choose your dare."

"That's not the rules," Nico argues, looking at Alex.

"Sounds fair to me, man."

"Cunt," Nico mutters, knowing that what's going to come next is going to be painful, either physically or just to his overinflated ego.

Toby's fingers slow as we all wait for Bri to come up with something, but as desperate as I am for him to finally make me fall, I also really want to see what's about to happen.

Bri holds his eyes, her face deadly serious as her plan plays out in her mind.

"Come here and get on your knees."

One side of Nico's smile increases.

"Any fucking time, Siren. You know that all you've got to do is ask."

He happily gets up, and after pushing the table back a bit, he drops to his knees before her, licking his lips in preparation.

He must be drunker than he looks because, there's no fucking way she's going to ask him to—

"Tell me she isn't," Toby pleads.

"No, she isn't. She's got him exactly where she wants him though."

Slipping her foot from her shoe, she lifts it and presses it to the middle of his chest.

"Worship my feet, playboy. Show me how good you are with those fingers." Her words drip with innuendo, and everyone sniggers around them as Nico glares daggers at Bri.

"Oh, you look disappointed, babe. Oh my God," she gasps innocently, covering her heart with her hand. "Did you really think I was going to dare you to give me head? Puh-lease. I'd sooner go and find a dead fish in that lake to get me off."

Alex, Theo, and Seb all fall about laughing at Nico's horrified expression, and Toby's body vibrates with amusement beneath me.

"Anyone would think you assume my best friend is a whore who gets her pussy out for just anyone, Nico," I quip, regretting my actions the second all eyes turn on me.

My cheeks burn as if the blanket covering us is

see-through and they're all able to see Toby's fingers disappearing inside me.

"I hate to break it to you, Jodie, but your best friend is a whore. Aren't you, Siren?" He takes her foot in his hands and presses his thumb into the arch.

Bri's eyes shutter and she sucks in a sharp breath.

"And by the time I've finished, I guarantee she'll be wet and begging me for it."

"As if," Bri spits. "I've got eyes on someone else tonight." Her attention moves over his shoulder toward Alex, who looks a little like a deer caught in headlights.

"I guess it's a good thing Alex and I are the perfect team then, isn't it? The things we could both do to you, Siren... it would blow your mind."

Suddenly, Toby seems to remember that he was in the middle of something. His fingers move as Nico drops his head and kisses a trail up Bri's foot toward her ankle. And the shameless slut she is, she parts her thighs for him, allowing him to see exactly what he really wants. I just hope she's wearing more underwear than I am.

"You're so fucking beautiful when you're falling apart for me, Demon," Toby growls in my ear as I continue to watch the show.

A moan rumbles deep in my chest as Bri fights to keep her composure while Nico's got his hands on her.

Something tells me that she's regretting this dare,

because Nico isn't the only one it's torturing right now.

"It's a damn shame the dare wasn't to get her off like this, cos I reckon I could do it," he announces arrogantly.

"Fuck off. You could barely even get me off when I gave you a road map to my clit."

We all know she's lying. Well, at least Toby and I do, because the way he made her scream when they've been together points toward the fact that he is more than capable.

"Sure. You keep believing that, Siren. None of my boys believe you anyway."

"All right, enough," Alex says eventually, calling time on the shameless flirting. "Spin, Cirillo," he demands.

Nico releases Bri's foot, but he doesn't get up from his spot between her legs. Ever the optimist.

Each spin of the bottle seems to take longer and make my heart rate rocket even more.

But it seems that fate is on our side again, because it comes to a stop in the exact same position it started in.

"Oh, Siren. How the table has turned. Truth or dare, babe?"

Without missing a beat, Bri squares her shoulders and firmly says, "Dare."

"If they start fucking, we're leaving," Toby whispers in my ear. "The only person I want to watch grinding down on a cock is you on mine."

"So romantic," I tease.

"Oh baby," he whispers, curling his fingers once more. "I know just how to treat you right."

"You'd have got me off by now if that was true," I sass.

"Delayed gratification, baby. Or maybe I'm just waiting for you to get so desperate that I get to dare you to ride me when it's our turn."

His eyes flash with heat at his words, and my muscles clamp down on his fingers.

"Don't pretend you wouldn't. We both know you love an audience. And you're not the only one." My brows pull together in confusion until I look over at Nico, who's now looming over Bri like a predator.

"I dare you to resist me."

"Oh Jesus," I moan, as Toby's fingers twist and Nico dips, burying his face in Bri's neck.

"You beg, moan, or make any move, you forfeit."

"What's the forfeit?" she asks, already sounding dangerously close to losing.

"This bottle of vodka," Alex says, thinking on his feet and placing a small bottle on the table.

It's not really a threat—Bri could probably drink that bottle for breakfast and barely feel the effects, but I'm not about to tell any of them that.

"Fine. Do your worst. Show me just how much I'm missing without you, babe."

"Finally," Alex barks. "We get to see how little game our boy has."

Everyone ignores him. I'm pretty sure that's

because everyone here knows just how much action Nico manages to get himself. I can't imagine he's one to keep his conquests to himself.

"You think she's going to beat him, Demon?" Toby asks, copying Nico's move and dipping his face to my neck.

The heat of his tongue burns up the side of my throat before he sucks on the sensitive patch of skin beneath my ear as he once again ups his attention on my pussy.

"God. Toby," I groan. "You need to let me come."

"I will, baby," he promises, his teeth grazing my skin hard enough to leave marks.

I'm too lost in him and everything he's doing to me to pay any attention to what Nico is doing to Bri, which is probably a good thing.

"Shit. Toby, please."

"Shh, Demon. Unless you want everyone watching you."

Ripping my eyes open, I find that no one is looking at us. Actually, it's only Alex and Calli who are watching anything, because while Nico continues to kiss across Bri's chest, both Emmie and Theo, and Stella and Seb are lost in their own little worlds.

Not caring about everyone around him, Nico pops open the buttons on Bri's blouse, exposing her bra beneath.

Her chest heaves as he continues, dipping his tongue into her cleavage, but apart from that, she's frozen, her eyes fixed on the house in front of her.

"Come on, Siren, you know you want to beg me for more. You're desperate for me to suck on your nipples, lap at your cunt," Nico growls shamelessly.

"Never," Bri says, her voice flat and void of the desire that's flooding her features.

"Hats off to her willpower," Toby says. "He might have bitten off more than he can chew with that one."

Alex smirks at the comment before Toby turns his attention back to me.

My eyes flutter closed once more just as Nico bites down on Bri's nipple through the lace of her bra and a very obvious moan rips through the air.

My eyes fly open, and I immediately find a furious Bri pushing Nico off her and covering herself up.

"I fucking knew you couldn't resist me, Siren."

He stalks back around to his seat with a smug-as-fuck grin on his lips and tented trousers.

"We'll finish what we started later," he promises, blowing her a kiss and rubbing himself through his jeans like the dog he is.

"We still playing or what?" Alex barks when the couples continue to have their own private parties around him. "Hey." Reaching over, he smacks Seb upside the head. "We're playing a fucking game, man."

"We're here, dude. Chill the fuck out."

"Aw," Stella coos. "Alex is feeling all left out. Give him a cuddle and make him feel better, Cal."

"Just spin the bottle, Siren," Nico demands. "The sooner this game is over, the sooner I can make good on my promise."

Toby pulls back on me once more, and my frustration shoots through the roof. My grip on his forearm tightens, my nails digging little crescents into his skin.

The second I see it's landed on Calli, my mouth and general irritation about how Nico thinks he even stands a chance with Bri gets the better of me, and I blurt a dare out without really thinking it through.

"Calli, I dare you to sleep in Alex's bed tonight."

"Oh hell yes, baby C."

"What the fuck? No. That's not happening," Nico argues.

"So I get to sit here and watch you suck Bri's tits, but I can't even share a bed with someone? Get fucked, Nico," Calli slurs, turning her attention on Alex and smiling at him in a way that's sure to make Nico's blood boil. "Just so you know, I prefer to sleep naked."

"Jesus fucking Christ," Nico barks, pushing from his seat and storming off.

"Bro, I thought you wanted to play."

"Fuck you," he shouts back before slipping into the house.

Toby's chest rumbles with laughter as Alex continues to stare down at Calli as if all his dreams have just come true.

"That was a joke," she states. "I never sleep

naked, and I have zero intention of doing so with you."

Alex reaches out and tucks a lock of hair behind her ear.

"We'll see."

Toby chooses that moment to bring me back to the edge once more, and I can't stop a moan ripping past my lips.

All eyes turn my way, including those who were previously distracted, and my cheeks burn.

"Ah, it seems like Jodie is feeling left out. Baby C, you wanna spin and get your own back?"

She shoves Alex's legs from her lap and reaches for the bottle as I fight to keep my eyes open.

Everyone knows what's going on now, so I guess I should just embrace it.

As if she'd planned it, the bottle stops on the two of us.

"Toby," Alex states with a naughty glint in his eye. "Finish what you've started."

Not missing a beat, Toby flips us, forcing me to lay back on the cushions before crowding me with his wide frame.

"I guess I've got little choice but to make good on that promise."

His fingers find that magic place inside me as his lips claim mine. I have no choice but to fall headfirst into everything he can offer me. I forget about our audience and where we are and just drown in him.

In only seconds, he's got me right back on the edge once more, but this time, he doesn't stop, and he finally lets me fall into a blissful release. I scream out his name, but he catches each syllable, swallowing down my cries as he lets me ride out every last second of it.

He pulls his fingers free of my body and lifts up from my lips. All I see when I open my eyes is his happiness staring back down at me.

"I love you, Jodie," he whispers, my heart tumbling at the sincerity in each word.

"I love you too," I finally say. It might not be the perfect time, or even the most appropriate considering our current situation, but fuck it.

Our world is messy, dirty, and full of unknowns. And after everything we've been through, I wouldn't have it any other way.

A door slams somewhere in the distance before Nico booms, "Last one in the lake naked is a fucking pussy."

I look up just in time to see his bare arse running toward the end of the garden.

Laughter and movement erupt around me, and Toby's warmth quickly disappears as he jumps at the challenge. I discover that the boys' competitive streaks are also strong enough that they follow suit.

"Surely you're not all going to—" When Stella and Emmie start joining in, stripping off their clothes, I realise that they are all serious.

"Come on, Demon. I thought you were up for the

wild night ahead." Toby pulls me from the sofa and drags my shirt over my head.

The cool night air rushes over my bare body, but it's soon forgotten as he throws me over his shoulder and runs toward the lake.

Cries of excitement and laughter follow before everything is cut off as Toby dives into the ice-cold water as if he has no cares in the world.

It's fucking everything.

16

TOBY

I might wake up with one hell of a hangover and what feels like a marching band inside my skull, but I've also got the widest smile on my face as I tighten my hold on Jodie and recall some of the less hazy memories from the night before.

Nuzzling her neck, I breathe in her scent mixed with my scent from the shower we shared after our short time in the lake.

A shiver rips down my spine at the thought of just how cold that water was. Fucking Nico and his stupid challenges.

"Morning," Jodie groans, pressing her body farther back into mine and grazing her arse against my morning wood.

"Morning, baby," I breathe, planting kisses across her bare shoulder.

"My head hurts," she complains, making me laugh.

"Yeah, same. You want some painkillers?" I offer, although the thought of getting out and finding them for her isn't exactly appealing.

"I can wait. This is nice." Her legs tangle with mine, connecting us in as many ways as possible.

"Hmm."

We lie there in silence for the longest time, both of us staring out of the huge windows that showcase the breathtaking views beyond.

I start to wonder if she's actually fallen back to sleep, she's so peaceful, but a few seconds later, she speaks. "When we get back, I think it's time to fully start over."

I don't respond, sensing that she's got more she wants to say.

"I want... I want you to follow through with your plan. Put your demons to rest and allow us all to move on with our lives."

"Are you sure, baby?"

"Yes."

"You don't want to—"

"My dad died in a fatal crash before Christmas. There was a leak on the fuel line and it went up in a fireball seconds after he collided with a tree. It was devastating. It is devastating. The man in your basement... he's not a man I ever knew. But he's one who has terrorised you, hurt you, abused you. He's made both you and those you love bleed, and for that, I want you to do what you need to do."

She flips over and allows me to see into her rich chocolate eyes, to see the truth within them.

"It needs to end, Toby. I know you're trying to do the right thing for me, and I really, really appreciate that. But this is weighing down on you. His presence is still affecting you, and it needs to stop.

"You need to wipe the slate clean and really restart your life. You've got an incredible family around you that would literally do anything for you. It's time to put the bad parts in the past where they belong and finally start embracing your future."

I wrap my fingers around the back of her neck and pull her closer so I can press my brow to hers.

"Do you want me to do it? Could you live with that?"

"I need you to do what you need to do. I need you free of those nightmares, Toby."

"That might take a bit more work than just pulling a trigger," I confess.

"I know. And I'm here for that. I'm here for whatever you need."

I nod against her.

"I don't deserve you, Demon."

"And you didn't deserve all that shit he dealt you, either. It's time to make it right. To move on."

"And what about you?" I ask, knowing that she's been fighting her own battle about her future recently.

She closes her eyes and sucks in a breath. The move makes my heart jump into my throat, and the kind of fear I hoped not to feel again for a while washes through my veins.

"I've had a place accepted at Imperial College Business School."

Shock floods me.

"W-what?" I stutter. "When did this happen? Why didn't you tell me?"

"I got the email when I was out with Stella on Friday. I just... I didn't quite believe it. I only applied on the off chance. I didn't really think they'd want me."

"Baby," I sigh. "Why the hell wouldn't they want you? You're amazing."

A shy smile twitches at her lips.

"There's nothing to be scared about, Demon. We'll do it together, yeah? We can be study buddies and pull all-nighters."

"The way you say that doesn't make it sound like we'll be getting much studying done."

"Can you blame me when you're this hot?" I ask, skimming my hand down over her waist and gripping onto her arse, dragging her body right up against mine.

"I still need to find a job. Something... useful, meaningful. I don't want to be serving coffee anymore."

"We'll figure something out."

The smile she gives me lights up the room.

"Yeah," she agrees. "We will. Everything seems less scary when I've got you at my side."

"Good, because that's how I feel with you."

***

"**O**h look, they didn't fuck off in the middle of the night and leave us with all the mess," Seb quips when we finally make it down to the kitchen a little over an hour later.

"Leave them alone," Stella snaps, slapping him around the head. "You two want coffee and breakfast?"

"Tell me you made pancakes," I beg.

"You know it, Bro. Take a seat." She lifts her chin toward the table where everyone else is sitting, and I pull a chair out for my girl, making Nico snort in amusement.

"From your attitude, I'm assuming you never got to follow through on your promise," I tease.

Nico crosses his arms over his chest while Brianna laughs at the other end of the table.

"We're not allowed to talk about it, apparently," Alex explains with a smirk. "But I've got money on him not being able to get it up, or get her off."

"Shut your fucking mouth, Deimos," Nico snaps.

"Whatever happened," Theo adds, "he certainly didn't get laid."

"I fucking hate you lot having girlfriends."

"Well, if you weren't such a pig, maybe you could have one of your own," Bri offers.

"What the fuck is this? Pick on Nico day?"

"Sure, why not," Alex quips. "Seems as good a day as any for it."

"Aw," Stella says, bringing two mugs of coffee over while Calli trails behind with two loaded plates. "Leave poor Nico alone." She wraps her arm around his shoulder and drops a kiss to his temple. "It's not his fault he couldn't find the right hole."

She shrieks through her laughter and jumps back when he stands.

"You're all a bunch of pricks," he barks and storms from the room.

We all watch his retreating back and wince when the door slams.

"Maybe you should just go suck his cock. Cheer him up a bit," Jodie suggests, damn near making me choke on my mouthful of coffee.

"He's got a perfectly good right hand. I'm sure he can cope."

"He's just pissed because he found Calli in Alex's bed this morning," Seb announces.

My eyes find a very sheepish-looking Calli.

"You didn't," I gasp.

"What?" she asks incredulously. "I didn't sleep with him."

"Not sure Nico cares about the details, baby C," Seb points out.

"Well, fuck him. And you too," she spits, pointing at Theo to cut off any opinion he might have about this before he gets a chance to say anything. "I was drunk. Alex was... bearable."

"Thanks, babe. I just about managed to put up with you too."

Calli flips him off before dropping into the empty chair beside him.

I watch them with interest as Alex leans into her and whispers something in her ear that makes her giggle.

I don't have any kind of issue with something happening between them, but I can understand why Nico does. She's his little sister, and we've watched her grow up from that little girl in pink tutus and playing with her Barbies. But he needs to accept that she's no longer a child. She's a woman. A beautiful, funny and intelligent one at that. Alex would be fucking lucky to have her, if that's what she wants.

"They're cute together," Jodie whispers in my ear.

"Yeah, they are."

Our conversations move on from the revelation of Calli and Alex spending the night together, and before we know it, we're knocking on Nico's door and telling him that we're leaving with or without him.

"I'll meet you out in the car, Demon," I say to Jodie after carrying our bags down to the front door. "I want to talk to Stella before we leave."

I don't need to say more. Jodie knows what I want to talk to my sister about, and she's more than happy to not know about the details.

She drops a kiss on my lips and follows Emmie and Theo out the door.

"Stel," I say as she and Seb go to move past me.

"Is everything okay?" she asks, reading something in my expression.

Wrapping my hand around her upper arm I pull her to the side of the stairs and explain what I'm planning on doing when we get back.

"Do you want to be there?"

"Aw, Toby. You're such a sweetheart," she teases.

"Do you or not? Because you won't get a second shot at this."

"Do I want to watch the life drain from that cunt's eyes? Hell yeah, I do."

"Something's wrong with you, Sis."

"Takes one to know one," she quips.

"Jodie is going to see Sara. I'll come and knock once she's gone and we can..."

"Okay, sounds good. I'll polish my gun." She winks.

"It's going to be over," I promise her.

"About fucking time. You should have done it weeks ago. Could have saved both you and Jodie a whole heap of pain."

"I know," I mutter, taking a step back from her. "But here we are."

"Ready, Princess?" Seb calls.

"Yeah, let's get this show on the road."

"Thank you for this weekend, it was perfect," Jodie says, wrapping her arms around my waist and laying her head against my chest.

"You're welcome, baby." I drop a kiss to the top of her head and hold her a little tighter.

I don't feel ready for what I'm going to do next.

I've avoided going down to the basement, I've avoided seeing him since things got serious with us, because Jodie deserves to have my full attention and focus. In some ways, I've managed to put him behind me. I've been able to shove at least some of the nightmares he's given me under a steel door and lock them in.

But I know she's right. As long as he's still with us, he'll have a hold over me, and we both deserve better than that.

"Are you sure about this?" I whisper, a huge part of me hoping that she'll say no, or even tell me not to do it.

"Yeah, I'm sure. It's time, Toby," she says confidently, stepping back from our embrace and holding my eyes.

She continues staring at me, and I swear all she can see is the scared little boy who lives inside me. The one who would rather hide and cower in a corner than deal with his father.

But that isn't who I am now.

He trained me, moulded me. Made me a soldier. A damn good one, too.

I now hold all the cards. And it's time for me to make the last play.

Nodding, I lower down, capturing her lips with mine and reminding myself of all the good that has come out of so much pain.

Having her makes it all worth it.

"Call me when you're done. We can do whatever it is you usually do after... a job."

"Fuck, I love you."

Capturing her face in my hands, I steal another kiss before finally allowing her to back up toward the door.

"I love you too. Lay your demons to rest, Toby. I'll be waiting on the other side."

She's gone long before I'm ready. Silence surrounds me and my chest aches.

Scrubbing my hand down my face, I force my legs to move and strip my clothes off as I make my way down the hallway and to my bedroom.

My head is still lost in the weekend. I need to find that switch inside me that can turn reality off so I can just focus on what needs to be done.

Turning the shower to cold, I step under the freezing spray, reminding myself of years that have passed.

I had my own bathroom under his roof, and cold showers were a regular thing. Apparently, it taught me resilience, strength. For weeks on end, he would shut the hot water off to my bedroom. My only relief was showering at school after football training.

My skin prickles as my memories build up in my mind. The shower, the basement, the control. The fear.

Faster than I thought possible, the hate that I was once consumed by flows through my veins once more.

I fight it, desperate to just drown in the solace that is Jodie. But I need this. For one final time, I need this poison in my veins to help put an end to it all.

My entire body is shivering when I finally cut the water and step out. Gone is the guy who spent the weekend loving his girl and laughing with his friends. In his place is the man who *he* trained me to be.

I dress on autopilot, pulling on my black suit as if it's armour.

Only ten minutes later, I march back through my flat with my mask firmly in place, ready to go and knock for Stella and get this done.

But just before I get to the front door, my phone starts ringing.

Pulling it from my pocket, my brows pinch at the sight of Daemon's name on my screen.

My armour slips and guilt twits up my insides that he wasn't there with us this weekend. But it's a little late for worrying about that now.

"Hey, how's it going?" I ask, my attempt at

happiness sounding nothing but fake even to my own ears.

"Uh... we've got a problem," he confesses, his voice dark and terrifying.

My heart jumps into my throat, and Jodie's smiling face from this weekend pops into my mind. Dread fills my stomach like concrete as silence continues down the line.

"W-what's wrong?"

"You need to get down to the basement. Now."

I'm out of my flat before I've even realised my legs have moved.

"I'm coming. Fuck," I bark before hanging up the phone.

He might not have told me what the problem is, but I know. Deep down, I know, and it's a fear I've had but refused to acknowledge all this time. Just another reason why I should have just fucking killed him that first night.

But then you never would have found her.

"FUUUUCK," I boom as I blow through the doors that lead to the stairs, needing to keep moving and not stand uselessly in the lift as it descends.

In only minutes, I'm running down the hallways deep beneath our building that lead to our holding cells. I round the corner and damn near crash right into Daemon, who stands there staring at exactly what I feared.

An empty cell.

17

JODIE

Everything feels wrong as I walk away from Toby and make my way down to my little sporty Abarth. It might look like a baby sitting next to Toby's BMW, but the similarities are uncanny. From the black paintwork to the red flashes of colour that make it stand out, there's no question that the two of them belong together. It makes me wonder if people think that about the two of us when they see us standing side by side.

I sigh, ripping my eyes from my car and back over at the lift I've just stepped out of. Everything inside me screams for me to go back, to tell him that I'll stand by his side through whatever he needs to do next.

But I can't. Despite seeing the fear in his eyes, I know this is something that he needs to do alone. Or, not so much alone, but without me. And for my own sanity, I need to stay the hell away from it all as well.

What I said to him this morning was true. The man he's about to go and see isn't someone I know. He's a stranger. And I need to keep it that way.

I've been mourning my father since we had the call about that accident. It doesn't matter how real that might have been. What I felt, the grief I still feel for the caring, loving man I lost is still there. He died that day, and that's the way I need to deal with that.

The monster that has haunted Toby and Maria for entirely too long is a different person.

Forcing myself to move, I pull my door open and breathe in the scent of a new car that hits me before I fall into the bucket seat that wraps around me like it's giving me a hug.

I sigh, needing to feel Toby's arms around me again.

Steeling my spine, I bring my car to life, telling myself that I'm doing the right thing leaving him. I know I am. He needs space to be able to do what he needs to do and then time to process it after. Celebrate even.

Although I sympathise with everything he's been through, I'll never truly understand how he feels, his need for revenge. I know first-hand just how hot that burns through his body.

I've had a good life. Good—albeit one mostly absent—parents. The only suffering I've ever really known has been recent with the loss of Joe and then Dad. I've been loved, cared for, had everything I could ever ask for. There's no way I could ever truly understand how Toby feels about his childhood. And that's without adding the whole mafia side to it.

Hearing his stories about how he was made to make his first kill, the things he's both done and seen from such a young age... It by no means excuses what he did to me, how he tried to use me, hurt me, but hell if it doesn't make me understand, allow me to forgive.

Shaking my head, I force myself to think about better times, about the weekend and the fun and laughter. Once this is over, we can have more of that. I'll, hopefully, be able to see Toby lose that final bit of weight that's always pressing down on his shoulders knowing that the man who haunts his nightmares is no longer breathing, no longer able to hurt those he loves. And I want that for him. I do. I want him to have that freedom to just live his life without worrying what's happening behind closed doors at home and how much his mum might be suffering, how much he might suffer when he returns.

I come to a stop at a junction as I prepare to return to the hospital to see Sara when the screen flashes with an incoming message. Being away from Jesse killed me yesterday. But I also can't lie—a day without being inside that depressing place was good for me, even if I never really forgot, if my chest never stopped aching with more impending loss.

· · ·

Mum: Can you stop by the house? I've made cookies for Jesse. x

A smile twitches at my lips. She's just as worried about Sara as I am. She went in my place yesterday to stop me feeling so guilty and sat with her for an hour, holding her hand, talking about memories she has of the two of us from when we were little in the hope that wherever Sara is right now, she's able to remember those times. Those seemingly endless summer days and the full belly laughs until we were sick.

Good times.

I quickly send back a thumbs up emoji before changing my direction and taking a right toward home.

The unsettled feeling in my belly never quits. In fact, as I close in on the only house I've ever lived in, the knot seems tighter.

Is that because I subconsciously know what Toby could be doing right this second? Is it just worry, concern that he's not going to get the freedom he seeks from all of this? Or is it more? A sixth sense that shit is about to hit the fan yet again?

The curtain in the dining room twitches as Mum peeks out to see if it's me already. Shoving down my anxiety over what's happening back at the guys' building, I head toward home, pulling my keys from the depths of my bag as I get closer.

The second I slide my key into the lock, something settles inside me.

Pushing the door open, the familiar scent hits me and I relax further.

But my hackles quickly rise once more when I push the door closed and hear nothing.

Mum was waiting—I saw the curtain move. It's unlike her not to call for me almost immediately.

"Mum?" I shout, a quiver in my voice that I don't like.

Dumping my bag on the unit, I go in search.

"Mum, what's wrong?" I ask as I turn into the dining room, finding her sitting in her usual spot, but her eyes are wide and her face is pale. Something is wrong. Very fucking wrong.

My stomach knots as my heart pounds so erratically in my chest, it's the only thing I can hear.

A whimper falls from Mum's trembling lips, her eyes shooting toward the open door behind me.

"Mum, what the hell is—"

A shadow falls over me and my heart plummets into my feet. A second before I get a chance to run, a cold hand wraps around my face, cutting off any kind of noise that might have been about to rip from my throat, and an arm wraps around my waist, pinning me back against a body.

Tears spill down Mum's cheeks, but she never

reaches up to wipe them away. I can only wonder why not.

Despite the fact that there's no chance of it helping, a scream rips up my throat. I act on instinct and slam my heel into his foot.

A loud grunt hits my ear, but his grip on me doesn't falter.

"Aw, come on, sweetheart. That wasn't really the welcome home I was hoping for." The voice that once used to fill me with joy and comfort now makes my stomach turn over and causes bile to burn up my throat.

"Get the hell off me, you arsehole."

Mum gasps, I guess realising that I'm not shocked by who is standing behind me.

"You'd better wish you had died in a fucking car crash, because when they get their hands on you, they're going to make you regret every second of your lying, poisonous life," I hiss.

"Oh my girl," he sighs sadly. "He really has got inside your head, hasn't he?"

"He's told me the truth," I spit, desperately trying to get out of his hold. "He's told me what a monster you really are."

"You don't actually believe any of those lies, do you?" He tsks as if I'm the one in the wrong.

"Every single fucking word, *Dad*," I sneer. "You've been lying to me since the day I was born. You're nothing but a liar and an abusive cu— Argh," I scream and he releases me with such force I fly across the room, colliding with the wall with a painful thud.

"Jodie," Mum cries, her chair scraping across the wooden floor as she tries to get to me.

"Don't move, Joanne," Jonas commands, and I watch in absolute horror as she does as she's told.

Holy shit.

I'm frozen for a moment as I wonder if he's always had that kind of control over her, or if this is just a result of the shock of him seemingly coming back from the dead.

I hate to admit it to myself, but history tells me that it's always been right in front of me. I was just too blind and stupid to notice it. Just like Jesse and the Wolves, and the warning signs at the beginning with Toby.

"No," I cry when Jonas marches over to her, twists his fingers in her hair and drags her head back so she has no choice but to look up at him. "Let her go."

"You're glad to have me back, aren't you, sweetheart?"

Mum swallows nervously, but after a beat of silence, she nods as much as his grip allows. "I'm so happy to see you, honey," she breathes with such sincerity, making me want to vomit on my own feet.

Fuck, I hope she's lying.

Please, for the love of God, be playing him at his own game.

"We've got a second chance now. Just the three of

us together again," Jonas continues. "It's how I always wanted it to be."

He grazes his knuckles down her cheek as if she's the most delicate thing in the world as I manage to climb back to my feet once more, the entire right side of my body burning from the collision.

"They're going to realise you're gone, and they're going to find you," I warn.

"They don't even know I'm gone, sweetheart. And where does your precious Toby think you are right now?"

Clearly, my face must give me away, because he smiles at me, revealing more than a few missing teeth. Unexpected pride washes through me, because I know deep down that Toby did that.

"They'll notice. Toby will find me, and they will kill you."

His smile widens.

"That pathetic piece of shit doesn't care about you, sweetheart. He only wants to hurt me. I'm the only one who loves you."

I stare at him in utter disbelief as my heart fractures at his words.

"No," I argue. "That's not true."

"He's using you, Jodie. As soon as he's got what he wants, he'll drop you as fast as he found you."

My hand lifts to the padlock around my neck. My heart doesn't believe a word of it, but my head? That little bitch can be easily swayed at times.

"No," I spit, but he ignores me and turns back to Mum.

"We're going to go away, aren't we, sweetheart? We're going to start over. Be a family. Just like we always should have been."

"What about Joe?" I ask, desperate to just keep him talking. The longer I can drag this out, the more chance we've got.

Toby will go down to the basement with the intention of killing him, and when he learns the truth, he'll come for me.

Jonas scoffs. "He was a dead weight. He didn't have what it took to really be an Ariti."

My chin drops at the fact that he can talk about his own son like that.

"You killed him," I cry. "You killed your own son. My brother." Mum whimpers, but it doesn't stop me. "Her son. Her firstborn. You set him up. You put him in that stupid fucking MC and you set him up."

"I didn't kill him," he scoffs. "That stupid cunt's kid did."

"No. Stella was defending herself and those she loved. You killed him."

Jonas shakes his head, not giving two single shits about his involvement in Joe's death.

I glare at him and he lifts Mum from the chair, her hands still locked behind her back.

"Let her go," I demand.

"We're leaving," he says, completely ignoring that

I've even said anything as Mum allows him to move her around the table as if she's fine with all of this.

"I'm not going anywhere with you, and neither is she."

The second she's in reaching distance, I grab her upper arm and try to pull her from his grip.

"Jojo, please. Don't," Mum begs quietly.

"No. I'm not letting this happen. I'm not letting him manhandle you like this. Haven't you heard any of the things Toby or Maria have told you about him?"

"They're lying, Jodie."

My chin drops in shock.

"W-what? You can't actually be saying this to me right now. He broke them. He hurt them. He—"

"Jodie, please?" Mum begs, her eyes boring into mine. "Just do what he says."

I hold her stare, my heart racing and my blood whooshing past my ears.

'Please,' she mouths. 'Trust me.'

"Joanne," Jonas growls, the grip on her hair tightening until she yelps in pain.

"Shit," I hiss, rushing forward, digging my nails into Jonas's hand and trying to release his grip on her. "Let her go, you fucking psychopath."

He moves too quickly, and the next thing I know, my cheek is burning and I just about manage to lift my hands to stop my head from colliding with the wooden floor as I stumble back.

"Jodie," Mum screams.

"You fucking hit me," I gasp in horror, holding my hand to my cheek.

Still holding Mum in his unrelenting grip, he leers at me. His eyes are almost as black as his soul, and it sends a bolt of fear racing through me. But I refuse to cower. If the last few weeks have taught me anything, it's never to cower. Instead, I summon all my strength and dig up my inner bad-arse.

What would Stella do?

"Do not disrespect me."

"Why?" I hiss. "Will you lock me in the basement to teach me a lesson, like you used to do with Toby?"

"Don't," he roars, spittle flying from his lips as his gaunt, previously pale face turns red with anger. "Don't even mention that scumbag's name. He's nothing. And once we're free I'm going to make sure there is nothing left of him but memories."

"No," I cry, scrambling forward, but I only make it a few inches before he presses his boot to my hand. "Do as you're told, sweetheart. Listen to your daddy."

My stomach turns over once more. "You're not my daddy. You're a fucking monster."

I snatch my hand away before he decides to break all my fingers.

He stares nothing but pure hate at me as I stand once more. My legs tremble, and I'm forced to reach out for the wall to steady me. His nostrils flare and his chest heaves.

He looks better than he did that day through Toby's tablet, but he's far from healthy.

"We can do this the easy way or the hard way," he warns me. "But we are leaving this house as a family, and we're never going to look back."

"You're delusional if you think for even a second I'm going anywhere with you."

"Fine," he says calmly. Too fucking calmly. "We'll do it your way."

Mum is discarded, thrown to the floor like she's nothing. Unlike me though, she isn't fast enough, and her head collides with the floor with a bone-chilling crack.

"Mum," I race forward but he catches me, his hand covering my face once more—but this time, it's not his skin that touches me, it's cloth.

My arms flail and my nails scratch down his arms, taking chunks of skin with me as my legs kick, but nothing I do loosens his grip, and it's not long before my body starts to get sluggish, weak, and my eyes start to drop, the claws of darkness beginning to wrap around me and threatening to drag me under.

"No," I cry, panic flooding my system as I try to stave off the inevitable.

I can't go under. If I do, I'll have no idea where he takes us. I'll have no way of getting to Toby.

Jonas is going to take us, and he's going to...

"Toby," I whimper.

"You're not listening to me, are you, sweetheart? He isn't coming. He doesn't want you, not really. He just wanted revenge, and I guess your pussy was good enough to keep around a little longer than required. You just couldn't see it. But then, I guess you always were irritatingly naïve."

T he scent of decay is the first thing that hits me when the darkness begins to lift. My nose wrinkles and my lip peels back.

The second thing I'm aware of is the cold. The bone-chilling cold that makes my teeth chatter.

Where the fuck am I?

Forcing my eyes open, I'm greeted by more darkness.

My heart races and my head spins as I try to make out anything of my surroundings.

"Mum?" I whisper as panic begins to set in.

"Yeah, Jojo. I'm here."

Relief floods me and I push to sit. A move I quickly regret when the contents of my stomach decide they want to make a reappearance.

Drawing in a deep breath through my nose, I close my eyes once more and will my stomach to settle. The smell is already bad enough—the last thing I need to do is puke.

When I think I've got things a little more under control, I finally sit upright and look around praying that I might be able to make out something, anything to give us a clue as to where we are.

"Mum?" I ask again in the hope that something louder than her breathing will lead me closer to her.

"Over here," she says softly.

"Are you okay?" I ask, falling onto my hands and knees so I can attempt to search her out.

The floor is ice cold beneath my palms, and another shiver races down my spine.

"I... um..." The hesitation in her voice makes my heart drop into my feet.

She's hurt. I just wish I could see her and know how bad.

My own face aches, but I refuse to feel sorry for myself because the man my father really is has revealed himself to us. What I really need to do is figure out where the hell we are and a way out.

I need to somehow get to Toby, to let him, or any of them know where we are. They'll be here in a heartbeat. I know they will.

Jonas doesn't know what he's talking about. He cares. He loves me. I know he does. And I can't wait for him to be proved wrong.

Hate for the man I always used to look up to burns through my veins. The memory of the way Mum submitted to him, the way he touched her.

My stomach rolls once more as I pray that earlier was the first time he's ever been that rough with her.

"What's wrong, Mum? Did he hurt you?"

"I'll be fine, baby. You don't need to worry about me." The tremor in her voice tells me otherwise.

I breathe a sigh of relief when my fingers brush some fabric before I find her thigh.

Her gasp of shock pierces the air.

"It's okay, it's just me," I assure her.

In only seconds, we're in each other's arms.

Tears cascade down my cheeks as I try to keep myself together. Falling apart right now like Mum isn't going to get us anywhere.

"It's going to be okay. He'll come for us. He'll get us," I promise her, praying that my faith in Toby is worth it. If Jonas is right, if this thing between us isn't real, it'll break me.

I've believed his apologies. I've embraced his darkness, his regrets, and I've taken his words as the truth, even after seeing what he's capable of. Have I actually learned nothing? Am I as naïve as I've ever been?

"You knew he was alive, didn't you?" Mum asks me, and despite it being so dark in here that I can't so much as make out a single shape in front of me, I can see the expression on her face as clear as day in my mind.

"Yes. The night I found out the truth, I discovered he was still alive, that it was all a cover-up."

"And you didn't tell me." Pain laces her voice, and I wish I could see into her eyes to give me some kind of clue as to why. Is she glad he's still alive? Or is it just because I lied? Surely it can't be the former, after the way he was with her earlier?

I find her hand, squeezing it in both of mine as the pounding in my head slowly gets worse.

"What good would it have done? He was meant to be... dealt with. He was as good as gone."

"Well, it doesn't seem that way right now," she mutters.

"What happened, Mum? When did he—"

There's a loud crash at the other side of the room, and suddenly, light floods in around us while a long, haunting shadow covers the floor.

I squint as I look up at the man responsible for all of this.

He stands there in the doorway, trying to exert as much power and control as possible, but his body is weaker and frailer than I've ever seen, he falls a little from the mark. Or it might just be that now I know the truth, I know he really is nothing but a monster. A monster I refuse to cower away from.

"Ah, good, my girls are awake. Are you both hungry?"

"Where are we, and what do you want with us?" I demand, trying to pull my hand from Mum's grip so I can stand and face him, but she holds on too tight and I'm only able to get to my knees. Not the kind of height disadvantage I wanted.

"It doesn't matter where we are," he says softly, making me feel like a little girl again when he used to read me my favourite bedtime stories. "We're together. That's the only thing that's important right now."

"Not by choice. We don't want to be here with you. You should be dead," I scream, losing the thin grasp I have on my sanity.

"Come on now, sweetheart. We both know you don't really mean that."

Finally, I manage to slip my hand out of Mum's grasp and I stand before him, holding my head high and throwing my shoulders back.

"Yes," I spit. "I do. I hate you, you're a monster."

His lips press into a thin line and his jaw tics as he glares at me.

"What are you going to do, Dad? Are you going to hit me again? Or are you just planning on locking us in here until we start complying? If that's the case, I can tell you that that is never going to happen. I'm never going to listen to—" His arm shoots out and he backhands me across the same cheek as before.

"Jonas," Mum screams while I cradle my face, blood filling my mouth.

"I hope they make it hurt when they kill you," I seethe quietly, my voice full of venom.

"I was going to take you upstairs and give you both dinner," he snarls before plunging us into darkness and slamming and locking the door behind him.

Silence follows before the thundering of heavy feet on stairs clues me in to at least one fact about our location. The cunt really has locked us in a basement. But where?

As I navigate my way back toward where I think

Mum is in the darkness, I can't help but wonder if he's taken us back to his house. Are we in the same basement he used to lock Toby in?

Surely not. That would be too obvious.

If my instincts are right and Toby is out there right now searching for us, then he'd think to go back to his family home. Wouldn't he? He would find us.

"He was going to let us out," Mum says through what I'm sure are gritted teeth.

"You wanted to go and eat dinner with him?" I ask, dabbing at my split lip.

"Jodie," she sighs. "Sometimes you've just got to play the game."

I narrow my eyes at her despite the fact that she can't see me.

"Getting angry and pissing him off isn't going to get us anywhere. We need to know where we are, and being locked in the dark isn't going to give us any clues."

I drop down on my arse with a huff. She's got a point, but the last thing I feel like doing right now is being compliant.

Resting my head against her shoulder, I search for her hand.

"I'm sorry I never told you he was alive."

"I'm sorry too. For everything."

"We're going to get out of here."

Mum sighs, but she never agrees—and that only makes the dread sitting heavy in my stomach worse.

18

TOBY

My fists clench and unclench as I pace back and forth in Theo's penthouse. The others are all sitting on his sofas, watching me as if I'm about to explode at any second.

"He can't just have got out. It's not fucking possible," I mutter to myself.

It's been ten minutes since I stood in that doorway beside Daemon and stared at an empty cell, and I still can't believe it.

There's no way.

The security system installed down there is better than most prisons. There is no way he just decided one day that he was fed up being our little toy and opened the door and walked out.

"It can't be a coincidence that it happened this weekend," Seb muses as Theo furiously taps away on his laptop, trying to pinpoint a time for all of this happening via the security feed that runs twenty-four-seven around this place.

At some point, we'll be able to see him leave. We'll know how he managed it, and hopefully, it'll give us a lead.

It has to. There is no other option.

"Have you got hold of Jodie yet?" Stella asks from the edge of the sofa where he's watching me with concern.

"No, her phone just goes to voicemail. She's at the hospital."

"We should go over there. Make sure she is and that she isn't about to get intercepted by—"

The blood that rushes past my ears at her words stops me from hearing whatever follows the beginning of that statement.

"Go," I boom. "Get her the fuck back here and lock her down," I demand.

If he gets even within a mile of my girl then... my heart begins to race. My lungs pump, but they're unable to drag in any air.

Stella's warm hand landing on my upper arms startles me. I stare into her blue eyes, seeing my own fear reflected back at me.

"Just breathe, Toby." Her grip on me tightens as she directs me to just suck in a deep breath before blowing it out once more. "We'll get her, okay? Seb's already called Dad. Mom is fine. They're both safe and on high alert."

"They should come here," I tell her. "It's safer here."

Stella nods. "I'll call him on the way to the hospital. We'll get them all safe, and then we'll find him," she promises me.

My lips twitch in acknowledgment of her words, but by no means do I feel the smile.

"Come on, Princess," Seb says, wrapping his arm around her shoulders and dragging her away from me.

I want to reach out and stop her, but I know that Jodie needs her more than I do right now.

"Look out, the cavalry has arrived," Seb shouts loudly from the front door, and two seconds later, Damien and Charon come storming into the room.

We were expecting the boss. Theo called him the second Daemon and I dragged him down to look at the empty cell. But I could really do without seeing my so-called grandfather.

Anger surges through me at the memories of the last time I saw him in Damien's office. When he stood there, completely unfazed by the fact he knew his cunt of a son treated Mum and me the way he did.

"No," I boom, moving across the room faster than I expected. My fingers curl in Charon's suit jacket before I slam him back against the wall.

I pull my arm back and am just about to commit the ultimate sin by planting my fist into his traitorous face when a hand locks around my upper arm.

"Careful, soldier," Damien warns, his fingers digging into my bicep until it hurts.

"He's not welcome here. He was probably the motherfucker who let him out."

My grip on his lapel never loosens, and Charon's cold stare never breaks from my eyes.

"I can assure you, Tobias, that if I were going to free him, I'd have done it long before now," Charon says calmly. "I know you think I'm to blame here as well, and partly, I could well be. But I have not done this. I will, however, help you fix it and put an end to the situation for good."

"You want to lay him at my feet so I can put a bullet through his head?"

He nods once, and my body relaxes a beat.

"Fine. But if he hurts either of them in the meantime, you might just find yourself leaving this world with him."

"That won't be necessary."

Tension crackles between us as I stare at him. The man who was only ever a good role model to me. I want to believe he's not entirely guilty in all of this. But I stand by my opinion that he had to have known more than he let on.

"Shall we—"

"Got it," Theo barks, turning all our attention to him.

Releasing Charon and shrugging out of Damien's hold, I rush over to where Theo and Nico are staring down at the screen.

"Who the hell is that?" I bark, watching in horror as two men in balaclavas just unlock the fucking door and let him walk free.

"Fucking dead, that's what they are," Nico growls, sounding almost as unhinged as I feel right now.

"Who's been guarding him this weekend?" Damien barks, shooting his death glare at Daemon, but he doesn't give him a chance to talk. "Get them here. Now."

"What do you mean, she's not there?" I bark into my phone as we all wait down in the basement for the guys who were tasked to keep Jonas alive this weekend.

"Jesse hasn't seen her, Tobes."

The fear in Stella's voice makes my heart drop into my feet.

"No, that can't be right. She was going straight there."

"Did she leave here? Did you watch her get in her car and drive away?"

My eyes meet Theo's as he watches my reaction closely.

"No," I confess, remembering that I let her walk out of the flat without having a single concern for her safety. "Theo, get the feed from the garage. We need to see Jodie leaving."

He nods, opening his laptop and resting it on one hand as he taps at the keys.

"We're going to Joanne's."

"I'll meet you there."

"No, you need—"

"Don't," I growl. As much as I might want to string the pair of cunts who let this happen up by their balls, my biggest concern right now is Jodie and getting her safe. "Did you talk to Galen?"

"They're on their way."

"Good. I'll meet you there." I end the call before she gets a chance to say anything more. "Jodie never made it to the hospital," I explain despite them probably already guessing.

"She left here alone, and as far as I can tell, no one has followed her," Theo adds, much to my relief.

"She probably just swung by home and is probably on her way to the hospital now. Track her," Nico suggests.

I already have and it showed her as driving toward the hospital as I was expecting. But I figure there's no harm in checking again.

My hand shakes as I wait for her location to update.

"She's at home," I state, finally seeing her little blue dot not where I was expecting it to be.

"Let's go then, bro. You got this here?" Nico asks Theo, Alex, and Daemon before taking off toward the stairs.

"You fucking know it. Those cunts aren't walking

out of this place until they've squealed everything they know."

"You should stay," I say to Nico, assuming that all of us turning up at Joanne's door is going to be total overkill when we find the two of them drinking tea and eating cookies. But even as I think that, something deep inside me knows it's not going to be the case.

"Fuck off. You need me, I'm there, bro." He reaches for me and messes up my hair as we race toward the garage.

I have my car unlocked before we even get there, and the second my arse hits the seat, I'm spinning it out of the space and gunning it across town.

"Watch her tracker," I bark, throwing my phone at Nico.

"This hasn't updated in over ten minutes," he points out, making my stomach knot with worry.

"Maybe the battery died," I offer, needing some kind of lie to convince myself that everything's going to be okay.

We're two minutes out when my phone rings through the speakers.

"You got her?" I bark as Stella's call connects.

"No one is answering the door."

"She's there, her phone is there."

"There doesn't seem to be anyone here."

"Shit. Shit." I slam my palms down on the wheel before taking the final turn up their street. "We're pulling up now."

I abandon my car in the middle of the road with the engine still running.

Racing toward the front door, I hammer my fists down on the dark wood.

"JODIE?" I bellow. "JODIE? JOANNE?"

But there's nothing.

"Look in the window," I demand.

Nico rushes over but Seb just stares at me, compassion filling his eyes.

"I have, man. There's no one in there."

"B-but... her car is there. Her phone is here. She has to be. JODIE?" I scream, trying again, desperate for her to open the goddamn door and prove to me that I'm overreacting.

"What the hell are you—"

Stella doesn't get to finish her question as I back away from the door a few steps before I run full pelt at it in the hope it'll give.

It doesn't so much as creak under my weight. My shoulder, on the other fucking hand, screams in pain.

"A little fucking help?" I ask, looking at Seb and Nico, who are wearing matching frowns.

"We're not gonna—"

My palms collide with Nico's chest before he can continue that argument. He stumbles back in shock, but he soon comes back at me, more than ready to be my punching bag if I need it.

"So you're just going to stand there and do fucking nothing? He's got her, man. He's fucking g-got—" The words get stuck in my throat as fear like I've never known threatens to rip me in two.

Hearing her voice on the phone while the building burned around her was bad. Running in there to get her was fucking terrifying.

But I could do something then. I could make a difference. I could help. Right now, I'm useless.

"If he touches her—"

"Then we'll gut him like a fucking fish. We'll find her," Nico promises, taking my face in his hands and pressing his head to mine. "We'll fucking find her."

His amber eyes stare into mine, darkening with promises of pain and retribution with each second that passes.

"Let's get that door down," Seb says, clamping his hand over my shoulder. "Something has to point us in the right direction."

The three of us line up as Stella backs away, her face twisted with concern and helplessness as we slam our combined weight into the door.

It groans and creaks, teasing us. But we don't give in until it finally swings open and the three of us crash to the floor in the hallway.

"Get your fucking elbow out of my balls," Nico barks.

Ignoring him, I climb from the top of the pile and race farther into the house.

Everything looks exactly as I would expect it to, apart from one thing. The sight of the overturned chair in the dining room makes my blood run cold.

"He was here," I breathe.

"Shit," Seb says, stepping up behind me and taking in the room.

"There's got to be something. Anything. Search the place."

I spin on my heels, ready to check the living room, and I run straight into Nico.

"Get the fuck out of my way."

"This might be a trap," he says, sounding way more serious than he usually does about anything.

"If he wants to jump out and try to take me on right now, then he's more than fucking welcome," I spit. "Move." I shove him aside, and thankfully, he lets me go this time.

"You really think he's planned this enough to start setting traps?" Seb asks.

"He managed to escape from a high-security cell," Stella says sarcastically. "He has a fucking plan."

"Someone let him out," Nico adds as I search the room, keeping one ear on their discussion.

"Tobes, you did all his background checks. Who did he have in his back pocket that could have helped pull this off?"

"It would probably be easier to ask who he didn't have in his back pocket, from what I can tell," I mutter, rejoining them when I find nothing suspicious.

"Who would want him back? What benefit did he serve to your enemies?" Stella asks.

"He was probably selling us out left and right. Everything that has ever gone wrong was probably his doing."

"Fight night, the Halloween party. I bet he even knew about the fucking Lovell riot," Seb lists off.

"Well, it can't be Luis or Ram," Nico argues.

"They had plenty of loyal followers, though. No reason why it couldn't be any of them."

Nico, Seb, and I share a look.

"What?" Stella demands, having seen our silent conversation.

"Let's check the rest of this place out and head back, see what they've managed to beat out of those two guys," Seb says bravely. "Ow, fuck," he cries when Stella grabs his nipple through his shirt and twists.

"Start fucking talking, Papatonis," she growls. "You do not leave me out of this shit anymore, remember?"

"We'll leave you with that," Nico says, shoving me toward the stairs. "He should just be glad that wasn't his balls."

"Pretty sure she's already got them stored safely in her handbag," I quip as I try to push aside the fact that I'm about to walk into Jodie's room, be surrounded by everything that is her but not know where the fuck she is.

But as bad as I know it's going to be, it's still nothing compared to the reality of stepping inside her room and breathing in her sweet scent.

"Fuck," I grunt, lifting my hand and fisting my shirt right over the pain in my chest. "Baby, where are you? Where's he taken you?"

My eyes scan the room as if the answer is going to jump out at me. But there's nothing. Nothing but pain, loss, and regrets.

Dropping down onto the end of her bed, I hang my head as all the things I should have done differently with her float through my mind.

I shake my head, my fists curling until my nails dig into my palms as I refuse to believe that he's going to beat us. Beat me.

He trained me better than this. I should be able to see through his plans.

Squeezing my eyes closed, I think back to that video call when he was talking to her all those weeks ago.

He told her that they'd be together again. That they could be a family again. Is that what this is about? Has he just run off into the sunset with them?

Shit.

A thought hits me, and I bolt upright.

No. Surely she didn't know about this?

"What's wrong?" Nico asks, appearing in her doorway.

"Do you think she wanted this?" I ask, my heart sinking further with every second that passes.

"No," he states without even missing a beat. "There's no way. She just told you to kill him," he reminds me.

"But she might have known he was going to have been gone."

"Nah, man. You're reading too much into it. There's no fucking way she'd ever choose him over you."

"You can't say that. You've never seen him with her."

Hell, I've never seen him with her. But I've heard the way she used to talk about her dad before she found out the truth, and she only believed he was her stepdad then.

"What if she never forgave me and all of this has been—"

"You're talking shit. That girl fucking loves you, man. Stop letting your fears overrule you."

He stands before me, giving me little choice but to crane my neck to look up at him.

"I'm not, I'm just—"

"Being a fucking pussy. Jodie isn't a liar. She isn't her father. You're it for her, bro. And right now, both her and Joanne need you fucking fighting for them."

I stare at him, my eyes narrowing in suspicion.

"When the fuck did you get so wise?"

"I didn't. I've just spent the past few weeks watching you two sappy shits fall deeper in love with each other. Stop questioning whether you're good enough, whether she wants the real you. Because you are good enough."

"I'm not sure I like you like this," I confess. "But I fucking appreciate it."

Pushing to my feet, I wrap my arms around him and slap him on the back in an attempt to keep it manly.

"Fucking love you, man. I'd do anything to keep that smile she puts on your face."

"I guess we'd better go and figure out how to find her then."

19

TOBY

Cries of agony hit our ears long before we get down the stairs to the basement. And when we do finally round the corner, we find Damien, Charon, Theo, and Alex all watching Daemon as he presses a branding iron into the skin of one of the guys they've got strapped naked to the two chairs in the middle of the room.

Both are barely recognisable, their faces swollen and bloody from the beatings and torture they've already endured.

I can only assume that it hasn't been enough, because from the dark cloud surrounding Daemon, I don't think he has any intentions of stopping anytime soon.

The scent of burning skin makes my stomach turn over a beat before Daemon pulls the red-hot brand back, revealing his artwork.

"I have a question," I say, stepping forward to stand beside the dark devil himself.

Everyone's attention in the room follows me as I stare dead into the swollen eyes of our captives.

"How much did the Italians promise you to pull this off for them?"

Both of them sit motionless, and I'm sure that if their faces were in any state to show a reaction, they wouldn't.

Stupid backstabbing fucking cunts.

Both of them have been with us for years. Or at least, we thought they were on our side. Turns out, they're about as corrupt as the arsehole Wolves we've recently taken down.

"I really hope that you both thought this through before you allowed them to manipulate you into doing their dirty work. You both have families, right?" I ask, having done a little research on the drive back over here thanks to Theo's intel. "Wives. Kids. It would be a real shame to have to make them suffer because of your stupid fucking choices."

Still, neither breaks.

"So I can assume that the Marianos have your loved ones somewhere safe. Or are you both so fucking arrogant that they're sitting at home right now, none the wiser that you've sold us out?"

Both Nico and I know the answer to that question, and so do they.

Finally, one of them gives me the reaction I was

hoping for as the quietest of whimpers rumbles in the back of his throat.

"What was that?" I ask, leaning a little closer but regretting it the second the stench of piss hits my nose.

Nothing.

"I think we should probably go and pick them all up now, don't you, Boss?" I ask, turning to look at Damien, who's watching me with something that I'm sure is pride in his eyes.

"Sure. Alex, Seb, take Stella and Emmie with you. Bring them here peacefully," he orders.

"Sure thing, Boss," Alex agrees before a pained cry finally cuts through the air.

"No, no. Leave them out of this."

Surging forward, I wrap my fingers around the cunt's throat hard enough to cut off his air supply. His eyes widen in panic, but I don't let up.

"Then you need to start fucking talking," I seethe, spitting in his face with every word. "We shouldn't need to be lecturing you on the fucking importance of family loyalty, soldier. You both know you're dead because of this fucking stupid stunt, but your families' lives are very much hanging in the balance right now. I really hope they made it worth your while."

Silence fills the room, and my grip on his throat only tightens. But despite his earlier protest to protect his family, no further argument falls from either of them.

Until Alex, Seb, and Stella make a move to leave.

"No," the other cries. "They promised us new lives away from here if we let him free."

I bare my teeth as I continue to stare at the scumbag in my clutches. His lips are beginning to turn blue, but he still isn't doing anything to fight me off.

"Is life with us really that bad?" Damien asks, stepping up beside me and finally getting involved.

"No, Boss. I just want more for my children."

"A life of wealth, power, and the protection of a whole family not enough for you, soldier?"

"I owe my wife more," he says, his voice giving away the fear he's trying so hard to hide.

"And you think a life that is now going to be without you is better than this one with her husband alive?"

"T-they promised i-it would b-be easy."

"Well, yes. I guess leaving a door open is fairly easy. But you seem to be forgetting something," Damien states, his voice as hard and cold as always. "The Italians are stupid, power-hungry fucks. Did you really think you'd get away with this? You were the last two to see him alive. Toby, release him," Damien demands. "You need them both breathing a little longer yet if we're going to find your girl."

The guy before Damien pales.

"Oh, I'm sorry. Did you really think that Jonas was going to skip off into the sunset and leave us all to our happy lives? I'm sorry to break it to you, but this life isn't like that. And we had him down here for a goddamn good reason." His voice deepens, getting more and more deadly by the second.

The guy I'd almost strangled to death heaves in hungry breaths as he tries to get enough oxygen back into his system. He'd better make the most of it, because as soon as we have all the information we need, the pair of them are fucking dead.

"Now," Damien says, his eyes lifting to his son and beckoning him over. Pulling a switchblade from his pocket, he hands it to Theo, whose eyes blaze with bloodlust. "Are we going to do this the fun way or the easy way?"

Theo clearly doesn't give a shit about the answer to that question, because the second he wraps his fingers around the knife, he drives the blade straight into the back of the guy's hand that is strapped to the arm of the chair, making him howl like a wild beast.

"I'm not really feeling easy tonight, Boss," Theo says casually, pulling the weapon back out of his hand and wiping it clean on the guy's trousers as he whimpers.

"Fair enough. So... where has Jonas gone?"

"We don't know, Boss," the guy I was strangling rasps.

"Not good enough," Damien roars, his booming voice making me flinch.

"W-we didn't ask questions, Boss."

"Theo," Damien offers not a beat before the knife finds a home in the guy's thigh. "We can keep doing this for days. Keep you on the edge of death for longer than you would believe. And the longer it takes, the closer we get to your kids. Do you think they'll scream as much as you?"

He groans as Theo pulls the knife free and looks down, blood spilling from the wound. There's a lot, but not enough for it to be an artery.

"He's leaving the country."

"Tonight?"

"No. He wanted to get his family first."

"Her tracker still hasn't changed," I say, staring down at the thing as if it'll magically move and tell us where she is if I pray hard enough.

"Tell us again why you thought it was a good idea not to put a tracker in her necklace?" Theo asks me, his brow quirked as if he genuinely can't understand why I wouldn't have done it.

"Because, arsehole, I didn't want to treat her like a fucking dog." I shoot a glance at Emmie, knowing full well that he fucking chipped her not so long ago.

"We would know where she was right now if you had."

Surging to my feet, I drag him from the sofa by his shirt.

"You think I don't fucking know that?" I boom, our noses so close they're almost touching.

My chest heaves as pure desperation rushes through my veins.

He could have taken her anywhere. He could be doing anything to her.

My stomach turns over at the thought of him laying a hand on her. Of him treating her even similarly to how he did me.

"Toby." Mum's soft voice filters through my ears, and it makes me relax even before she rests her hand on my shoulder.

She and Galen were up here in my flat waiting when we came to a dead end with the two cunts down there.

We left them for the night groaning in pain and coating the floor in their blood, letting them believe that their families would have a less-than-pleasant wake-up call in the morning if they didn't come up with something we could use.

"We'll find her."

I release Theo with a shove, he falls back to the sofa as I wheel around on Mum.

"How?" I bark. "How the fuck are we going to find her? He could have taken her anywhere."

My voice is loud and deadly, but she doesn't so much as flinch.

"He's not going to leave quietly," she tells me, her voice even and steady as if she knows this for a fact. Which of course, she doesn't. But she's put up with enough of his bullshit over the years to know how he works. Hell, I should know this too, but the only thing I'm capable of right now is fear. Bone-chilling fucking fear that he's going to hurt my girl.

I used her against him. And now he's going to repay the favour.

"He was always about the glory, the gloating. He won't leave until he's twisted that blade he pushed through our hearts all those years ago."

I fight to drag in the air I need as the meaning behind her words hits me square in the chest.

"If he hurts her—"

"We will find him, Toby. And we will kill him before he gets the chance."

"What if we don't?" I ask, my voice weak and terrified.

"We will," Stella says, stepping up beside me and wrapping her arm around my waist as Galen comes to stand beside Mum.

"We're all behind you, Son," he says, not helping the unrelenting ache in my chest. "He will not beat us now," he promises me.

My fists curl at my sides. Barely restrained anger surges through me, locking my muscles up tight as movement behind Mum's shoulder catches my eye.

"This is cute and all, but Toby needs to come with me," Nico states, able to see what the others fail to.

"Where are you going?" Stella asks, totally affronted.

"Don't worry your tits over it, Princess. I'll keep him

safe. Call us if anything happens and we'll be straight back up," he says with a smile. "Go get changed," he tells me before pulling his phone from his pocket.

Silence falls around the room, and it's everything I need to know that I can't stay in here with this oppressive tension weighing down on me.

Stepping forward, I wrap my arms around Mum, breathing in her scent and praying that the words she just said to me are true and we'll figure out his next move before it's too late.

In only minutes, I have a pair of sweats on and a tank, and I'm jogging down the stairs to our basement gym right behind Nico while the others continue trying to figure shit out in my flat.

Damien and Charon have gone to meet Evan and Stefanos to fill them in on what's happening. Stefanos has been heading up the intel with the Italians since they tried encroaching on our territory on their side of the city before Christmas. So if they've left any loose thread with this, then he should be able to pull it and watch it unravel.

It's not a real surprise that they're in bed with Jonas. They were the ones who started the fire that fight night, claiming that it was a direct order from us. Or whatever bullshit they tried to spew. They tried to warn us that night that we had a snake in our Family —little did we know just how fucking slippery he would turn out to be.

The second we push through the doors to the

gym, Nico selects a playlist on his phone and jumps into the ring, holding his arms out at his sides.

"Bring it on, baby," he taunts, making me see red with just those four words.

With a loud roar that I'm sure any wild animal would be proud of, I fly at him, pummelling my fists into any bit of his body he leaves unprotected. His returning blows are just as brutal, but I use the pain he leaves me in to fuel my movements. Acting on instinct, using the skills I was taught from such a young age that they're now almost as natural as breathing, allows me to empty my mind, to push the worst of the anger and desperation out for just a short while.

I have no idea how long we fight for, but when Nico's ringtone fills the space around us, I've got sweat pouring from my body and blood dripping from my fists, I'm sure covering almost every inch of my body.

"Break," Nico barks, wiping his brow with his arms and ducking under the ropes to answer his phone.

"Yeah. Yeah. Basement. Yeah. Yeah."

I stare at him as he hangs up and walks toward the fridge, throwing me a bottle of water not a second later.

"Who was that?" I ask, twisting the top and immediately drinking half of it down.

"No one who has any answers."

I've just upended the bottle over my head when

the door to the gym opens and a distraught-looking Brianna comes rushing in.

"You're a fucking cunt," she barks, storming toward Nico and swinging her handbag at him.

My eyes widen at her savagery as whatever she's got in there collides with Nico's head with a painful thud.

"What the fuck, Siren?" he barks.

"You don't fucking text me to tell me my best friend is fucking missing, you massive fucking cunt waffle."

"Would you rather not know?"

"You're a fucking prick. I don't know why I ever thought spending time with you was a good idea."

She waves him off and turns to me.

"Jesus, you look a mess."

I quirk a brow at her.

"What's happening? Have you found her? Who has her?"

My eyes lift from Bri to Nico, who just shrugs in exasperation.

"Didn't you tell her anything?" I ask.

"No, he told me Jojo was missing. That was it. No other fucking details. Where is she, Toby? Is she okay?"

"Fuck," I hiss, shoving my bloody fingers into my dripping wet hair. "We don't know where she is, Bri. Jonas has her."

"J-Jonas?" she stutters, a deep frown marring her brow.

"Starting to figure out why I didn't lay it all out in a fucking text message now?" Nico grumbles behind her.

"Fuck you," she shoots over her shoulder before turning back to me. "Please, continue."

"Jonas isn't dead. Our boss faked his death. We've had him locked in a cell for the past few months."

Her mouth opens and closes like a goldfish as she tries to process the CliffsNotes of this whole clusterfuck of a situation.

"He's escaped. We can't find her or Joanne."

"Shit, Toby. This is fucking insane," she says, throwing her hands up in exasperation.

"Welcome to our world, Siren," Nico says.

"Are you still fucking here?" she snaps at him.

"Hell yeah, you know I love it when you get all feisty."

"My best friend, my cousin, is fucking missing. Can you lay off the jokes, maybe?"

I shake my head at the two of them as I swipe a towel from the top of the pile in the corner and rub it over my head and face. When I pull it away, the bright white cotton is tinged red.

"Everyone is up in my flat. Come on," I say, marching past Bri, more than ready to take a shower and hear if there have been any breakthroughs.

Everyone turns to look at us as we storm through my flat. Mum gasps in horror at the sight of the two of us, but I'm not sure why she's so surprised. It's not the first time she's helped patch us up after we've gone at it a bit too hard as we've fought to banish our demons.

"Anything?" I bark, my eyes locking on Theo.

Everyone is still here apart from Daemon, who's disappeared.

"Boss and Dad are digging into shit at the office. Daemon's gone to the Italians' compound to see if he can get some intel," Alex explains.

"He thinks he's going to randomly overhear something?"

"Fuck knows what he thinks or what they've got going on," Alex mutters, clearly feeling a little pushed out with whatever their dad and Daemon are working on.

"I'm going to shower," I grunt, taking off through my flat and toward the solitude of my bedroom.

With each step I take, the tight grip that I've had on anything but my anger over this begins to loosen.

A huge ball of emotion crawls up my throat, and as I push through into my bedroom, all I can see is Jodie sitting in the middle of my bed, my sheets twisted around her naked body. My heart shatters into a million pieces as memories of our time together play out in my mind.

I promised her that I would always protect her. That I would never let anything or anyone hurt her. But now fucking look. I can't even find her.

"FUUUUCK," I roar, swiping my arm across the top of my chest of drawers, watching as the bottles of fragrance and a couple of photo frames tumble to the floor. "FUUUUCK."

Tears fill my eyes as I fight not to just crumble into a million useless fucking pieces.

I push my fingers into my hair until it hurts enough that I'm sure I'm about to rip it all clean out of my scalp.

A warm palm touches my shoulder and I wheel around, my fist clenching once more, ready to take out whoever it is standing there and witnessing me break.

"Bri," I breathe a second before I throw what would probably have been the most regretful punch of my life.

"I'm sorry. I'm so s-sorry. I j-just— fuck," she whispers, her tears spilling over her lashes.

"Fuck. Me too. Me fucking too."

Forgetting about the fact that I'm covered in sweat and blood, I pull her into my body and wrap my arms around her as she cries.

"We're gonna find her, Bri. I fucking promise you," I say into her hair, praying to anyone who might listen that I'm not lying again.

Fuck. I have to find her. There is no other choice.

"I'll do whatever you need me to do," she says honestly, holding me as tight as I'm holding her. "But I'm going to kick all your arses once all this is over for lying to me about Jonas. Why the fuck is that cunt still alive?"

"Good fucking question," I mutter, finally

releasing her. "I'm going to regret not killing him sooner for the rest of my life. I know that for a fact."

Walking away from her, I pull my tank off and throw it toward the laundry basket before pushing my sweats and boxers over my hips and storming into the bathroom, slamming the door behind me.

I turn the dial down and stand under the ice-cold water until everything is numb and my teeth are chattering.

It's the least of what I deserve for fucking all this up so badly.

20

JODIE

As much as I hate to admit it, doing what Mum suggested and complying with Jonas's crazy-arse demands did allow us some sort of freedom.

He did feed us, although it was barely worth the effort of chewing. And we both did get to have very quick, accompanied, trips to the bathroom. Trips that involved us being blindfolded so we couldn't get a sense of where we were.

All I know is that there are two flights of stairs to get to the bathroom, and inside there's one small boarded-up window. The room itself is old—a similar size to ours but with a slightly different layout.

I craved to stand under the shower in the dirty old bath and feel hot water rain down on me.

I was filthy, my hair was gross, my skin dry and itchy. Those things are the only way I could tell how long we'd been locked up for. I can usually pull off two days without washing my hair. At this point, we've definitely been down here for at least four.

My hopes of Toby finding us and getting us out of this hell are starting to wane.

We have no idea where we were; how the hell was he meant to figure it out?

Clearly, we're not in their family basement where Toby used to be locked up. He'd have tried that. He'd have looked there. I'm fucking sure of it.

The man who's escorted me to pee rips the blindfold from my face, and a large palm presses between my shoulder blades, shoving me forward. I manage to make it down the first few steps before my foot catches and I stumble, crashing to the ground with a pained cry.

"Jodie," Mum gasps, rushing forward as the man at the top of the stairs laughs. The deep evil rumble flows through the air around us before the heavy door swings shut and the locks engage.

"I'm okay," I breathe, pain shooting up my arm. "I'm okay," I try again, hoping that at some point, I might just start believing my words.

I manage to get myself up, and I curl up with Mum on the makeshift bed we've made for ourselves.

"This isn't working," I hiss. "He's not getting complacent, we're just feeding his need for control."

"He's going to slip up. He has to."

"And what if he doesn't?" I snap. "If we can't find a way out of here, and they can't find us, then what?"

"I don't know," Mum whispers, sounding more defeated than ever.

"You know him better than anyone. You've put up with this... bullshit all your life. You have to know his weakness."

"He hasn't got one. Not while he's got us both under lock and key. We're the only thing he wants in the world. And he's got us right where he wants us."

"Surely his game plan isn't to keep us down here forever? He's going to have to let us out eventually."

The look on her face asks, *does he?* but I refuse to believe that's the truth.

He's had months to plan this, and he's clearly had some help. I've identified two different men who have escorted me to take a piss. But who are they? And why do they feel the need to help that cunt?

The minutes tick by, the ache in my arm only getting worse. At least we've got light now. Not that it allows us to see anything good.

Everything down here is cold and dank. The concrete floor is black with damp, and it's slowly growing up the dirty grey walls. At some point, Mum started coughing, and I have no doubt it's the spores that are causing it.

We have no concept of time down here, nor whether it's day or night outside. The window has been so well boarded up, there isn't even a slither of light that comes through it. And I've tried everything in my power to pull it down. But with nothing down here but a few thin blankets and my own fingers, escaping is far from a possibility.

I have no idea how much time passes again before the sound of heavy footsteps pounds above us.

My stomach knots, knowing that he's back. Dread seeps through my bones as we wait. We're always his first port of call when he reappears, coming to greet us as if we've been waiting for him to return from a hard day's work.

He gets closer, my heart picking up speed in my chest before the locks release and the door is swung open.

"My girls," he announces. "I've got a treat for you tonight." His smile that follows is manic, and it sends fear shooting through my body.

"That sounds wonderful, darling," Mum breathes, smiling sweetly up at him. Her fake happiness sets my teeth on edge. But while I might not agree with her plan to pacify him into fucking up, I also don't have a plan B. Kicking off and screaming in his face is a sure-fire way to ensure our stay in the basement only continues.

"Come on, then. I've got dinner for us all."

"You want us to come up there and eat with you?" I ask, my brows pulling together in confusion.

He hasn't let us out without a blindfold yet, so why would he suddenly want to have a sit-down family meal?

Mum pushes to her feet and I hesitantly do the same, curious as fuck as to what he's playing at.

With each step I take up the stairs, I expect him to laugh in our faces and slam the door once more.

My stomach aches where it's so empty, and as I hit the top step and the scent of food hits me, I forget all about this being a setup and begin moving faster, desperate for what he might have for us on the other side of the door.

"What the fuck?" I mutter under my breath as I get a look at the house we're being kept beneath.

I blink a few times, looking around in disbelief.

It's our house. Only... it's not.

But the walls, the furniture, even some of the photographs, they're identical to our house.

This is seriously fucked up.

"I've got our favourite," he says, gesturing toward the kitchen diner.

We walk inside ahead of him and find the table covered in everything to make tacos.

My mouth waters at the sight of all the food after only existing on dry bread and lukewarm water for... days.

"What did we do to deserve this treat?" Mum says softly behind me, her tone making me cringe.

"I thought it was time for us to be a family again."

"Why?" I ask, the question falling from my lips before I even realised I was going to say it out loud.

"Because I want to do something nice for my girls."

I spin around and stare at him. He looks better than he did the first time I saw him in our home, however many days ago that was. Being free is obviously good for him.

"We're starting over. Just me and my girls. I've planned everything and we're going to be so happy."

My eyes narrow at him, but I manage to keep my thoughts to myself.

"That sounds wonderful, darling. Why don't you tell us more about it?"

Jonas's eyes never leave mine as he leads Mum toward the table.

"Where are we going to start over?" I ask, realising that he's suspicious of me and needing to follow Mum's plan to make him think we're on his side.

"We've got tickets booked for a couple of days' time. I've got the most incredible house waiting for us. It's near some fantastic universities, you're going to love it."

"Where is it?" I ask, my heart racing.

If he gets us out of the country, we're royally fucked.

"You don't need to worry about that right now. Sit, eat. You both must be starving."

Yeah, no thanks to you.

Jonas pulls Mum's chair out, and the second she's seated, he begins filling her plate.

I'm not quite so keen despite just how loudly my stomach is growling, and it's not until he finally sits and begins eating that I follow suit, figuring that he's not about to poison himself after setting all this up.

"This house looks wonderful," Mum says.

"I've been having it remodelled for weeks," he confesses, lifting his first taco to his mouth. "I missed home so much. I missed you both so much," he says, reaching for Mum's hand and holding it tightly. "It's all I've been able to think about. Us being back together."

"We missed you too, darling," Mum purrs like a good little wife.

Her act turns my stomach, and I can't help but wonder if there's a very good reason why she's so good at it.

She's told me time and time again that she's loved him with all her heart, and I believe her, but I can't help but wonder if there's so much more to their relationship, possibly more than she even realises.

He stares at her with hunger in his eyes, and as much as the idea that hits me disgusts me, it gives me the only hope I've had in days.

If she could distract him, use that weakness he has for her against him, it could give us the window we need to find help, to gain the upper hand, to escape.

"It's so nice to see that smile on your face again, Mum," I add, playing along with the charade.

Jonas's eyes light up.

"I always knew we'd be back together." He grins widely at her as I force myself to eat. I'm starving, but I'm also worried that the second this hits my stomach, it's going to immediately come back up again.

"I'm so sorry about everything you'd been through while I've been away," he says, almost sounding genuine. "But everything is going to be okay. We have everything we could possibly need. And where we're going... they'll never find us."

Ice slowly forms around my heart. We can't allow him to follow through on this plan. We can't end up somewhere random. Not only will they never find us, but we'll never be able to get out.

"Everything is planned," he says, pushing his chair back and walking out to the hall.

My eyes collide with Mum's, and immediately, I see that she's on the same page as me.

'Let me help us,' she mouths as Jonas rummages through something just outside the door.

Scanning the room, I look for anything in touching distance that I can make use of.

His need to mimic our house has done me some favours. There's a heavy vase on the unit that I'm sure would do some damage, although it's not like I can really hide that up my shirt. But sitting on the kitchen counter is a knife block.

Deciding it's worth the risk, I jump out of my chair and pull the smallest one free.

Her eyes watch me with concern as my heart jackhammers in my chest and fingers curl around the cool metal of the weapon.

"Ah ha." Jonas's deep voice booms through the air as he finds what he's looking for, and my arse hits the chair just as he steps back inside. "Here we go," he says, dropping three passports onto the table. "Everything we need for a clean escape."

Bile burns up my throat as I tuck the knife up my sleeve.

"Are these new?" Mum asks innocently.

"Sure are. New. Fake. No one will know we've slipped out of the country until it's too late."

"You really have thought of everything," Mum mutters.

He beams at her praise like a little kid, and I can't help but shake my head, disgust for this abusive, violent man making it hard to breathe.

"I'm so excited to have you back." Mum smiles up at him like he hung the moon, and I swear his chest swells with happiness.

How fucking deluded is this sick prick?

"We need a photo," he declares.

"A photo?" I blurt.

"Yes. This is a new beginning for us, for our family. It's important."

"Sure, darling. Whatever you want," Mum says, the sweetness in her voice setting my teeth on edge. How doesn't he notice it's fake?

Because he's used to it, a little voice says at the back of my mind. *You just never noticed before, you naïve bitch.*

I blow out a long breath, hating myself for not seeing more in the past. I was content to believe they were both happy, that everything was as it should be. But I'm starting to realise that was far from the truth. He's brainwashed her, controlled her, turned her into his little lapdog. I just hope that she doesn't fall straight back into his trap, because I would really hate to have to walk out of this without her.

"Come on then," Jonas says, pulling his phone from his pocket and unlocking it. With the same passcode he's always used, I notice. "Jodie, come over here," he encourages.

Keeping the knife securely tucked up my sleeve, I do as I'm told, hoping that this charade will be over soon. The last place I might want to be in the world is locked down in that cold and dank basement, but I'm starting to think it's actually preferable to this.

If I didn't think there was a chance of getting the upper hand, or at least an escape plan by finally being allowed up here, then I'd be locking myself back down there.

A loud creak sounds out from above us as Jonas leans in and takes photograph after photograph of us. I wince every time the shutter closes, because I look like hell. The cuts and bruises from his brutal hits are more than obvious in each image. It makes me sick to think they've been caused by my father. Someone who's meant to protect me above all else.

That's all he's tried to do all my life, it seems. Protect me.

Has he decided that now I know the truth, all bets are off? He can now treat me as badly as everyone else in his life?

Is it that he's lost Maria and Toby as his punching bags, so now he's going to turn that on us instead?

Another loud creak makes me look to the ceiling in question.

"Oh, it's just my buddy. He's been helping me out."

"Who is he?" I ask, breaking away from our huddle and backing toward the door.

"No one you need to worry about. Well, unless you cross him," he warns darkly.

"This has been so lovely, Jonas. Thank you," Mum says, pushing to her feet and running her hands up his chest. Folding them over his shoulders, she looks at me. 'Go.'

"Is it okay if I use the bathroom?" I ask, not wanting to risk running out on him.

"Of course, sweetheart. But don't try running. All the doors and windows are securely locked."

"I just need to pee, *Dad*," I force out through gritted teeth.

He looks back at me and smiles in achievement.

Thankfully, Mum quickly distracts him and I'm able to bolt from the room.

"I've missed you so much, darling." I retch as Mum's purr filters up to me.

"I've fallen asleep every night wishing you were beside me."

I don't bother going for the doors. He might be a pathological liar, but I'm pretty sure that was the truth. He's put too much work into this for one of us just to be able to walk free. And anyway, if the door was wide open right now, I'd never leave Mum with him. When we get out of this place, we get out together.

My eyes sweep to the front door. The light coming through the glass panels calls to me, but when I finally move, it's in the direction I told him I was going.

My body aches and my muscles pull as I climb the stairs. Days going without food have left me weaker than I think I've ever felt before.

Each step is a colossal effort, but I know I need to do it.

I scan the hallway when I finally haul my heavy limbs to the top, trying to figure out where I should try first.

Someone is up here, and if he catches me doing anything other than going for a pee, I'm screwed— and I'm sure any chance of being allowed back for something as 'normal' as a meal with my parents isn't going to happen again.

I need to make this count, and I need to bank on Mum being able to keep Jonas distracted.

A shudder of disgust rolls through me as I think about what new lows she might have to stoop to in order to give me this chance.

Finally, I decide to head to the bathroom as I said I would. If shit is about to go down, then I don't need to be busting for a pee throughout it.

I push into the small room and shut the door

behind me. It's the first time I've had that privilege since being here, and it's a heady feeling, knowing that I don't have someone's eyes on me as I lower my arse to the toilet.

After doing what I need to do, I make quick work of rummaging through the cupboards in the hope of finding more weapons, but disappointingly, each one is empty apart from a new toilet roll, and I really don't think that's going to be a whole lot of help.

"Shit," I hiss when I try the window and find it as firmly covered as the one in the basement.

Stealing a calming breath, I prepare to slip out of the room and search through whatever other rooms are up here.

The second I step foot in the hallway, a loud, obnoxious snore cuts through the silence.

A smile twitches at my lips as I follow the loud noise toward the room at the end of the hall.

The door is ajar, but the room inside is dark, just like the ones downstairs despite the obvious daylight through the front door.

My breath catches in my throat when I find the beast of a man laid out on the bed in just his jeans, his hairy gut hanging over the waistband.

My top lip curls back at the stench of stale old man sweat and something else gross that I don't even want to try to identify as I sneak deeper into the room, looking for anything useful.

It's not until I'm standing right behind him that I spot exactly what I want.

His phone is poking out the top of his pocket.

'Fuck,' I mouth, clenching my fists to stop my hands from trembling.

If this guy is a light sleeper, then I'm beyond fucked. But if he's not, if I can pull that free without him realising it's our way out.

Letting the knife slip from my sleeve, I wrap my fingers around it and hold it tight above the guy's throat.

Our lives are literally on the line here. If Jonas catches me doing this, then... fuck, I don't even want to think about what the consequences would be.

I squeeze my eyes closed for a beat and channel my inner bad-arse.

I have to believe that Toby is out there fighting for me, and I need to do exactly the same.

If this goes badly, and I wake him... well, I've gotta protect myself. And I will just have to find a way to live with that later.

Blowing out a breath, I force any thoughts out of my mind and count down.

Three.

Two.

One.

21

TOBY

I sit on the edge of my sofa with my head in my hands.

Bri's concerned eyes burn into the top of my head, but I don't have any words of comfort anymore.

It's been five days.

Five fucking days and we're still no closer.

Our rats might have squealed a name about who is helping Jonas, but that hasn't been any fucking help because we can't find him either.

The motherfucker must have been planning this the whole time he was down there. And here we were, thinking that he was too weak to do anything.

I thought I'd felt hate burning me up inside before, but what I feel right now has nothing on anything he's done in the past.

Hurting Mum was one thing, something he deserved to die a painful death for. But taking my girl from me? That's something else entirely, and if he's hurt her...

Fuck.

I'm going to fucking destroy him.

The need for violence, for blood, bubbles up inside me until I'm not sure I'm going to be able to contain it any longer.

My entire body trembles with pent-up fury, fury that fighting with Nico now only barely takes the edge off.

Nothing short of pushing a fucking blade through that cunt's heart and twisting it as I watch him die at my feet will lessen it.

I need him dead before me and my girl in my arms, and then I might just be able to see through the red haze that has descended.

Everyone else is either out searching or at school. Stella and Emmie are doing their best at keeping up appearances while Daemon is heading up the search alongside Stefanos, and the guys flit between working and being at school.

Damien wanted me to go, to sit in fucking class and pretend like nothing is wrong in the world. But fuck that. How is that even possible when my fucking world has been ripped away from me?

I understand his concern, that Jonas might be watching and that we need to look like we're not going to raise hell to find him, but I can't... I just can't.

"Let's go to the house again," Bri suggests.

She's the only one who's stuck by my side through this agony. I know the others are here for me —I know they haven't abandoned me and that they're doing what's needed of them. But Bri hasn't so much as stepped outside my flat unless she's right by my side. I appreciate it more than she could know. But equally, I hate looking into her terrified eyes multiple times a day.

I have no fucking clue what excuses she's made to get out of her life, but her support hasn't wavered once.

"We've been there every day this week," I grit out, not lifting my eyes from my feet.

"I know, but... There's a clue there. I know there is. It's where she went last. It's where he took her from. There has to be a clue."

In the past four days, we've turned their house upside down looking for this magical piece of evidence that Bri is convinced is right under our noses. But we've found nothing. Not a fucking scrap of anything other than the last place her phone tracker registered before she went off grid.

Finally, I lift my head, although I'm nowhere prepared to look into her eyes once more. But before I'm forced to, my phone pings.

I rush to pull it from my pocket as my heart jumps into my throat.

Please, please, I silently beg.

Just give us a clue, baby.

When I pull it in front of me, my eyes damn near pop out of my head.

"Fuck," I gasp, my hand trembling violently. "It's her."

Bri crashes over the coffee table in her need to see, and she lands beside me as I open the message.

Jodie:

"There's nothing there," Bri cries, seeing the same disappointment as me. "She's got signal though. Check her tracker."

"Shit."

The wait for the app to load is the most agonising few seconds of my entire life. But what I can't prepare for is just how fast my stomach plummets when it finally does load and I get to see where she is.

"Motherfucker," I bark, jumping to my feet.

We've searched my old house almost as thoroughly as we have Jodie's, but there was no sign of anyone being there since the day Nico found me on the roof.

I'm at the front door with my shoes on before my brain has even registered the move.

"Wait," Bri calls from somewhere behind me. "You're not going alone."

"I'm not taking you there," I growl.

"Where is there?"

My phone pings again and my stomach knots.

Jodie: He wants you to come alone.

My teeth grind as I picture exactly where she's going to be.

But I don't give a shit. If it's me he wants, then he can fucking have me—as long as he lets her go free.

"Hell," I state, pulling the door open, ready to follow that motherfucker's orders. Something I promised myself that I'd never do again. But I never expected this. I never thought I'd have to save her from her own fucking father.

"Just stay here," I warn her. "And if we don't return, then you know where we are."

"No, Toby. I'm not letting you do this. Call the others. Take someone."

I head off, leaving her shouting behind me.

Without looking back, I take the stairs as quickly as I can, knowing that she's going to follow if I'm not fast enough.

I don't remember the drive across town. It's a route I've taken time and time again, but it's not familiarity which makes the sights outside of the windows pass me by. It's pure fear for what I'm about to find that blinds me.

She hasn't been there all this time. We searched that entire house from top to bottom, so I know he didn't take her there.

But they've gone back. Why?

Why is he risking moving her around? Giving her the opportunity to reach out?

My stomach churns with the fear that that message wasn't from her.

It could just as easily be him leading me into something.

My palms sweat against the wheel, my grip making my hands cramp as the house comes into view.

Dread sits heavy in my stomach, but the possibility that she's got hold of her phone, that it's her on the other end keeps me going.

Just before I pull the car to a screeching halt outside the front door, my phone starts ringing and Nico's name flashes up on the screen.

Ignoring him, I grab my keys and take off, leaving my car running and Nico's call ringing through the bluetooth.

I skip the front door in favour of walking around the back of the building.

There are cars parked out the front, but that was the same the last few times I've been here. Left and abandoned as their owner rotted in hell—or at least that was what I thought was going on.

My heart thumps against my ribs as I come to a stop by the back door and push the handle down.

It's locked. But I'm not sure if that's a good thing or not.

I slide the key into the lock, cursing as it cuts through the silence around me before pushing the door open.

Everything is silent, peaceful as I walk through

the utility room and into the kitchen. Nothing is out of place, and I quickly decide that this is a trap just like I feared on the drive over here but was stupid enough to ignore in case I was wrong.

I take two more tentative steps toward the hallway just to convince myself nothing or no one is here before I can take off and find whatever is going on that I'm being distracted from, but the second a voice hits my ears, everything changes.

"Toby," she calls.

Hearing her after the hell I've been through this week is like taking a bat to the chest, and all the air rushes out of my lungs as I race forward, forgetting any consequences.

"Jodie?" I call back. "Where are you, baby?"

"Toby," she cries again, but it's quieter this time and I spin around, my heart dropping to my feet as my eyes land on the basement door.

"No," I breathe.

I didn't go down there when we searched the place—Nico did it for me to save me the pain. But there's no escaping it this time.

Swallowing down my fear, I pull the door open and face the darkness.

My hand shoots out to where I know the light switch is, but despite flicking it on, nothing happens.

"Toby." Her voice is louder, more pained this time, and I forget all about being able to see as I fly down the stairs, muscle memory from the number of times I've descended them taking over as I fumble with my phone to put the torch on.

I'm almost at the bottom before the small light finally brightens the space up.

I gasp as screens suddenly illuminate around me, and I scream like a fucking girl when the door at the top of the stairs slams with a bone-chilling bang.

"NO," I bellow, panic rising within me as my heart rate picks up.

I look around, my eyes barely focusing as I look at the video feed of Jodie sitting around the table in the dining room at her house with Joanne and Jonas.

"No, baby." I rush forward, focusing on her instead of my situation as I take in the cuts and bruises on her face.

He's hurt her. He's raised a fucking hand to her.

A sob rips from my throat as I'm forced to continue watching them there playing happy families, although the look in Jodie's eyes is anything but happy.

I jolt as her voice comes from somewhere behind me. "Toby will find me, and they will kill you."

"That pathetic piece of shit doesn't care about you, sweetheart. He only wants to hurt me. I'm the only one who loves you."

My stomach turns over, and I'm powerless but to vomit up the contents, which is little more than the whiskey from last night.

"No," she argues. "That's not true."

"He's using you, Jodie. As soon as he's got what he wants, he'll drop you as fast as he found you."

"No," I scream. "No."

Another screen flickers to life, and I find an image of Jodie and Joanne curled up together in what I can only assume is a dark basement.

"Jodie," I cry. "Fuck. FUCK."

I stumble back against the wall, completely useless.

My chest heaves as I stare at the screens showing the same video clips on repeat as her begging voice comes through a speaker, quickly followed by him trying to convince Jodie that I don't care about her. That she's only a game to me. A way to hurt him.

Sliding down the wall, my arse hits the floor and I drop my head into my hands as red-hot tears burn my eyes.

I've failed her. I know there's no getting out of this basement. I've tried enough fucking times. I also know that he's put a signal blocker down here, so I can pray for a miracle all I want, but it's fucking pointless.

No one ever saved me down here before. No one is going to save me now.

22

JODIE

I don't believe I've done it until I'm resting back against the closed door of the bathroom with his unlocked phone in my hand.

Excitement and fear duel within me.

I might be one step closer to getting out of here, but there's still a way to go yet.

A cry comes from downstairs, turning my blood to ice as I race to get help.

They'll be able to trace this number, and they'll be able to find us.

I'm barely able to hit the numbers, my hands are shaking so badly. But I've got this far. I need to see this through. I need to get help before whatever that sick fuck's plans play out.

I hit call on Toby's number and lift the phone to my ear.

But nothing happens. It doesn't ring. It doesn't even go to voicemail.

Shock rocks through me as Jonas's words come back to me from the day I walked to Mum's house to find him waiting for me.

"He's using you, Jodie. As soon as he's got what he wants, he'll drop you as fast as he found you."

No. I refuse to believe that.

He's out there looking for me. He is. They all are.

Dialling the other number I remember without even having to think about it, I hope and fucking pray that this one connects and that she's able to get help.

"Jodie?" Bri's panicked voice rings through the line.

"It's me."

"Holy shit, Jojo. Where are you? What's going on? What—"

"Shut the fuck up, Bri, and listen to me. You need to get one of the guys to trace this number. It'll lead you to me."

"Oh my God, okay. I'm with Nico. He's ringing Theo."

"Where's Toby?"

"Uh..."

"Brianna, is he okay?"

I don't get to hear her response because there's another loud scream from downstairs before footsteps begin thundering closer to me.

"Oh shit. Don't hang up," I demand before shoving the phone in my bra and rushing toward the basin to wash my hands.

"Jodie?" Jonas booms, making my heart catapult into my throat.

My hands shake as I try to scrub off the evidence of what I've done, but I fear it's going to be too late in about thirty seconds.

His footsteps get louder, but I can barely hear them over the blood racing past my ears.

The door crashes back against the wall and I squeal in fright, despite knowing it was coming.

"What did you do?" he booms, surging toward me and grabbing me by the hair.

"Get off me." I reach for the knife that's still in my back pocket. Pain sears down my neck as he drags me forward and out of the bathroom.

The evidence of what I did not so long ago is more than obvious on the cream carpet that lines the hallway.

Thankfully, he doesn't notice that I'm armed— well, not until it's too late and I plunge the knife into his side.

He roars in pain, spinning around to see what I've done a few steps from the stairs.

"You stupid, stupid bitch."

The pain on my scalp gets worse to the point I think he's just ripped my hair clean out before I go tumbling down the stairs.

"Jodie," Mum screams in horror before my head finally collides with the wall at the bottom of the stairs with a sickening crack before everything goes black.

The first thing that comes back to me is my sense of smell, and it turns my stomach.

"Please, Jonas. Please, don't do this," Mum begs, the fear in her voice sending a shiver down my spine.

Darkness threatens to drag me back under again, but I fight it. I fight it so fucking hard.

A loud slap rings through the air before Mum whimpers.

My stomach convulses and I lean to the side, vomiting all over the floor.

"Oh good. Jodie is awake to play now as well."

His voice is dark and deadly, and the image of it the second before I blacked out comes back to me.

"You're sick," I spit, ripping my eyes open and glaring right at him.

"Me? Nah, sweetheart. You're the one who's been fucking my son."

"He's not your son. He's a good man. You're a monster."

"Is that why he lied to you? Played you? Used and abused you?"

"He did that because of you. Because of all the years of abuse you forced him to suffer. He loves me. And he's coming to save me."

"Because of this?" He laughs darkly, holding up the blood-stained phone.

I gasp in realisation that he found it stuffed in my

bra a second before he launches it at the wall. I wince as it shatters. I just pray that Bri and Nico managed to get what they need.

I have no idea how long I was out for. It could have been minutes or it could have been hours. And if it was the latter, why aren't they here?

He isn't right. He isn't. Toby is coming. They'll get us.

"Just let us go. You can run. It's not too late," I say, changing tack.

"I'm not leaving without either of you," he states coldly.

"If you stay, they will kill you."

His dark chuckle turns my blood to ice, and in a moment of clarity, my stomach bottoms out as I finally figure out what the smell is.

"No," I breathe. "No, you can't do this."

The corners of his mouth turn up into a sinister grin.

"Oh but I can. You stop me from leaving with my family, and I'll ensure we're together forever."

Holy shit.

If I ever needed proof that everything Toby ever told me about my father was true, then here it is in the form of this fucking raving lunatic who's about to blow us all to kingdom come.

Mum's swollen eyes catch mine, and I hate that I see resignation in their depths.

Tears flow down her cheeks, washing the dried blood and dirt away. My chest aches for what she might have gone through while I was upstairs and then out cold.

'I'm sorry,' she mouths, making the lump in my throat grow ever larger.

Tearing my eyes away when she begins to sob, I look around the room, noticing differences from the room we ate in.

"W-we're at home?"

"Home isn't a place, Jodie. Home is where those you love are," Jonas tells me as if he actually fucking believes that being anywhere near him is a fucking blessing.

"You need to stop this."

"Do I?" he asks, taunting me as he pulls a lighter from his pocket, flipping it between his fingers.

"Please, Jonas. Don't do this," Mum sobs. "That's your little girl. Take me. Do what you want to me, but let her go. She's got her whole life to live."

"With him?" he spits.

"You've already told me he doesn't want me," I force out, my heart not believing a word of it despite the fact that his call didn't connect. Surely, he's worried. Surely, he's looking for me. "So what's the harm?"

"It's not just him though, is it? You've found yourself at home with all of them. With her."

"Stella?" I ask, feeling fiercely protective after what he did to her.

He scoffs at just hearing her name.

"You're threatened by her, aren't you?"

"She's nothing. A worthless piece of shit, just like her brother. I should have strangled them both the moment they were born."

Mum's startled gasp rips through the air.

"Did you think that about us? Because we didn't have enough Greek blood running through our veins? Is that why you sent Joe to the slaughter by convincing him to join that gang? Is that why you never wanted to claim me? Because you're ashamed?"

I have no idea what the fuck I'm saying. All I know is that I've got to keep him talking. Bri will fix this. Nico, Theo, Toby, Stella. All of them are out there right now. I just need to keep him distracted, because the second he flicks that lighter, we're all fucking dead.

23

TOBY

Jodie's pleas and Jonas' vicious comebacks about how I don't love her and never did taunt me as I sit with my back against the wall, my arms locked around my legs.

She's at home. At fucking home and having a nice family meal. How have we missed them? We've searched every inch of that goddamn house. Where the fuck are they?

Surely, he's not risking moving them in and out. Anyone could see that and alert us to it. Bri has spoken to more than a few of the neighbours and they're aware we're looking for them.

He can't just move around like the ghost he should be, not when he has two captives with him.

A loud bang from upstairs rattles the wall I'm leaning against, and a small, pathetic whimper rips from my lips.

I hate that he has the power to reduce me to a

terrified mess when we don't even know where he fucking is.

My entire body trembles, my stomach churning with dread that I might be forced to watch him walk down those stairs in a few seconds.

Things are different now. You can take him, a rational voice tells me. Yet despite knowing it's true, it doesn't help. But fear of this place overrides everything.

There's another loud, terror-inducing bang before the door to the basement is heaved open.

Scrambling to my feet, I back up into the darkest corner in the hope of either hiding or being able to get one up on him when he descends, I have no idea.

"Toby." Jodie's voice rings out again before feet get closer.

"Tobes? What the fuck is going on?"

Nico.

It's Nico.

Relief floods me as I run from the shadows.

"She's at—"

"Home," he finishes for me.

"How do you know that?" I ask over my shoulder as I race up the stairs, the fear that was consuming every inch of me only seconds ago draining from me.

"She called Bri. Theo tracked the number," he states behind me, but there's something in his tone that I really don't like.

"Is she okay?"

Only silence greets that question.

Spinning on my heels, I slam straight into his body.

"Tell me what the fuck is going on," I demand.

"There's no fucking time for this. Get your arse in the fucking car. Your girl needs us." His fingers wrap around my upper arms and he damn near drags me out of the house as my heart thrashes to a reckless beat inside my chest.

My legs take on a life of their own when I spot Nico's car out the front of the house with Bri sitting in the passenger seat. Being pissed about her obviously following me when I told her not to doesn't even register as I throw myself into the back.

"What's going on? Is she okay?"

Bri looks around. Her eyes connect with mine, and the expression on her face says it all.

"She's fighting, man. She's fighting so hard to get back to you," Nico says, wheelspinning out of the driveway and racing down the street.

"That doesn't make me feel all that much better. Tell me everything that's happened."

"The guy we can't find is with them. She stole his phone, called Bri to get us to track the number. Jonas must have got wind of something happening, because he came and dragged her out of the bathroom where she was hiding."

"Fuck," I breathe, red-hot fury filling my veins.

"We're pretty sure he threw her down the stairs."

"Jesus fucking Christ," I boom. "She's his fucking daughter. Get us there now, Nic. Go fucking faster."

"The others are there," he says, handing me his phone so I can see their tracking dots.

"Why the fuck are they outside still?"

Nico and Bri share a look.

"They're listening in. He's pulled the fucking gas pipe and is threatening to let it go up."

"No," I breathe, all the air rushing from my lungs at the severity of this whole situation. "He wouldn't. He loves them too much."

"He threw Jodie down the fucking stairs, Toby," Bri says, although it's completely unnecessary. I've seen her. Sitting around that table with cuts and bruises marring her face.

"I know," I mutter. "How the fuck are we gonna get them out of there?"

"Boss has a plan," Nico says, damn near overturning his car as he takes a corner way too fucking fast.

"It better be a fucking good one," I mutter, holding onto the back of the passenger seat as if my life depends on it—which it absolutely fucking does with the way Nico is driving.

"Thank fuck," I bark the second Nico starts slowing to a stop at the end of Jodie's street. I don't wait for him to pull to a halt. Instead, I jump out and start running toward the small crowd of dark figures hiding in the shadows. Every normal member of the public would probably miss them. But I'm far from fucking normal.

"Boss, what's happening?" I ask, coming to a stop in front of Damien.

He stares at me, compassion and deadly determination warring in his dark eyes.

"He's threatening to blow the house."

"I fucking know that. I want to know what's happening to stop him from doing it."

"We're trying to get a shot at him. Take him out before he flicks that goddamn lighter."

Dread washes through me. "Is that a good idea?" Because a bullet and gas sound like a really fucking bad one to me.

"We're going to get your girl out, Toby. Trust us."

Damien lifts his hand to his ear, where I assume he has an earpiece, before nodding.

"The second you've got it, take him down. We're ready."

"W-who are you talking to?" I ask, looking around to see who's here.

"Stefanos and Daemon. All the guys are in those bedrooms, waiting for the shot." He jerks his chin in the direction of the houses directly opposite Jodie's as Nico and Brianna come to stand with us. "Daemon has the best vantage point."

I glance back at the windows, but I can't see him. I can't fucking see anyone.

I trust my brothers with my life, and I trust Jodie's with them too. I just fucking hope it's enough, because if that house goes up with her inside it, then I may as well just run in there too and go with her.

"Here," Evan says, handing me and Nico earpieces so we can get in on the action.

I hesitate, unsure if I really want to know any of this, but equally aware that I'm about to do whatever it takes to get her out, to wrap her in my arms and never fucking let her go.

"You all in position?" Daemon's cold voice crackles in my ear.

Damien and Evan start pointing and we scatter, following orders.

Half go around the back of the terrace buildings while the rest of us head for the front.

Dropping to our hands and knees, we crawl up the street, ensuring we're hidden by the short walls in front of all the houses before we come to a stop and wait for the signal.

My heart thumps so hard it's all I can hear as the seconds stretch out. With each one that passes, I know we're only closer to him losing his patience and flicking that lighter. As much as I want to think he's not capable of killing the love of his life and his own daughter, I know he is. Just look at what he did to Joker. It might not have been in person like this, but he knew exactly what he was setting him up for by pitting him against us.

Come on, Daemon, I silently beg.

I'm almost at the point of storming the fucking house alone and taking him by surprise when Daemon's deep voice suddenly booms through the earpiece.

"Go."

I move on instinct as the window before me shatters.

I dive through it, not giving a single shit about the glass or the potential explosion that could follow that shot. My only thought is Jodie.

I land on the shards of glass, but before I get a chance to feel anything, Jodie's screams hit my ears and I dive for her.

"Oh my God," she cries as I spot a discarded lighter on the floor at the feet of the man who's bleeding out before me.

"It's over, Jonas. You lose."

Movement right alongside me is all I need to know that my brothers have Joanne, and I trust my judgement as I climb out of the window, ignite the lighter and throw it back into the house.

With the window now out, I don't really expect it to do much other than hopefully burn him to ash, so I'm shocked as fuck as I'm swept off my feet and the two of us are thrown across the street.

Despite free-falling, I manage to spin us so that when we collide with a car, I'm the one who takes the impact as I cradle Jodie's body against mine.

My back hits the car, all air ripping from my lungs as we crumple to the ground.

"I love you, Jodie. I love you so fucking much."

24

JODIE

I wake with a start as the echo of an explosion rocks through me, but I don't sit up. I can't. There's a dead weight over my waist, holding me down.

Where the fuck am I?

"It's okay, baby."

That voice.

That fucking voice.

"Toby?" I cry. My eyes fly open and immediately flood with tears.

I find him laying beside me, propped up on his elbow, staring down at me.

His face is covered in ash and dried blood, his brow and lip are split, and a tender-looking purple bruise covers his jawline. My brows pinch at the state of him before my eyes lift to his messy hair before locking on his dark and haunted eyes.

"It's over, baby. You're safe. He's gone. It's over."

285

"Oh my God," I sob, my tears spilling free as I lift my arms, wrap them around his neck and pull his entire weight down on top of me.

It hurts, but it's nothing compared to what I've been through the past... however long.

He's here, and he's in my arms.

He came for me. Jonas was wrong.

He came for me and—

"I love you, Jodie. I'd have given my life to get you out of there, I hope you know that."

"Toby," I sob, unable to get the words out that I want to say to him as I hold onto him tighter.

My entire body trembles with the strength of my sobs, but I'm powerless to stop them.

Toby shifts us so that I'm sitting in his lap with my face tucked into his neck.

Memories of the past few days. The desperation I felt at being so helpless. The fear that Jonas was right and that he wasn't out there looking for me. All of it just comes flooding out in red-hot, ugly tears.

I soak his shirt through but he doesn't complain. He just holds me, his strength and comfort unwavering as I slowly begin to relax.

"Where's Mum? Is she okay?" I ask, my voice rough with emotion.

"She's fine, baby. She's in my guest room."

"We're—" I pull my face from his shoulder and blink a few times as I look around at his bedroom.

"I brought you both home, baby. You're safe here, and you can stay as long as you need to."

"O-our house?"

Toby winces, giving me the answer I already knew.

"Shit."

"You and your Mum are safe. That's all that matters right now."

"Is everyone else okay?"

"Yeah, you have nothing to worry about."

I hang my head, wishing that were true.

"I killed someone," I whisper, hardly able to believe what I did in that bedroom when the fat guy began to wake up as I pulled his phone from his pocket.

"I know, Demon. And I'm so fucking proud of you."

My brow creases. "B-but—"

"If you didn't do that, we might not have got to you fast enough."

I nod, trying to accept his words. I hope that one day I might, but that's not going to be happening anytime soon.

"He was helping Jonas, baby. He was a bad man. He'd helped organise all of that. He deserved it."

I know this. I know all of it, but it doesn't make it any better.

"Can I see her?"

"Of course."

Placing me down on the bed, he climbs off and takes my hand.

"Can you walk?" he asks with concern pulling at his brows.

I want to say no. I want him to sweep me off my feet and hold me as if he's never going to let me go. But that's not what falls from my lips.

"Yea—"

"Fuck that," he mutters, doing exactly as I silently crave and lifting me into his arms.

"Toby, you're hurt too," I argue lightly.

"It'll take more than that to stop me taking care of you, baby."

My heart tumbles in my chest at his words.

"Thank you. Thank you for coming for me."

"Anything, Jodie. I'd go through fire for you and you know it."

"Sara," I gasp, realisation slamming into me. "How's Sara?"

"Same. No better, no worse."

"Shit," I hiss, really hoping that something good might be waiting for me at the other end of this.

"I'll take you to see her when you're strong enough."

I nod, curling myself into his warm body once more as he carries me across the hall.

"Jodie," Mum breathes, her voice hoarse.

"Shit, Mum," I gasp, taking in her battered and bruised face.

"I'm okay, Jojo. Gianna's been looking after me like a queen." I glance at the woman she nods to who is hovering in the corner.

"Hi, sweetie," she says with such a kind smile that my tears threaten once more.

"Gianna is Alex and Daemon's mum," Toby tells me as he lowers me to the bed beside Mum.

I immediately fall into her open arms, and the emotions I'm trying to keep a lid on erupt once more.

"Come on, Toby. Let's go fix them some breakfast and give them a few minutes."

I'm vaguely aware of them both leaving and the door being closed, but I'm too lost in my meltdown to really register it.

"I'm so sorry," I force out through my sobs. "I'm so sorry I didn't tell you. I'm sorry you had to go through... that," I say, not really knowing what she had to endure to keep him busy, distracted while I escaped upstairs.

"I'd do anything for you, sweetheart." She takes my face in her trembling hands and wipes my tears with her thumbs.

Her eyes are swollen and bruised, and she has a sore-looking cut on her lip. But she's been cleaned up and the cut on her arm bandaged.

"Anything," she repeats. "And I knew he'd come for you. That boy loves you something fierce. We just had to bide our time and find a way to let them know where we were."

I nod.

"You did so good, baby. You saved us."

"I—" I hesitate. "They saved us."

"Consider it a group effort."

"Where were we, before I woke up back at home?"

Mum lets out a pained laugh.

"Next door."

"W-what?" I blurt, hardly able to believe it.

"He'd been planning this for a while, it seems. He —someone—had knocked through the cupboard in the spare room and he dragged us through it."

"He... He'd made it look like a replica." She nods. "Why?"

"Other than because he was mentally unstable?"

"Well..." I wince.

"It was all a game, Jojo. He was trying to play God, and he failed." I swallow the lump in my throat as I hold her eyes. "But it's over."

I bite down on my bottom lip, not wanting to ask my next question but knowing I need to.

"Has he ever hurt you before?"

"Not physically, no. But I knew he was capable of it. His anger always had a very loose switch and he could flip on a dime. But he was controlling. More so than I think I ever really saw. But having him back in front of me, watching him try to poison your mind with lies about Toby, I saw it. I saw all of it for the first time. All the things he'd convinced me to do over the years that were seemingly for my own good. None of it was for me. It was all for him. A way to hide the person he really was. I may have known about his other life, his wife, but that was all I knew.

He worked very hard to keep us as far away as possible."

"I wish you'd gotten us out earlier. You deserved a better life than that."

"I've had a good life, Jojo. Despite all of that, things could have been worse—"

"You could have been Maria," I interrupt.

"Yeah," she says sadly. "It's time for a new start, baby. You've got your place at uni, an amazing boy out there who would go to the ends of the earth for you. Everything is going to get better."

"What about you? You've just lost everything," I say sadly, mourning all the memories that were held inside that house.

"They were just things, Jodie."

"I know, but—"

"Everything will be okay. We will be okay."

"But where will you live? What will you do?" She shrugs, the darkness in her eyes making my heart ache in a whole new way.

"I'll figure it out."

A soft knock sounds on the door, and it opens a beat after Mum calls out for whoever it is to enter.

I can't help but smile as I take in the relief in Toby's eyes when he steps into the room and sees me here.

"Hey, you hungry?" My gaze drops to the tray in his hand, and my stomach groans at the sight of the piles of pastry.

"Starving," I say, pulling my aching body up the

bed a little so I can rest back against the headboard. My eyes catch on my bare legs that are poking out from the hem of one of Toby's shirts.

"What's wrong, Jodie?" Gianna asks, placing coffees down for each of us. "Are you in pain?"

"N-no," I lie, because the reality is that every inch of my body aches like a bitch. "I'm just... how didn't I break anything?" I ask, astounded that I made it out of that house with only a few cuts and scrapes. "He... he threw me down the stairs."

"Here," Gianna says, passing me two little white pills and a glass of water. "I can see it in your eyes, sweetheart."

"Thanks," I whisper, taking them from her and eagerly swallowing them down.

"You were very lucky, from what your mum has said."

"Lucky? I'm not sure that's how I'd describe it."

"Give it a week or so and the evidence of the past few days will have faded. Hopefully, that will help you be able to process it all and find a way to move forward." She looks away from me to Mum. "Do you need anything, Joanne?"

Mum takes my hand in hers. "No, I have everything I need right here."

"The pastry, you mean?" I joke, making a genuine smile spread across her lips.

"What can't a pain au chocolat fix?" she asks, plucking one from the tray that Toby's lowered to the bed between us.

I watch her in amusement as she takes a bite and groans in delight. Maybe she's right. Maybe everything will be okay and this really is just a total fresh start for us.

I eat until I'm pretty sure I'm going to explode, and when I glance over at Mum, I find that she's barely able to keep her eyes open.

"We should let you sleep," I say to her after nodding at Toby to clear up the tray.

She immediately sinks down in the bed and pulls the covers up around her.

"I love you, Jojo. And I'm so proud of you," she murmurs before her eyes completely close and her breathing evens out.

"I love you too, Mum," I say before Toby wraps his arm around my shoulder and guides me out of the room, letting me use my own slightly wobbly legs this time.

"There's someone waiting for you down in the living room," he tells me, steering me in that direction.

"Jodie," Bri breathes, throwing her mug in excitement and launching herself at me.

"You fucking bitch," Nico barks, his lap now covered in what I assume is burning coffee.

Toby snorts a laugh beside me as I'm rugby tackled by my best friend.

"Fuck, Jodie. Do you have any idea how terrifying that was?"

"I'm okay, Bri. The guys saved me."

"Nah, girl. You were a fucking bad-arse. You did that. You got you and Joanne out of that."

I shrug, not really feeling worthy of any of her praise.

"The others were here too, but I finally managed to convince them to go home and leave you to rest," Toby tells me.

"Thank you," I breathe as Bri continues to squeeze me as if she's afraid I'm going to disappear in front of her eyes.

My gaze catches on Nico as he pulls off his jeans and throws the sopping wet fabric across the room.

"No," Gianna cries when his hands go to the waistband of his boxers to get rid of them too.

"You're a nurse, G. Surely you've seen enough cocks to be able to look past it."

"Not one that small," Toby quips.

"Nico," I gasp when he drops his underwear without a care in the world.

He stalks over, cupping his junk in one hand, slapping the other on Toby's shoulder.

"I'm borrowing some clothes, bro."

Toby's chin drops as we all watch his bare arse stalk toward Toby's bedroom.

"There is something wrong with him," Bri mutters, finally releasing me.

"You should know," I point out. "You know him way more intimately than us."

"Oh I don't know. From what I've heard, Nico and your boy are pretty close," Bri teases.

"We ain't that fucking close."

"I should probably go before I hear something I can never forget," Gianna says, interrupting us.

"Oh, G," Nico shouts before reappearing in a pair of Toby's sweats. "If you ever need the gossip, I am your man. I know all your boys' dirty secrets."

"I think I prefer living in ignorant bliss. But thank you for the offer," she says politely, a smirk twitching at her lips.

"That really is a shame, G. The things I could tell you about what they get up to."

"What the hell do you know that I don't about Daemon?" Toby asks.

Nico barks out a laugh. "He doesn't just kill people and worship the devil, you know? He also jerks off over—"

"And I'm out. Call me if you need me," Gianna says before damn near running for the front door.

"You were saying?" Toby prompts after the sound of the front door slamming rings through the flat.

He just shrugs. "Fuck knows what gets the devil hard. I was making that shit up."

"You're a horrible, horrible person, Nico Cirillo," Bri hisses.

"Come and tell me that while you're sucking my cock, Siren."

"Un-fucking-likely, arsehole," she hisses.

"Aw, I love it when you two get along. It warms my heart," Toby teases, making me wonder what it's been like between them while I've been gone.

"What day is it?"

"Saturday," Toby says solemnly.

"Shit. Really?" I guess that explains why I feel so dirty and gross.

"Really."

"I need to shower."

"I'll say," Bri says teasingly. "I'm going to go. He is too," she says, pointing to where Nico is getting comfortable once more on Toby's sofa. "And leave you to relax. To talk."

"Thanks, Bri," Toby says sincerely. "For everything."

"More than welcome. As long as you look after my girl right."

"You got it."

"I'd give you a hug, but you're all gross and shit," she says, looking him up and down with her top lip peeled back.

"You hugged me," I argue.

"Yeah well, Toby has cleaned you up. He's still covered in fuck knows whose blood."

I glance back at Toby and raise a curious brow.

She shoots me a grin and he pulls me into his side.

"Nico," Bri barks, grabbing her bag from the sofa. "Move your fat arse."

"What have I told you, Siren? You only get to order me around if you're willing to open your legs for me."

She flips him off before blowing me a kiss and

disappearing around the corner shouting, "Love you, Jojo."

"So?" Toby says, glaring at his best friend.

"What?" he asks innocently.

"If you're quick, you could catch her in the lift," I suggest.

He thinks about it for a second before deciding it's a decent enough suggestion and bolts from the flat.

The door slams closed a few seconds later and Toby spins me around and captures my face in his hands.

"Alone at last," he whispers. "What shall I do with you?" he teases.

"How about you tell me whose blood you're actually covered in and why you look like you've been fighting."

"Come with me," he says after dropping the sweetest kiss to my lips. "And I'll tell all."

Ignoring his bedroom, he leads me to the final door in the hallway and swings it open.

The scent of coconut fills my nose before Toby stands aside to reveal flickering candles and a tub full of bubbles.

"Toby," I breathe.

"I can't take the credit. Bri got it ready for you."

I shake my head, my emotions getting the better of me.

Reaching behind his head, he drags his shirt up

his body, revealing dark purple bruising across his ribs.

"What the hell?" I rush forward, gently brushing my fingers over the marks.

"It's nothing, baby," he argues, tucking his thumbs into his waistband and shoving his sweats to his ankles, leaving him deliciously naked.

"That is not nothing. What the hell happened?"

He kicks off his trousers before stepping up to me and wrapping his fingers around his shirt that's hanging around my thighs.

Peeling it up my body, he throws it behind me.

"I'm never going to be able to explain how it felt to think I'd lost you, Jodie," he says, his own frayed emotions making his voice deeper with every word as he wraps his hand around the back of my neck and pressing his brow to mine. "I've never felt so helpless in all my life."

As I slide my hands up his bare chest, his entire body shudders at my innocent touch.

"You got me, baby. I'm right here, and I'm not going anywhere."

"Fuck. I'm so sorry."

"Stop," I demand, pressing my fingers against his lips to cut off any more words that might want to fall free. "It's over. We're free. We're going to focus on the future. Right after you tell me why my boyfriend is black and blue."

"I'll tell you everything."

"Me too," I promise.

25

JODIE

Turns out, after Toby brought me home and made sure I was actually okay, he and the guys headed out to the Italian soldiers' hangout and raided the place in retaliation for what they helped Jonas do—and a whole host of other things that I didn't ask too many questions about. I figure that while I might want Toby to be open and honest about his work, I also don't need all the dirty details.

All I know about that night was that he took a arse-kicking—although he assured me that the three Italians on the other end of the fight came out worse —and that they now have two important members of the Mariano Family hostage somewhere. Somewhere that is thankfully not the basement below where we're living.

It's been a week since Toby dragged me out of that house and away from the psycho that was threatening to blow us all to pieces. A week since he was able to shed the lingering demons that he was constantly battling, knowing that the reason for his years of abuse and torment was still alive.

Although we have a lot to work through in order to rediscover who we really are after everything we've been through—both individually and as a couple—I wake up every day feeling a little better, a little lighter. And know he feels the same. I can see it in his eyes, feel it in his touch.

Swiping some lip gloss on, I stare at myself in the mirror. My makeup hides my lingering bruises. Anyone who doesn't know they exist wouldn't see them now. Not having to stare at them every time I catch my reflection is helping me move on. Although I'm not sure the memories of those few days locked in that basement will ever fully leave me, I can already feel some of the less memorable parts fading. Maybe one day it'll all vanish and I can forget about the fact that I pushed a knife through a grown man's throat and was forced to listen to his gargling breath as he died. Possibly wishful thinking, but whatever.

Happy with the face looking back at me, I spin around and head out to find some clothes.

Toby went back to school two days ago. As much as I hate him going. I know he can't keep putting his life on hold for me. He has to achieve his grades if he's going to get his place at uni, and I'd never forgive myself if I fucked that up for him.

The sight of our messy bed makes me smile as I

step into the room. I straighten it out and grab a couple of pillows that have fallen on the floor, probably not long after we fell into it, a tangle of limbs and heated kisses last night.

Mum might still be recovering across the hallway, but it hasn't really stopped us. I just seem to spend a lot of time with Toby's hand over my mouth as I scream out his name and lose myself in the mind-numbing pleasure he's able to offer me.

A pink sticky note beneath my phone catches my eye, and when I walk over, I find his handwriting on it.

Put some shoes on and grab your mum. I've got a surprise for you.

A smile twitches at my lips as memories of the last time I found notes like this float through my mind.

Grabbing a pair of Converse from the wardrobe, I rush across the hallway and knock on her door.

"Everything okay?" she asks when I push inside.

"Yeah. Put some shoes on, we've got to go somewhere."

Mum sucks in a breath at my words.

She might think she's doing a good job at covering up how she's really coping after everything, but I can see deeper than I think she believes. It also hasn't escaped my notice that she's yet to leave the flat. Like me, her injuries are now easily covered by makeup, but it seems that's not enough to give her the confidence she needs to step back out into the real world.

I've told Toby that I'm going to give her until the end of the weekend, and then I'm forcing her to come out with me. Although, it seems that he might be taking matters into his own hands.

"Oh? Where?" she asks, trying to cover her trepidation.

"I don't know," I confess, holding the note up. "It's a surprise."

Throwing her shoulders back, she stands from the bed where she was reading one of the magazines Maria brought for her. "Well, I guess we'd better not let him down."

A smile tugs at my lips that she's willing to push past her fears. That she trusts him enough to just do as he says.

Maria and Stella went out shopping for both of us the day after Toby took us both in to make sure that we had everything we could possibly need, seeing as everything we used to own got blown to smithereens a week ago.

Pain slices through my chest as I think about the things we lost. I know Mum's right. They are only things, but it still hurts to lose pieces of my childhood, my life, like that.

"Any idea what this is?" Mum asks as she follows me down the hall toward the living area.

"No clue," I mutter, spotting the next note almost instantly on the coffee table.

"Go to the lift."

"Well, this is fun," Mum says with a smile. "I hope there's cake at the end."

"We can only hope. I found my car last time he played this game."

"Oh, maybe he's going to lead us to a mansion."

My chin drops and I turn to look at her.

He wouldn't do something that insane... would he?

"You don't need to look so worried, sweetheart. If it's a surprise for you from Toby, then I'm sure it's nothing but sweet and thoughtful."

I just about manage to smother the snort of laughter that wants to erupt as I think about how sweet and thoughtful he was last night when he handcuffed me to the bed, stuffed my knickers in my mouth, and teased me to within an inch of my life, getting me right on the edge time and time again before he finally sunk deep inside and me let me come around his cock.

Oh yeah, good ol' sweet Toby.

"Yeah," I force out. "I'm sure it's fine."

"Come on then, I'm excited," Mum says, bouncing on the balls of her feet.

Following her out, we let the front door fall closed behind us and head toward the lift. We find another sticky note with 'press me' and an arrow pointing at the button, just in case it wasn't abundantly clear what he meant.

It's already on our floor, so the doors open in a

heartbeat and we step inside, finding a box waiting for us.

"Go down a floor," I say, reading it out loud. "Then open me."

Mum presses the button and we descend the short journey through the building.

The second we step out, I pull the lid of the box off.

"Find 1401." Mum and I share a look, but we push forward and I follow the instruction written beneath to unwrap the tissue.

There's another small box with a note on it.

Open me, then use me. But remember, it's my first time. Be gentle.

"What the fuck?" I bark.

Mum spins around and looks down at the note.

"What the hell is that boy playing at?" But as she asks the question, I think we've both already guessed. And I love him even harder for what I think we're about to discover.

Opening the final box, I find a key staring back up at me. Although seeing as there's a biometric scanner beside the door of number 1401, it seems kind of redundant.

"Go on then," she encourages. "Just go slow and gentle. It might be tight."

"Mum," I gasp before falling about laughing.

"No need to play innocent with me, young lady. The walls of that flat upstairs aren't completely soundproof, you know."

"Oh my God," I mutter, forcing the key into the lock rougher than instructed.

Pushing the door open, I step inside, my feet sinking into the plush carpet as the scent of fresh flowers fills my nose.

A sticky note catches my eye on an oak unit and I rush over.

Welcome home, baby. Make yourselves comfortable.

"No," falls from my lips despite the fact that I know it's true. I knew it long before I got into the lift. I just didn't want to believe it.

"What is it?" Mum asks, stepping up behind me.

"It's ours," I say, passing her the note.

"Shit."

"Yeah."

"I guess we'd better check the place out then, see if it's good enough."

"Mum," I gasp. "We can't accept this."

"Sweetheart, they haven't bought us a house. This building is an apartment block. They'll just be loaning it until we get back on our feet. I'm sure they'll want rent and all the other usual stuff."

I stare at her unblinking, once again reminded of where my naivety has come from.

"What?" she asks innocently.

"Even if that is true," although I already know it's not, "we can't afford rent on a place like this. I mean, look," I say, waving my hand toward the floor-to-ceiling windows at the other end of the vast room.

"It's incredible."

"Yeah," I breathe, walking farther into the flat and taking it all in.

It's not as big as Toby's upstairs, but it's still huge and over the top and everything anyone could want for a home. And the views over the city, even on the opposite side to Toby's, are breathtaking.

"We'll figure it out. We've got his money. What better way to spend it than to put it back into the Family bank?"

"Well, I guess when you put it like that," I mutter, staring out at the city below in total shock.

"Come on, let's check the rest of the place out," Mum says, looping her arm through mine.

I want to refuse and call Toby to rip him a new one for this over-the-top gesture. But he's in class, and I also kind of don't want to. The smile on Mum's face and the excitement in her eyes is everything. This is the beginning of our new start, and I really want her to have this. Her own place, somewhere she can make a home and rebuild her life. And I know that we don't need to worry about Jonas anymore, and she'll be safe here. We'll be safe here. And Toby is right upstairs along with the rest of his friends, who are quickly becoming almost as important to me as he is.

Each room is better than the next, and by the time we're standing in the master bedroom, both staring at the view once more, I swear my heart is going to explode with happiness.

He did this. He did this for us, for Mum.

"You picked a good one with Toby, Jojo."

A smile tugs at my lips as I think of him.

"He's really something," I whisper, thinking of the guy in question.

As if he knows we're talking about him, my phone starts buzzing in my pocket.

"Is that him?" Mum asks when I pull it out.

"Sure is."

Swiping the screen, I walk out of the room, leaving her to get acquainted with her new bedroom.

"Tobias Doukas, what the hell have you done?" I bark down the line as I move into the living area and lower my arse to the sofa.

"Do you like it?"

"Toby," I sigh, my fake irritation disappearing with that one simple question. "It's stunning, of course I like it."

"Good. Although really, I'm more concerned about your mum's opinion, because I don't intend on you spending a lot of time down there."

"Oh, moving me somewhere else, are you?" I ask lightly, my heart taking flight in my chest.

"You belong one floor up, baby."

"Are you asking me or telling me that I'm moving in with you?"

"Uh... bit of both," he confesses. "I was hoping to make a bit more of a gesture out of it than just a conversation down the phone, though."

"Are you really sure it's okay for Mum to have

this place?" I ask, concerned that he's doing too much for us.

"It's more than okay."

"The rent is going to be extortionate."

"There is no rent, Demon."

"Oh, no. You're not doing that. We're not living here for free."

"Jodie," he says a little more sternly. "As much as I'd love to take all the credit for this, it wasn't just me. The boss actually suggested it." My mouth pops open at his confession. "And everyone else agreed. The guys and I have been doing everything we can to keep this building ours since before we all moved in. Having family here is exactly what we didn't know we were holding out for."

"Family," I breathe, a smile playing on my lips.

"Yeah, baby. You're a part of all of this now. And none of us are going to be letting you go. Either of you."

A giant lump forms in my throat, stopping me from responding for a few seconds too long.

"Jodie?" he asks quietly.

"Yeah, sorry. I'm still here."

"Is everything okay? Are you mad at me for this?" he asks, doubt evident in his voice.

"What? No. I'm not mad, Toby. I'm overwhelmed. Blown away. So fucking in love with you that I don't even know what to say."

"That'll do it, baby. I love you too. I'm taking you out tonight," he tells me.

"Oh? What did I do to deserve all this?"

"Just being you," he breathes, making me swoon hard. "I need you to be ready for five-thirty, okay?"

"Uh... yeah, sure. What do I need to wear?"

"I've got it all covered, baby. All you need to do is go back up to our flat when you're ready and you'll find everything you need."

Our flat.

"You, Tobias, are—"

"Perfect. Mysterious. Hot?" he offers.

"I love you," I laugh. "And yes, you're all of those things and I wouldn't have you any other way."

"Good. Be ready, okay? You're in for a wild night."

"I hope it's going to be reckless," I tease.

"Would I plan anything else?" he quips before telling me he loves me again and hanging up.

Mum appears around the corner after I lower my phone, having obviously been eavesdropping.

"Everything okay?" she asks, coming to join me on the sofa.

I can't help but smile as she studies me.

"Yeah. This place is yours, Mum. Rent free for as long as you want it."

Her lips part to respond before my words really register.

"My place?"

"Toby's asked me to move in with him."

She chuckles at me, happiness still shining bright in her eyes.

"I'm so proud of you, Jojo."

"Even if I did manage to find myself in the middle of this life despite everything?"

"I never had anything against this life. But I've always been an advocate for following your heart, and I'm pretty sure yours has led you to exactly where you're meant to be."

"I just hate that it took so much loss to get here."

She reaches for my hand and holds me tight.

"Joe would have liked Toby too," she tells me honestly.

"Shame he had to try to kill his sister though, huh?"

"Yes, that was... unfortunate." Sadness washes over her. "But I firmly believe he wasn't really to blame for that."

"I know, Mum. Deep down, Joe wasn't the kind of man who would ever do that. It's all on Jonas. All of this falls on his shoulders."

Mum shakes her head.

"Things can only get better from her on out, baby girl. I think I'll be buying a new hat soon, too."

I try to laugh that off, but it's harder than I expect as the comment hits me right in the heart.

I've never really thought all that much about serious relationships and marriage. But here I am, suddenly wondering what it might be like to walk down an aisle toward the man I'm more than ready to spend the rest of my days with.

"Who knows what the future holds? I certainly

never thought we'd be right here only a few weeks ago."

"Same, sweetheart. You fancy going out? We can visit Sara, get some lunch and then stop to buy something nice for this place."

"Sounds good. I just need to be back for—"

"Oh. I know," she teases.

"You know?"

"I'm sworn to secrecy. Come on."

26

JODIE

I knew the day was looking up even more the second Mum and I walked into Sara's room and Jesse's face lit up like it was Christmas.

The doctor had just been in with news that she was once again making progress.

Jesse's reaction to that was everything, and it made my heart even lighter with newfound hope that Sara was going to find a way back to us. The road is long, but with more positive news, it's starting to feel like a dream that we really can start hanging on to.

By the time I step into Toby's—our—flat a few hours later after leaving Mum on her floor with her massive new house plant she picked out, my excitement is threatening to bubble over.

Everything looks exactly as I left it as I make my way through the living area, but the second I step into the bedroom, I know he's been here—or at least, someone has.

Walking over to the wardrobe, I pull the sticky note free.

Time to get dolled up, baby. I'm about to give you the best night of your life.

"No pressure," I mutter to myself. He's already given me some pretty memorable ones.

Dropping the note to the bed, I turn toward the bathroom and strip off to shower.

I wash, scrub, and shave every inch of my body in preparation for what's to come.

A gasp rips from my lips when I step out of the bathroom and find a dress laying on the bed that wasn't there when I entered.

Wear me.

Tingles race down my spine as I stare at the elegant, slim-fitting black dress before me. On the floor is a pair of heels and beside it is a clutch and a stunning set of lingerie. Just the thought of Toby's face when he looks at me while I'm wearing it makes my thighs clench.

I make quick work of drying myself off and pulling on the underwear. It fits like a glove and makes my arse and tits look insane.

Lifting the dress from the bed, I hold it up, the designer label taunting me.

I can only imagine how much this cost.

Spinning it around, I find another note.

Wait... there's a robe hanging on the back of the door. Wear it and go to the living room.

A chuckle falls from my lips as desire pools in my

belly.

Please let him be out there waiting for me.

Doing as I'm told, I pull the door open and walk barefoot down the hallway.

"Oh my God," I gasp when I find Stella, Emmie, and Calli waiting for me.

"Surprise."

"You," I say pointing at Stella, knowing that she's the one who planted all the notes and the clothes.

She shrugs, a beaming smile on her face

"Anyway, we're here to make you look killer for your boy," she says, pushing to her feet.

"Well, they are. I'm just here because they told me I had to be," Emmie says with a smirk.

"Oh shut up. You love all the girly shit and you know it."

"At least it's not a spa."

"Which you've now admitted to enjoying. You're full of shit, Mrs. Cirillo."

Her smile grows as Stella flips open a massive makeup case and Calli reaches for a hairdryer and curling tongs.

"Take a seat and relax. Emmie's going to get you a drink to get the night started."

With a roll of her eyes, Emmie heads toward the kitchen, and only a minute or two after a loud pop sounds out, she appears with a glass of bubbles for each of us.

"To the Cirillo princesses," Stella says with a smile, holding her glass in the middle of our group.

"To being bad-arse bitches," Emmie counters.

"Yeah, that too," Stella laughs. "For bringing the bad boys to their motherfucking knees."

"Even better."

But as they laugh, my eyes catch Calli's sad expression.

Sensing my attention, she glances up, quickly covering whatever hurt is lingering. She plasters a smile on her face before lifting her glass to clink against ours.

"Right, we've got an hour to make you look better than you've ever looked in your life."

By the time they're done with me, the bubbles have gone to my head and my need to finally see Toby and find out what he's been planning is bordering on obsessive.

"Go get dressed, it's almost time to go."

"Go where, exactly?" I ask Stella, knowing that she's fully aware of the plans.

"You'd have to kill me first."

Rolling my eyes at her, I disappear down to the bedroom and pull on the dress, zipping myself into it and standing in front of the mirror.

"Whoa," I breathe in shock at the woman staring back at me.

I stand taller than I think I ever have before and raise my head higher in confidence.

The past few weeks have been painful as hell, but I don't think I've ever learned so much, not just about my life but also about myself. I've discovered that I'm stronger than I ever could have believed I was, and that I'm resilient, and powerful, and determined. I've found my flaws, my naivety, my ability to see good in everyone, and I've learned from it—or at least, I hope I have. But even if I haven't, I know I've got people around me who would literally do anything for me. And that in itself is priceless.

I might have lost a lot recently, but I've also gained a lot. A whole new family and people who I know are going to be a part of my life for the rest of my days here.

Reaching up, I toy with the padlock hanging around my neck. I had to take it off for a few hours last weekend while Theo had a tracker installed into it.

I felt naked for the short time I was without it. It was my lifeline when I was locked in that basement. It was a part of Toby, a part of us, that I was able to cling onto and the words he said to me when he gave it to me.

I appreciate why he didn't put a tracker in it to start with, and I love that he wanted me to have my freedom when both Seb and Theo did the exact opposite, but I also wish he'd just done it. He'd have got to me faster, rescued me before I was forced to do something as drastic as kill one of the Italian freaking mafia.

A shudder rips down my spine as I remember it. I'm pretty sure the sight of that knife slicing into his throat is going to haunt me for the rest of my life. But

I stand by the decision I made. If I didn't do that, we might not have made it out.

Toby, Theo, and even Damien have all assured me that there will be no repercussions to what I did, but that doesn't reassure me in the way I'm sure it should. And I hate that they're now dealing with the fallout. Toby has explained that the issues they have with the Italians have been going on for a while now, and this is just the latest in a whole heap of shit they've been landed with. I just have to take his word for it and let them do their thing.

The only people who know the truth about how one of their own lost his life is us. Everyone else believes he went up in the same explosion as Jonas. Something I'm more than happy for them to think.

Pushing my feet into the red-soled shoes, I grab the clutch from the bed, flipping it open to slide my phone inside.

A smile forms when I find another sticky note inside.

You look beautiful. I can't wait to tell you in person.

A million butterflies take off in my belly as I tuck my phone safely inside and head out.

The girls' chins drop when they see me.

"Whoa, Toby has taste. Who knew?" Emmie mutters.

"Well, he chose me so I'm assuming you had a clue," I counter, making all three of them bark out laughs.

"Touché, Jodie."

"Here," Stella says, passing me another note.

There's a car waiting for you downstairs. I'll see you soon, baby.

"Right, well... I guess I should go then."

I'm halfway across the room before Stella blurts, "Good luck."

"What the hell do I need luck for?" I ask as guilt covers her face.

"N-no reason," she stutters as Emmie hits her upside the head, muttering, "Idiot."

"Should I be worried?" I ask, turning back to focus on them.

"No, ignore her. Go have fun," Emmie assures me.

"Okay, well... see you later then, I guess."

"Later," Emmie promises, and I swear I see a little evil twinkle in her eye.

Oh yeah, I should definitely be worried.

"Miss Walker," the driver greets the second I step out of the building and find a black SUV waiting for me. The windows are as dark as the paintwork, and I can't help but hope that I might find my man hiding behind them.

Sadly, that isn't the case. When I poke my head inside, I find the back of the car disappointingly empty.

"Where are we going?" I ask a beat before the driver closes the door, shutting me inside.

"Can't possibly say, Miss." He winks, and I roll

my eyes. "I hope he's paying you well," I shout before he closes the door, and I swear I hear him chuckling before it slams.

I've had ideas about what this night might hold since Toby first said he had a surprise on the phone earlier, but as we make a couple of more than obvious turns through the city, one becomes more and more insistent. And the thought of us heading there has my entire body buzzing with excitement.

I want it. I want to go back and do that all again so bad. And I know he's aware of my desire to experience it all once more.

By the time we pull up outside the club that holds so many crazy, yet still slightly hazy memories for me, my hands are trembling and my need to see my man is almost all-consuming.

My driver gets out, and not a second later my door opens. Only, when I step out and look up to thank him, I don't find my amused driver but Toby.

"Oh my God," I gasp, leaping into his arms and slamming my lips down on his, forgetting all about the blood-red lipstick Stella painted on my lips.

We kiss out on the street right in front of Hades as if it's the last chance we'll ever get, and when we finally part, my entire body is aching with need.

"Miss me, baby?" Toby teases, reaching up to tidy up my lipstick.

"Please tell me we're going in there," I demand, much to his amusement.

"Fuck, you're perfect," he groans, pressing his brow to mine.

"So... are we?"

"You're already ruining those pretty little knickers I got you at just the thought of stepping back inside there, aren't you, Demon?"

"Toby," I warn, squirming with need.

"Toy," he counters, his pupils blown and his cock hard between us, pressing insistently against my stomach. "Yes, we're going in there. But I've got a surprise for you before the real fun starts."

I pull back a little and look him dead in the eyes.

"What have you done, Tobias?"

"Wait and see. There's someone inside who wants to meet you."

"I'm not sharing you," I argue, planting my feet firmly on the pavement when he tries to pull me toward the entrance.

"Oh Demon, you've got nothing to worry about there." He drops our joined hands to his crotch and presses my palm against his solid dick. "This is yours. And only yours."

I nod once and finally let him tug me inside.

"Why isn't there a queue? Friday nights are usually manic."

"Says the expert," he quips, descending into what seems to be a deserted club.

Unlike the last time we were here, there's no deep, pounding music to make the steady beat of my clit even more demanding, and there's no dark mood lighting making the place seem even more illicit than I'm sure it really is.

The bar is almost as incredible in the light as I remember it being in the dark. All of the gold fittings and accents damn near sparkle under the spotlights, and the glossed black surfaces make the entire space modern and exclusive. Exactly what it is, I guess.

"Toby," a woman announces happily, her black sky-high heels clicking across the polished black floor as she comes to greet us with a wide smile on her face.

My stomach knots as I take her in. She's beautiful. She'd probably look more at home up on a runway than she does in here in her slim-fitted suit that I'm sure cost more than I used to make in a month at the coffee shop.

Remembering what Toby said upstairs about not sharing him, I plaster a smile on my face and try to stuff my anxiety inside the box it belongs in.

"And you must be Jodie. It's so wonderful to meet you at last."

At last?

"Uh..." I stutter, lifting my arm to shake her hand when she gives me little other choice.

"Jodie, this is Hera. She's the manager of Hades."

"Um... hi, it's... uh... nice to meet you."

I look between the two of them, thoroughly confused as to why we're here instead of heading to one of the back rooms.

My cheeks heat as my thoughts head down a road I'm sure they shouldn't be right now.

"Come and take a seat. Would you both like a drink?"

"Sure," Toby says, pressing his hand into the small of my back and guiding me to follow Hera. "Trust me," he whispers. His fingers slide down until he squeezes my arse hard enough to make me gasp. His grip locks on my hip, and the second I come to a stop, he presses his front to my back, letting me know that I'm not the only one thinking about what else we could be doing down here right now.

Hera says something, but I have no idea what as I grind my arse back against his, my blood boiling with need.

"Please, take a seat. I won't keep you long. I'm sure you have other plans for the evening," she says with a soft smile that makes her appear a little more approachable.

"I'm sorry, but what's going on right now?" I ask, unable to keep my mouth shut any longer as a young waiter delivers a tray of drinks. Vodka, by the looks of the bottle.

He pours us each a measure before disappearing out through a hidden door behind the bar.

"You haven't told her," Hera tsks.

"I thought a surprise might be more fun."

"Men," she mutters before turning to me. "I'm looking for a trainee manager to help me run this place. A little birdie told me that you might be interested."

My chin drops so low, I swear it hits the floor.

"Y-you... uh... you want to offer me a job?" I stutter, unable to believe what I'm hearing.

"Toby has told me that you've secured a place at Imperial College and given me a copy of your CV."

I turn to the man in question and scowl at him.

All he does in response is smirk and sip his drink.

"I understand you're at a loose end before you start later in the year and are looking to begin your career, maybe get some experience. Well," she says, holding her hands out, "I can't promise you the best hours, but I can promise you a wild ride, hands-on experience—excuse the pun—and the best job of your life, assuming you can cope with a little nudity here and there."

"Uh..." I hesitate, my mind spinning with everything she just said.

"You're seriously offering me a job?" I blurt. "You don't even know me."

Hera looks at me with amusement before knocking back her vodka in one go with not so much as a wince at the burn.

"I know enough. Toby and a few others have vouched for you."

"A few others?" I ask, a deep frown forming between my brows.

"A good friend of mine assures me that you're a hard worker with managerial potential. He was disappointed to have to lose you, but someone," she shoots a glare at Toby, "ripped you away from him."

"Matt?" I breathe.

She nods once to confirm my suspicions. "You don't have to decide right now. I'm aware that this has just been sprung on you out of the blue, and I'm also aware that things have been... difficult for you recently. Take a few days, think on it, and give me a call." A black and gold business card appears on the table and she pushes it toward me with one perfectly black-painted finger.

"Now," she says, pushing to her feet. "I've got a rare night off, and I don't intend on spending it at work. Make sure you lock up on your way out, Tobias. I'd hate to let the riff-raff in. Call me," she says, shooting me an Oscar-winning smile before she glides across the room and disappears through the same door the barman did not so long ago.

"What the fuck just happened?" I bark, turning to Toby the moment we're alone.

The smile that spreads across his face almost has me forgetting all about the past few minutes in favour of allowing the alcohol flowing through my system and my libido to take over.

"Thought you might be interested in what she had to offer," he says, his voice deep, his eyes dropping to my lips and then lowering to my cleavage before his tongue sweeps across his bottom lip.

"Do you think maybe you should have run it by me first?"

"I took my chances. Something tells me you'd be all over this opportunity." As he says that, he runs his hand down the centre of his body, bringing it to a stop over the bulge in his trousers.

Lord, give me strength.

"And you'd be okay with that? Me working here?"

"My girl managing one of the most exclusive clubs in the city and coming home at night to fuck me in my bed? Hell, yeah, baby. I'm good with that."

"You're a dog," I mutter.

"I'll be whatever you want me to be if you get up on that stage over there and make the most of that pole."

I let out a little puff of air at his words. This place really does turn my sweet Toby into the devil. And from the state of my underwear right now, it seems my inner whore likes it. A lot.

"You want me to dance for you?"

"It's what you've fantasised about, isn't it? Getting up on stage. Being the most powerful person in the room. Bringing me to my fucking knees."

"Aw, baby," I coo, cupping his cheek and sliding closer. "I'm pretty sure I did that a while ago."

He throws his head back on a laugh. "Fair point. What do you say though? You gonna put on a show for me?"

"Is this place really closed? On a Friday night?"

"Yep." He leans forward until his hot breath washes over my ear and sends a shiver racing down my spine. "I hear they're having a private party," he whispers. "And they've got full run of the place. Manager's perks and all that."

"Huh, maybe this job does have some benefits."

"Oh, Demon. You have no idea. It's like a sinner's playground. And we already know I'm heading straight for hell."

My argument is right on the tip of my tongue, but the excitement and desire darkening his eyes at the idea of watching me up on that stage stops me.

Reaching out, I knock my drink back, wincing as the neat vodka hits the back of my throat before dragging my tight skirt up my thighs and straddling Toby where he's pinning me into the booth Hera led us to.

A growl rumbles in his throat as I lower myself onto his lap and press my hands to the cushion behind him.

"Demon," he groans as if he's in pain when I roll my hips, grinding my pussy over his hard length. "I thought I was getting a pole dance, not a lap dance."

"You complaining, bad boy?"

"Hell no. I'll take anything you have to offer, Demon."

"Red suits you, by the way," I say, lifting my hand and swiping what's left of my lipstick away from our kiss outside.

"That explains why Hera looked at me strangely."

"I'm sure she's seen worse in here than a man

with his girl's lipstick on his face," I murmur, dropping my lips to his neck and gently sucking on his skin.

"No doubt." His deep voice rumbles through me as his hands slip under my dress and grabs my arse. His grip is so tight as he drags me down harder that I have no doubt he'll leave bruises.

"Fuck, I can't get enough of you, Demon."

"That may be true, but you're not having me yet."

27

TOBY

She's gone before I've even realised that she's managed to twist out of my grip and I groan, pulling at the fabric of my trousers in the hope of giving my aching cock some space.

Suddenly, a low, sexy beat fills the space around us, and a smile twitches at my lips. Hera's parting gift for us.

Jodie pauses and glances over her shoulder. The look in her dark eyes is pure sex, and it makes every single muscle in my body beg for me to follow her, to bend her over the bar and fuck her until her voice is hoarse from screaming my name.

Or I could throw her over my shoulder, lock her back up on that cross. Add a few more images to my wank bank of her completely at my mercy. Or there's the swing... or the bed... a spreader bar...

Fuck. The possibilities are endless. I have every intention of trying out every single one and then a few more with my girl in the coming weeks, months, and years.

Right now, I need to lock my desire to take her down and let her finally get the chance she's always dreamed of. Getting up on stage and channeling all that sexiness she oozes, the confidence, her sinful fucking curves.

She starts moving again, swaying her hips to the music, making my gaze drop to her arse.

Fuck.

I bite down on the inside of my cheeks as I take her in. I knew that dress was going to be fucking dangerous on her from the moment I saw it. I've never spent such an obscene amount of money on one item of clothing before, but hell, it was worth every single penny.

She steps up onto the stage, wraps her fingers around the pole, arches her back, drops her head and swings around it.

Jesus. Fuck. This is going to be torture.

I tug at my trousers again, but it's pointless. There's nowhere near enough space down there for what I'm about to witness.

Her movements are fluid, totally in sync with the music. It's almost as if she's spent all week rehearsing, it's so perfect. Or maybe I'm just blinded by desire and the painful ache in my balls. Who gives a fuck if it is? As I watch her dip and roll her hips against the pole, the only thing I can think about is her, about how incredible she is, how strong she is, how literally every single thing she does blows me away.

Her skin is flushed with sweat, her cheeks are red from exertion, and it spreads down her neck, disappearing beneath the low-cut neckline of her dress. Her breasts are straining against the fabric covering them, desperate to be released.

I sit forward in my seat, more than ready to end this torture and go and drag her off the stage, but my movements pause when she reaches behind her and begins dragging the zip of her dress down.

Oh hell, yes.

Take it off for me, baby.

Resting my elbows on my knees, I lean forward as much as I can without crashing off the chair with my need to get closer to my girl.

The second the back of her dress is open, she lets the straps fall down her arms, teasing me with just hints of the black and red underwear I know she's wearing beneath.

"You're a tease, Demon."

"Isn't that the point?" she shoots back. "You don't seem to be enjoying yourself that much, bad boy. You almost look... composed."

A smirk curls at my lips.

"You want to see how composed I am right now, baby?"

"You know I do." She spins around, biting down on her bottom lip as she drops her eyes down my body. They linger on my crotch and flare with desire when I start stroking myself through the fabric.

I have to grit my teeth in an attempt to hold myself back, because just from watching her, I'm only a few strokes from coming in my pants like a teenager.

"Drop the dress then. Let me see what you're hiding beneath that dress, Demon," I growl, my voice full of desperate need.

Reaching above her head, she grips onto the pole and wiggles her hips seductively, allowing the dress to fall down her body until it pools at her feet.

"Oh fuck, baby," I groan, pushing to my feet and dragging my jumper from my body in one quick move.

Her eyes eat me up as I toe off my shoes and rip open my waistband, pushing both my trousers and my boxers from my hips in one quick move.

The second my cock springs free, I wrap my fingers around it and squeeze the base—anything to stave off the release that I'm already teetering on the edge of from her one-woman show.

Stepping up onto the small stage, I take her face in my hands, slam her body back against the pole and crash my lips to hers.

A groan of desire rumbles in her throat as I push my tongue into her mouth.

"Hottest fucking thing I've seen in my life," I moan into our kiss.

Lifting her thigh, I hook it around my waist,

allowing me to grind my aching cock against her soaked core.

"You liked dancing for me, didn't you, Demon?"

"Yes," she cries when I lower my hand to cup her breast, squeezing until she moans once more.

"You're dripping for me."

She gasps, when I suddenly lift my hand once more and collar her throat, pinning her back against the pole.

"Not sure I gave you permission to ruin these pretty little knickers, baby."

I skim one finger down the centre of her body as I speak, loving the way she shudders at my simple touch before pushing my hand inside the soaked lace that's covering her.

"Oh shit, Toby," she cries. My fingers collide with her heated skin.

"Fuck, baby," I groan, dropping my head to hers as I push two fingers inside her. "Tell me how much you need my cock," I demand.

"Fuck, yes. Toby, Please."

"Not good enough. I need you to be a good little toy, and tell me exactly what you need."

"Your cock," she gasps, and I fingerfuck her harder, grazing that spot inside her every time I dive deeper. "I need to feel your cock stretching me open."

"Out here? Or you wanna go back there?"

She thinks for a moment, her heaving breaths coating my face as I watch her.

"Have we really got all night here?"

"All night, baby," I promise.

"Then... r-right here. There's time for—"

Slamming my lips down on hers, I release her throat in favour of lifting her up the pole and wrapping her legs around my waist.

"Oh shit."

"Move your knickers to the side. I need you impaled on me right fucking now."

She rushes to do as I say and exposes her slick cunt to me.

My mouth waters to drop to my knees and have a taste of her, but the ache of my cock is too much to deny right now, and not a second after I've lined myself up at her entrance I thrust forward, sinking myself fully inside her in one move.

"Toby," she screams, her back arching as I stretch her wide, giving me exactly what she was begging for.

"Never gonna get enough, Demon. Fucking addicted to you. Have been since the first time I laid eyes on you."

"Oh God," she whimpers.

"You're so beautiful," I groan, kissing down her neck and grazing my teeth across her delicate skin. "So fucking sexy. Strong. Intelligent. You bring me to fucking knees, baby. And I never want to get up."

"I love you," she cries as my fingers dig into her arse as I fuck her harder.

Sweat begins to run down my spine as I let my inner demon out and give her everything my body craves. It's only the beginning of what I hope is going to be a wild night, and I have a feeling it's barely going to take the edge off. But that's fine. We've got hours and more places to play than fucking Disneyland right now.

Her body begins to tighten around me and her nails sink into my shoulders, no doubt drawing blood, but it only spurs me on.

"I need to feel you coming, Demon. I wanna feel you milking my cock and taking everything I have."

"Yes. Yes. Please," she chants.

Her head falls back and her eyes close as she absorbs the feeling of our bodies taking over.

"Look at me, Demon. I need you to see just how much you own me as we fall."

Her eyes pop open at my words and her body tenses as she cries out, her release crashing into her the second we connect.

"Fuck. Fuck," I bark, unable to do anything but fall right along with her.

"Toby," she whimpers as her body continues to convulse.

"I love you, baby. I love you so much."

"I love yo—" Her words are cut off by my lips and I kiss her until I'm once again hard inside her. Picking her up, I carry her over to the bar and lay her out on top of it, reluctantly slipping from inside her as I take a step back to study her.

"Damn, you should be on the menu every night, Demon."

She watches me as I prowl back toward her, dropping lower, keeping her exposed and running my tongue up the length of her cunt. The taste of both of us explodes in my mouth.

"Damn, we taste good, Demon."

"Shit, Toby. That's... hot."

I push two fingers inside her, dipping them into the cum I filled her with only minutes ago.

"Nah, baby. Knowing you're full of me... watching it drip from your body," I say, dragging my finger out. "That's fucking hot."

"You're filthy."

"You love it."

Any more conversation is cut off when I suck her clit into my mouth once more. She arches on top of the bar and I don't let up until she's screaming, her fingers twisted so tight in my hair that I'm sure she's about to rip it out.

The second she's down, I stand and drag her arse off the edge, filling her once more until she falls all over again.

"We should go clean up," I confess once we're both sweaty, our breaths heaving from exertion.

"I thought we had all night," she says, a small pout on her lips.

"We do. So there's no need to rush. We can have a drink, maybe," I suggest, walking over to where my clothes lie abandoned in a heap on the floor.

Pulling my phone out, I shoot off a quick message

before snatching Jodie's dress and dragging her toward the bathrooms.

Ignoring the sign for the men's, I take her straight to the ladies'.

"What are you doing?" she asks when I open the hidden cupboard beneath the basins and pull out a bag.

"I thought you might need replacements. Those," I say, glancing down to her knickers, "are a little damp, after all."

I pass her the bag and she looks inside.

"You really have thought of everything, huh?" she asks as she pulls out a matching pair to the ones she's still wearing.

"I've done my best."

We make quick work of cleaning up before I lock her hand in mine again and drag her back to the main bar.

We're about halfway there when a noise makes her pause.

"What's wrong, baby?" I ask with a knowing smirk.

"T-there's... people out there. I thought—"

"You thought we'd get away with this place to ourselves? Come on, baby. You know our friends better than that by now."

"They knew, didn't they?" she asks.

"Yep. I'm amazed they kept it a secret. Come on."

As we emerge from out the back, four sets of eyes turn our way.

"Jodie," Stella gasps. "You've messed up your makeup."

"In only the best ways," she explains, making both Stella and Emmie laugh.

Theo and Seb's eyes meet mine for a beat before turning back to their girls.

Oh yeah, I know that pain well, my friends.

"Drinks," Emmie shouts, nodding to the row of shots in front of her.

"This is going to hurt tomorrow," Jodie mutters.

"Then we'd better drink and party like tomorrow is never going to come."

Heading over, we take a shot each and the six of us throw them back with a collective groan.

"Let's get the party started then," Stella announces, grabbing Emmie's hand and dragging her toward one of the raised platforms.

"This, Tobias, is the best fucking idea you've ever had," Seb says, clapping me on the shoulder.

"Just remember the rules," I growl at him.

"Yeah yeah, no fucking your sister in the same room as you or letting you see her getting all kinked up." I lift a brow at him, sensing that he's not taking my warning about tonight seriously. "We'll see." He winks.

"Let your hair down, Tobes. We're all about fun tonight. Ain't no one judging fuck all," Theo adds.

"Where's Nico and Alex?" Jodie asks.

"Well, tonight had a couples only stipulation, and seeing as Alex is still moping over Calli, we thought it best not to invite him."

"He is not," Theo argues.

"Sure, whatever you say, Boss. I offered for Bri to come with Nico, but she said she'd rather pull her toenails off and eat them."

"Nice," Jodie says with a wince.

"Her words, not mine."

"Well," she says, lifting another shot. "Their loss."

The second she's finished it, she takes off toward the girls, hops up on the platform and begins dancing with them.

Resting back against the bar with my boys, we watch our girls grinding and laughing, having the time of their lives.

"They're gonna hate us for this," Theo says, handing out another drink each.

"Yeah, well. Maybe they should pull their heads out of their arses and let a girl in for once," I mutter.

"Oh, Toby, you're so fucking whipped," Seb says happily.

"Too fucking right. Now, are we going to just stand here watching them or are we gonna—"

"Let's go. Last one with his girl trussed up in one of the back rooms is the loser," Theo challenges.

"Oh, game on, bro. Game fucking on."

28

JODIE

I stretch my legs out, every single one of my muscles pulling, telling me that whatever went down last night was pretty intense.

Lifting my head from my pillow that is Toby's chest, I blink a couple of times to make my vision clear.

The second my surroundings come back to me, I gasp in shock as memories begin rolling through my sore brain from the night before.

The vodka. The dancing. The mindless pleasure Toby offered me as we experimented in almost everything this room has to offer before I'm sure the sun was beginning to rise outside our little sex haven.

I startle when I find other bodies strewn about before my eyes lock with Stella's across the room.

She smiles at me and I can't help but laugh at the state of her. Her hair is sticking up every which way, her makeup has been obliterated, and even from this distance, I can see the red hickies marring the skin of her neck and chest.

"Morning," she croaks.

"You look like you had a fun night," I say quietly so as to not wake everyone else who's still sleeping around us.

"Best night of my fucking life," she beams. "I don't think I'm going to be able to walk for a week."

"Woman," a deep voice grumbles before she's pulled back down once more. "Quit the fucking noise."

Chuckling to myself, I lie back down, but not before I take in the other couple cuddled up on the other bed in the room. Emmie and Theo are locked in their embrace, and I smile as I see the bad boy heir to the Family wrapped around his girl like she's the only thing that matters in the whole world.

"Should I be worried that you're checking out my boys instead of being down here with me?" Toby whispers, making me jump.

"Hell, no. I was just laughing at how bad-boy they look while cuddling."

"Oh, we're all plenty bad enough, Demon. There are only a very few select people who get to see this side."

"Well, I'm privileged," I say, snuggling back down beside him, hooking my leg over his hip and wrapping my arm around his waist.

"Hey," he says with a sleepy smile.

"Hey back. Last night was—"

"Amazing," he finishes for me.

"Yeah. It was," I agree.

"So, what do you think about the job? You wanna help run this place."

I shake my head. "This is crazy, you know that, right?"

"What part of my life isn't crazy, baby? It's time you hopped on for the ride." He thrusts his hips forward as he says it, letting his hard cock graze my more-than-tender core.

"How? I blurt. "How is that thing still working?"

"You're naked. It's got a one-track mind."

"You don't say."

"So about that ride?" he asks, wiggling his brows.

"I'm too sore and hungover for this," I laugh.

He rolls me onto my back and settles at my side with our legs tangled together as he stares down at me. The love pouring from his eyes makes my breath catch.

"I'll take a few kisses and a cuddle then," he smirks.

"Oh, will you?" I tease.

"I will."

Ignoring what I know is a horrendous case of morning breath, he presses his lips to mine and sweeps his tongue into my mouth.

The kiss is so sweet it sends tingles right the way to my toes.

And he doesn't stop, not until I'm squirming with the need for him to deepen it, my body proving my head wrong about being unable to take any more after the delicious overuse it had the night before.

When he finally pulls back, my chest is heaving and I wrap my hand around the back of his neck to drag him back to me, not ready to lose that incredible connection with him yet.

But he holds steady, content on just staring down at me with his swollen lips and puppy-dog eyes.

"Tell me that you're moving in with me, Demon," he almost begs. "My home isn't my home without you in it."

My heart soars at his words.

"Toby," I sigh, and he seems to take that as my hesitation to say yes, which it absolutely is not.

"Your mum will be right downstairs. You can escape me whenever you need to. And Bri is only a few minutes away in your car. I need you, baby."

I smile up at him, lowering my hand until it's pressed over his heart.

"There's nowhere else in the world I'd rather be."

All the air escapes his lips in a rush as if he was physically holding his breath for my answer.

"Yeah?"

"I love you, Toby."

"I love you too, baby. You saved me. Fixed me. You've reminded me of the person I really am and you've made him better. You're everything. Everything," he repeats as my eyes burn with tears.

"Can you do something for me?"

"Anything. Just name it."

"In the future, when you ask me something equally as important as moving in with you," he nods eagerly, and I know he's thinking exactly the same thing I am with the way his eyes twinkle in excitement, "maybe actually ask me instead of telling me."

"Meh. If it's not broke, why fix it?"

My response to that is cut off by another one of his knee-weakening kisses, and I close my eyes and allow myself to drown in this incredible guy who crashed into my life and changed it in more ways than I ever would have imagined.

Things might still be messy. But together, we can get through anything. I know we can.

Calli

Five days earlier...

My legs move as if I've got the devil himself chasing after me.

Well, to be fair, I pretty much do. He's just currently in no position to be running anywhere. I hope.

My heart pounds so hard in my chest, I swear I can feel it in my ears.

I don't look back.

I can't.

If he's there... if he wasn't as asleep as I thought he was, then I'm screwed. Royally fucking screwed.

I mean, I am anyway.

When he wakes up and discovers what I've done, he's going to hunt me down like a raging bull, I have no doubt.

I'm just hoping that I'll have had enough time to figure out how to deal with him.

Shit. How do you deal with the devil?

My hands tremble and my legs barely hold me up as I fly toward the lift and my escape.

I have no idea what I'm going to do once I get out of this building. I guess I'll figure that out once the cool spring air hits my bare legs.

All I know is that I can't stop.

I press the call button for the lift, bouncing on the balls of my feet in impatience, not noticing that it was already rising before I pressed it.

I should have noticed.

I should have taken the stairs and run from who is inevitably about to step out of it.

I can add that mistake to all the others I've made this weekend.

"Fuck," I hiss the second it dings, announcing its arrival.

I'm about to bolt to the right, knowing that whoever is in there can't see me like this. If any of them find out... if it's Nico.

Fuck.

But I'm too late.

"Calli?"

I spin back around the second the female voice hits my ears, and I breathe a massive sigh of relief when I find Brianna, Jodie's best friend, standing before me with a cake box in one hand and a bottle of rose prosecco in the other.

"Oh... uh... hey. I gotta—"

I nod toward the now empty lift and run toward it.

"Are you okay?" she asks, despite the fact she can clearly see that I'm not.

"Yeah, great. You never saw me, okay?" I beg. I have no idea how trustworthy she is, but I really, really need her not to go blabbing to Jodie and Toby the second she gets inside his flat.

"Uh-uh. No, we're not playing that game."

Before I know what's going on, she's walking back into the lift with me and hitting the button for the ground floor.

"I'm calling an Uber. Where are we going?"

"Home," I whisper, my bottom lip trembling as I realise that she's going to help me escape.

"Uh... here, put it in." She passes me her phone and with a trembling hand, I manage to get my address in so she can order a car.

"Was Alex really that bad a lay, huh? Did he even get you off, sweetie?"

"What? No. Yeah. Fuck," I bark, dropping my head into my hands as a sob erupts.

"Here," she says, and when I look over, she's got a

pair of knickers in her hand. "They're new, don't worry. They're my emergency pair."

I stare at her in confusion but decide against asking right now.

"And this." She hands me a face wipe the second I've pulled the knickers on. "Keep it together and own it. You fall apart when you get home and away from the waste of space who made the mistake of making you feel like shit."

Finally, she hands me a pair of ballet shoes that are rolled up into a little ball.

"Who are you, Mary Poppins?" I ask through my smothered sobs.

"Nah, I'm just a girl with a few more years of experience with this shit than you. Best advice I can give you? Stay the hell away from any guy who makes you feel as wrecked as you do now."

"It's not that easy," I whisper.

"I know. It never is."

The lift dings and thankfully, no one greets us on the other side and the Uber is already waiting for us by the entrance.

Bri holds the door open for me and shocks me by jumping in with me.

"Oh, you don't need to—"

"Let's go, man. We haven't got all day," Bri snaps at the driver before popping the top of her prosecco and handing it over.

I eye it suspiciously before she damn near thrusts it into my hands.

"Now, tell me how small Alex's cock really is and I'll laugh right along with you."

I blow out a pained breath.

"It wasn't Alex."

I watch as she thinks about who else lives on that floor, and her eyes widen in shock.

"No," she breathes.

A sad smile pulls at one side of my lips before I tip the bottle up and swallow down more mouthfuls of the bubbles than I really should.

But that's the least of my issues.

Dance with the devil and you're always going to get burned.

I guess the only question is, just how bad is it going to hurt?

Ready for Batman? Dark Knight is up next.
Have you read Call and Batman's prequel, Dark Halloween Knight?

HATE YOU PROLOGUE

Tabitha

I stare down at my gran's pale skin. Her cheeks are sunken and her eyes tired. She's been fighting this for too long now, and as much as I hate to even think it, it's time she found some peace.

I take her cool hand in mine and lift her knuckles to my lips.

"It's Tabitha," I whisper. I've no idea if she's awake, but I don't want to startle her.

Her eyes flicker open. After a second they must adjust to the light and she looks right at me. My chest tightens as if someone's wrapping an elastic band around it. I hate seeing my once so full of life gran like this. She was always so happy and full of cheer. She didn't deserve this end. But cancer doesn't care what kind of person you are, it hits whoever it fancies and ruins lives.

Pulling a chair closer, I drop onto it, not taking my eyes from her.

"How are you doing today?" I hate asking the question, because there really is only one answer. She's waiting, waiting for her time to come to put her out of her misery.

"I'm good. Christopher upped my morphine. I'm on top of the world."

She might be living her last days, but it doesn't stop her eyes sparkling a little as she mentions her male nurse. If I've heard the words 'if I were forty years younger' once while she's been here, then I've heard them a million times. She's joking, of course. My gran spent her life with my incredible grandpa until he had a stroke a few years ago. Thankfully, I guess, his end was much quicker and less painful than Gran's. It was awful at the time to have him healthy one moment and then gone in a matter of hours, but this right now is pure torture, and I'm not the one lying on the hospital bed with meds constantly being pumped into my body.

"Turn the frown upside down, Tabby Cat. I'm fine. I want to remember you smiling, not like your world's about to come crashing down."

"I know, I'm sorry. I just—" a sob breaks from my throat. "I don't know how I'm going to live without you." Dramatic? Yeah. But Gran has been my go-to person my whole life. When my parents get on my last nerve, which is often, she's the one who talks me down, makes me see things differently. She's also the only one who's encouraged me to live the life I want, not the one I'm constantly being pushed into.

That's the reason I'm the only one visiting her right now.

When my parents discovered that she was the one encouraging my 'reckless behaviour', as they called it, they cut contact. I can see the pain in her eyes about that every time she looks at me, but she's too stubborn to do anything about it, even now.

"You're going to be fine. You're stronger than you give yourself credit for. How many times have I told you, you just need to follow your heart. Follow your heart and just breathe. Spread your wings and fly, Tabby Cat."

Those were the last words she said to me.

29

HATE YOU CHAPTER ONE

Tabitha

The heavy bass rattles my bones. The incredible music does help to lift my spirits, but I find it increasingly hard to see the positives in my life while I'm hanging out with my friends these days. They've all got something exciting going on—incredible job prospects, marriage, exotic holidays on the horizon—and here I am, drowning in my one-person pity party. It's been two months since Gran left me, and I'm still wondering what the hell I'm meant to be doing with my life.

"Oh my god, they are so fucking awesome," Danni squeals in my ear as one song comes to an end. I didn't really have her down as a rock fan, but she was almost as excited as James when he announced that this was what we were doing for his birthday this year. Although I do wonder if it's the music or the frontman who's really captured her attention. She'd never admit it, but she's got a thing for bad boys.

I glance over at him with his arm wrapped around Shannon's shoulders and a smile twitches my lips. They're so cute. They've got the kind of relationship everyone craves. It seems so easy yet full of love and affection. Ripping my eyes from the couple, I focus back on the stage and try to block out that I'm about as far away from having that kind of connection with anyone as physically possible.

I sing along with the songs I've heard on the radio a million times and jump around with my friends, but I just can't quite totally get on board with tonight. Maybe I just need more alcohol.

"Where to next?" Shannon asks once we've left the arena and the ringing in our ears has begun to fade.

"Your choice," James says, looking down at her with utter devotion shining in his eyes. It wasn't a great surprise when Shannon sent a photo of her giant engagement ring to our group chat a couple of months ago. We all knew it was coming—Danni especially, seeing as it turned out that she helped choose the ring.

Shannon directs us all to a cocktail bar a few streets over and I make quick work of manoeuvring my way through the crowd to get to the bar, my need for a drink beginning to get the better of me. The others disappear off somewhere in the hope of finding a table

"Can we have two jugs of..." I quickly glance at the menu. "Margaritas please."

"Coming right up, sweetheart." The barman winks at me before his eyes drop to my chest. Hooking up on a night out isn't really my thing, but hell if it doesn't make me feel a little better about myself. He's cute too, and just the kind of guy who would give both my parents a heart attack if I were to bring him home. Both his forearms are covered in tattoos, he's got gauges in both his ears, and a lip ring. A smile tugs at the corner of my mouth as I imagine the looks on their faces.

My gran's words suddenly hit me.

Just breathe.

My hand lifts and my fingers run over the healing skin just below my bra. My smile widens.

I watch the barman prepare our cocktails, my eyes focused on the ink on his arms. I've always been obsessed by art, any kind of art, and that most definitely includes on skin.

I'm lost in my own head, so when he places the jugs in front of me, I startle, feeling ridiculous.

"T-Thank you," I mutter, but when I lift my eyes, I find him staring intently at me.

"You're welcome. I'm Christian, by the way."

"Oh, hi." A sly smile creeps onto my lips. "I'm Biff."

"Biff?" His brows draw together in a way I'm all too used to when I say my name.

"It's short for Tabitha."

"That's pretty. So... uh... how do you feel about—"

"Christian, a little help?" one of the other barmen shouts, pulling Christian's attention from me.

"Sorry, I'll hopefully see you again later?"

I nod at him, not wanting to give him any false hope. Like I said, he's cute, but after my last string of bad dates and even worse short-term boyfriends, I'm happy flying solo right now. I've got a top of the range vibrating friend in my bedside table; I don't need a man.

Picking up the tray in front of me, I turn and go in search of my friends. It takes forever, but eventually I find them tucked around a tiny table in the back corner of the bar.

"What the hell took so long? We thought you'd pulled and abandoned us."

"Yes and no," I say, ensuring every head turns my way.

"Tell us more," Danni, my best friend, demands.

"It was nothing. The barman was about to ask me out, but it got busy."

"Why the hell did you come back? Get over there. We all know you could do with a little... loosening up," James says with a wink.

"I'm good. He wasn't my type."

"Oh, of course. You only date posh boys."

"That is not true."

"Is it not?" Danni asks, chipping in once she's filled all the glasses.

"No..." I think back over the previous few guys they met. "Wayne wasn't posh," I argue when I realise they're kind of right.

"No, he was just a wanker."

Blowing out a long breath, I try to come up with an argument, but quite honestly, it's true. My shoulders slump as I realise that I've been subconsciously dating guys my parents would approve of. It's like my need to follow their orders is so well ingrained by now that I don't even realise I'm doing it. Shame that their ideas about my life, what I should do, and whom I should date don't exactly line up with mine.

Glancing over my shoulder at the bar, I catch a glimpse of Christian's head. Maybe I should take him up on his almost offer. What's the worst that could happen?

Deciding some liquid courage is in order, I grab my margherita and swallow half down in one go.

I'm so fed up of attempting to live my parents' idea of a perfect life. I promised Gran I'd do things my way. I need to start living up to my promise.

By the time I'm tipsy enough to walk back to the bar and chat up Christian, he's nowhere to be seen. I'm kind of disappointed seeing as the others had convinced me to throw caution to the wind (something that I'm really bad at doing), but I think I'm mostly relieved to be able go home and lock myself inside my flat alone and not have to worry about anyone else.

With my arm linked through Danni's, we make our way out to the street, ready to make our journeys home, and Shannon jumps into an idling Uber while Danni waits for another to go in the opposite direction.

"You sure you don't want to be dropped off? I don't mind."

"No, I'm sure. I could do with the fresh air." It's not a lie—the alcohol from one too many cocktails is making my head a little fuzzy. I hate going to sleep with the room spinning. I'd much rather that feeling fade before lying down.

"Okay. Promise me you'll text me when you're home."

"I promise." I wrap my arms around my best friend and then wave her off in her own Uber.

Turning on my heels, I start the short walk home.

I've been a London girl all my life, and while some might be afraid to walk home after dark, I love it. I love seeing a different side to this city, the quiet side when most people are hiding in their flats, not flooding the streets on their daily commutes.

My mind is flicking back and forth between my promise to Gran and my missed opportunity tonight when a shop front that I walk past on almost a daily basis makes me stop.

It's a tattoo studio I've been inside of once in my life. I never really pay it much attention, but the new sign in the window catches my eye and I stop to look.

Admin help wanted. Enquire within.

Something stirs in my belly, and it's not just my need to do something to piss my parents off—although getting a job in a place like this is sure to do that. I'm pretty sure it's excitement.

Tattoos fascinate me, or more so, the artists.

I'm surprised to see the open sign still illuminated, so before I can change my mind, I push the door open. A little bell rings above it, and after a few seconds of standing in reception alone, a head pops out from around the door.

"Evening. What can I do you for?" The guy's smile is soft and kind despite his otherwise slightly harsh features and ink.

"Oh um..." I hesitate under his intense dark stare. I glance over my shoulder, the back of the piece of paper catching my eye and reminding me why I walked in here. "I just saw the job ad in the window. Is the position still open?"

His eyes drop from mine and take in what I'm wearing. Seeing as tonight's outing involved a rock concert, I'm dressed much like him in all black and looking a little edgy with my skinny black jeans, ripped AC/DC t-shirt and heavy black makeup. I must admit it's not a look I usually go for, but it was fitting for tonight.

He nods, apparently happy with what he sees.

"Experience?" he asks, making my stomach drop.

"Not really, but I'm studying for a Masters so I'm not an idiot. I know my way around a computer, Excel, and I'm super organised."

"Right..." he trails off, like he's thinking about the best way to get rid of me.

"I'm a really quick learner. I'm punctual, methodical and really easy to get along with."

"It's okay, you had me sold at organised. I'm Dawson, although everyone around here calls me D."

"Nice to meet you." I stick my hand out for him to shake, and an amused smile plays at his lips. Stretching out an inked arm, he takes my hand and gives it a very firm shake that my dad would be impressed by—if he could look past the tattoos, that is. "I'm Tabitha, but everyone calls me Biff."

"Biff, I like it. When can you start?"

"Don't you want to interview me?"

"You sound like you could be perfect. When can you start?"

"Err... tomorrow?" I ask, totally taken aback. He doesn't know me from Adam.

"Yes!" He practically snaps my hand off. "Can you be here for two o'clock? I can show you around

359

before clients start turning up. I'll apologise now for dropping you in the deep end, we've not had anyone for a few weeks and things are starting to get a little crazy."

"I can cope with crazy."

"Good to know. This place can be nuts." I smile at him, more grateful than he could know to have a distraction and a focus.

My Masters should be enough to keep my mind busy, but since Gran went, I can't seem to lose myself in it like I could previously. Hopefully, sorting this place's admin out might be exactly what I need.

"Two o'clock tomorrow then," I say, turning to leave. "I'll bring ID. Do you need a reference? I've done some voluntary work recently, I'm sure they'll write something for me."

"Just turn up on time and do your job and you're golden."

I walk out with more of a spring in my step than I have in a long time. I'm determined to find something that's going to make me happy, not just my parents. I've lived in their shadow for long enough.

I look myself over before leaving my flat for my first shift at the tattoo studio. I'm dressed a little more like myself today in a pair of dark skinny jeans, a white blouse and a black blazer. It's simple and smart. I'm not sure if there's a dress code

—D never specified what I should wear. With my hair straightened and hanging down my back and my makeup light, I feel like I can take on whatever crazy he throws at me.

With a final spritz of perfume, I grab my bag from the unit in the hall and pull open my door. My home is a top floor flat in an old London warehouse. They were converted a few years ago by my father's company, and I managed to get myself first dibs. They might drive me insane on the best of days, but at least I get this place rent-free. It almost makes up for their controlling and stuck-up ways... almost.

Ignoring the lift like I always do, I head for the stairs. My heels click against the polished concrete until I'm at the bottom and out to the busy city. I love London. I love that no matter what the time, there's always something going on or someone who's awake.

The spring afternoon is still a little fresh, making me regret not grabbing my coat, or even a scarf, before I left. I pull my blazer tighter around myself and make the short journey to the shop.

The door's locked when I get there, and the bright neon sign that clearly showed it was open last night is currently saying closed.

Unsure of what to do, I lift my hand to knock. Only a second later, the shop front is illuminated, and the sound of movement inside filters down to me, but when the door opens it's not the guy from last night.

"Oh... uh... hi. Is... uh... D here?"

The guy folds his arms over his chest and looks me up and down. He chuckles, although I've no idea what he finds so amusing.

"D," he shouts over his shoulder, "there's some posh bird here to see you."

My teeth grind that he's stereotyped me quite so quickly, but I refuse to allow him to see that his assumptions about me affect me in any way.

"Ah, good. I was worried you might change your mind."

"Not at all," I say, stepping past the judgemental arsehole and into the studio reception-cum-waiting room.

"That's Spike. Feel free to ignore him. He's not got laid in about a million years, it makes him a little cranky." I fight to contain a laugh, especially when I turn toward Spike to find his lips pursed and his eyes narrowed in frustration. All it does is confirm that D's words are correct.

"Is that fucking necessary? Posh doesn't need to know how inactive my cock is, especially not when she's only just walked through the fucking door. Unless..." He stalks towards me and I automatically back up. I can't deny that he's a good looking guy, but there's no way I'm going there.

"I don't think so."

"You sure? You look like you could do with a bit of rough." He winks, and I want the ground to swallow me up.

"Down, Spike. This is Tabitha, or Biff. She's our

new admin, so I suggest you be nice to her if you want to stop organising your own appointments and shit. I don't need a sexual harassment case on my hands before she's even fucking started."

I can't help but laugh at the look on Spike's face. "Don't worry. I'm sure you'll find some desperate old spinster soon."

He looks me up and down again, something in his eyes changed. "Appearances aside, I think you're going to get on well here."

I smile at him. "Mine's a coffee. Milk, no sugar. I'm already sweet enough." His chin drops.

"I thought you were our new assistant. Why am I still making the coffee?"

"Know your place, Spike. Now do as the lady says. You know my order."

"Yeah, it comes with a side of fuck off!" He flips D off before disappearing through a door that I can only assume goes to a kitchen.

"I probably should have warned you that you've agreed to work around a bunch of arseholes."

"I know how to handle myself around horny men, don't worry."

After finishing my A levels, before I grew any kind of backbone where my parents were concerned, I agreed to work for my dad. I was his little office bitch and spent an horrendous year of my life being bossed around by men who thought that just because they had a cock hanging between their legs it made them better than me. I might have fucking hated that year, but it taught me a few things, not just about business but also how to deal with men who think they're something fucking special just because they're a tiny bit successful and make more money than me. I've no doubt that my time at Anderson Development Group gave me all the skills I'm going to need to handle these artists.

"So I see. So, this is your desk. When you're on shift you'll be the first person people see when they're inside, so it's important that you look good. But from what I've seen, I don't think we'll have an issue. I've sorted you out logins for the computer and the software we use. Most of it is pretty self-explanatory. I'm pretty IT illiterate and I've figured most of it out, put it that way."

D's showing me how they book clients in when someone else joins us. This time it's someone I recognise from my previous visit, although it's immediately obvious that he doesn't remember me like I do him. But then I guess he was the one delivering the pain, not receiving it.

"Biff, this is Titch. Titch, this is Biff, our new admin. Be nice."

"Nice? I'm always nice. Nice to meet you, Biff. You have any issues with this one, you come and see me. He might look tough, but I know all his secrets." Titch winks, a smile curling at his lips that shows he's a little more interested than he's making out, and quickly disappears towards his room.

It's not long until the first clients of the afternoon

arrive, and I'm left alone to try to get to grips with everything.

Between clients, D pops his head out of his room to check I'm okay, and every hour I make a round of coffee for everyone. That sure seems to get me in their good books.

"I think I could get used to having you around," Spike says when I deliver probably his fourth coffee of the day. "Only thing that would make it better is if it were whisky."

"Not sure the person at the end of your needle would agree." He chuckles and turns back to the design he was working on when I interrupted.

My first day flies by. D tells me to head home not long after nine o'clock. They've all got hours of tattooing to go yet, seeing as Saturday night is their busiest night of the week, but he insists I get a decent night's sleep.

Continue reading Tabitha and Zach's story
HATE YOU!

ABOUT THE AUTHOR

Tracy Lorraine is a *USA Today* and *Wall Street Journal* bestselling new adult and contemporary romance author. Tracy has recently turned thirty and lives in a cute Cotswold village in England with her husband, baby girl and lovable but slightly crazy dog. Having always been a bookaholic with her head stuck in her Kindle, Tracy decided to try her hand at a story idea she dreamt up and hasn't looked back since.

Be the first to find out about new releases and offers. Sign up to my newsletter here.

If you want to know what I'm up to and see teasers and snippets of what I'm working on, then you need to be in my Facebook group. Join Tracy's Angels here.

Keep up to date with Tracy's books at
www.tracylorraine.com

ALSO BY TRACY LORRAINE

Falling Series

Falling for Ryan: Part One #1

Falling for Ryan: Part Two #2

Falling for Jax #3

Falling for Daniel (A Falling Series Novella)

Falling for Ruben #4

Falling for Fin #5

Falling for Lucas #6

Falling for Caleb #7

Falling for Declan #8

Falling For Liam #9

Forbidden Series

Falling for the Forbidden #1

Losing the Forbidden #2

Fighting for the Forbidden #3

Craving Redemption #4

Demanding Redemption #5

Avoiding Temptation #6

Chasing Temptation #7

Rebel Ink Series

Hate You #1

Trick You #2

Defy You #3

Play You #4

Inked (A Rebel Ink/Driven Crossover)

Rosewood High Series

Thorn #1

Paine #2

Savage #3

Fierce #4

Hunter #5

Faze (#6 Prequel)

Fury #6

Legend #7

Maddison Kings University Series

TMYM: Prequel

TRYS #1

TDYW #2

TBYS #3

TVYC #4

TDYD #5

TDYR #6

Knight's Ridge Empire Series

Wicked Summer Knight: Prequel (Stella & Seb)

Wicked Knight #1 (Stella & Seb)

Wicked Princess #2 (Stella & Seb)

Wicked Empire #3 (Stella & Seb)

Deviant Knight #4 (Emmie & Theo)

Deviant Princess #5 (Emmie & Theo)

Deviant Reign #6 (Emmie & Theo)

One Reckless Knight (Jodie & Toby)

Reckless Knight #7 (Jodie & Toby)

Reckless Princess #8 (Jodie & Toby)

Reckless Dynasty #9 (Jodie & Toby)

Dark Knight #10 (Calli & Batman)

Ruined Series

Ruined Plans #1

Ruined by Lies #2

Ruined Promises #3

Never Forget Series

Never Forget Him #1

Never Forget Us #2

Everywhere & Nowhere #3

Chasing Series

Chasing Logan

The Cocktail Girls

His Manhattan

Her Kensington

Printed in Poland
by Amazon Fulfillment
Poland Sp. z o.o., Wrocław

90042275R00223